THE DEATH SCRIPT

dreams and delusions in naxal country

ASHUTOSH BHARDWAJ

FOURTH ESTATE · *New Delhi*

First published in hardback by Fourth Estate 2020
An imprint of HarperCollins *Publishers*

Building 10, Tower A, 4th Floor, DLF Cyber City, Phase II,
Gurugram Haryana - 122002, India
www.harpercollins.co.in

This edition published in India by Fourth Estate 2022

2 4 6 8 10 9 7 5 3 1

P-ISBN: 978-93-5489-351-3
E-ISBN: 978-93-5357-810-7

Cover design: Amit Malhotra

Typeset in 11.5/15.2 Arno Pro at
Manipal Digital Systems, Manipal

Printed and bound at
MicroPrints India, New Delhi

THE DEATH SCRIPT

The Death Script is a remarkable work of narrative non-fiction – closely reported, sharply insightful, richly readable. The landscape, dramatis personae and social consequences of the civil war in Bastar come vividly alive in this moving, empathetic, always courageous and sometimes chilling book. The narrator himself is a never intrusive but always reliable presence in *The Death Script* – trusted by the reader for his moral compass, and admired for his literary skills. – RAMACHANDRA GUHA

Ashutosh Bhardwaj was for many years a reporter in the 'red corridor' of central India, the adivasi land where Naxals and police forces have been locked in deadly combat for decades. In this book, he steps back to take a long view of all that he witnessed, and to reflect with both clarity and feeling on the unavailing inexorability of it. Only he could have written this moving, troubling and indispensable book. – HARISH TRIVEDI

A searing account of his journeys through murky and treacherous fields ... Ashutosh Bhardwaj has been assiduously impartial and has never given in to the temptation of becoming judgemental. The novelist and journalist in him have come together to create an essential document of an overlong struggle that urgently awaits a dignified and humane solution. – ADOOR GOPALAKRISHNAN

Dandakaranya is, literally, the forest of punishment. This is where, centuries ago, a palace intrigue is said to have banished Lord Rama on the eve of his coronation. The area, now the feared Naxal corridor, still remains primal: dark, full of whispers, unspoken treacheries, anger and a deep desire for justice. This young and gifted writer spent years here, exploring, connecting with the banished and hunted, and reporting on this irrepressible uprising in the heart of India. Readable, full of anecdotal and hard evidence, it forces the reader to rethink crime and punishment. – MRINAL PANDE

A searing and stunningly crafted narrative based on the author's reportage from India's so-called 'red corridor'. All sides in the conflict find voice in Bhardwaj's sensitive treatment, offering poignant reflections on the human predicament in a danger zone: fear and love, betrayal and violence, and above all the yearning for justice. – JURY CITATION, THE KAMALADEVI CHATTOPADHYAY NIF BOOK PRIZE 2021

In his arresting prose and the deft use of multiple literary devices, Ashutosh Bhardwaj brings before us his overwhelming experience of violence by the state and the Maoists. – JURY CITATION, THE ATTA GALATTA–BANGALORE LITERATURE FESTIVAL BOOK PRIZE FOR NON-FICTION 2020

One of the most original and interesting works of non-fiction from India in recent times ... a genre-bending book ... with its imaginative churn of fact and fiction, reportage and confession. This is a challenging and hugely impressive book, well worth your time. – THE HINDU BUSINESSLINE

A traumatized – and traumatizing – account of Naxal country ... the many threads in the book start to form knots of betrayal and revenge, of injustice and rage, knots that will ensure that the death script will continue to play out. By the end of the book, you realize the knots have found a home in your throat. No amount of swallowing can undo them. – THE WIRE

The Death Script is, instead, an exorcism ... the book draws its name from the most unbridgeable abyss of all: it is the living writer acknowledging his debt to death, and the dead ... By putting his own voice and life in the centre of *The Death Script*, and by comparing his project to a novel rather than to reportage, Bhardwaj makes the whole nasty affair personal: to him, to the newspapers that gave him his career, and to us. – MUMBAI MIRROR

A haunting account of the Maoist insurgency ... Every word in every sentence of this book speaks volumes about the hard work and perseverance put in by [the author] to ensure that nothing in this book is less than extraordinary. – MATHRUBHUMI

Though several informative and insightful books have been published in the past on the Maoist insurgency in general, and specifically in Bastar, the depth, sincerity and empathy of this latest addition far surpasses that of its predecessors ... An empathetic portrayal of poverty, death, and even a paean to the dangerous beauty of the uncharted forests of Abujhmad, it certainly is; but above all else it is, perhaps, the manifesto of the struggles of this author to find an equipoise from the often-contentious dualities present within himself as a journalist and a writer of fiction, of straddling two almost opposed worlds ... [It] raises the bar for contemporary Indian non-fiction. – JOURNAL OF COMPARATIVE LITERATURE AND AESTHETICS

The fat earth glistens, strewn with severed heads, hands and every other limb, forming heaps all jumbled together. Finding here familiar torsos, beyond reproof, now decapitated, and heads severed from their bodies, women lose consciousness. Placing a head with a torso, they look at them, confused, realizing to their distress, 'This is not his' but are not able to find another one in its place.

– *The Mahabharata*

How can I picture it all? It would take a god to tell the tale.

– *The Iliad*

Map of places related to the Maoist insurgency mentioned in the book

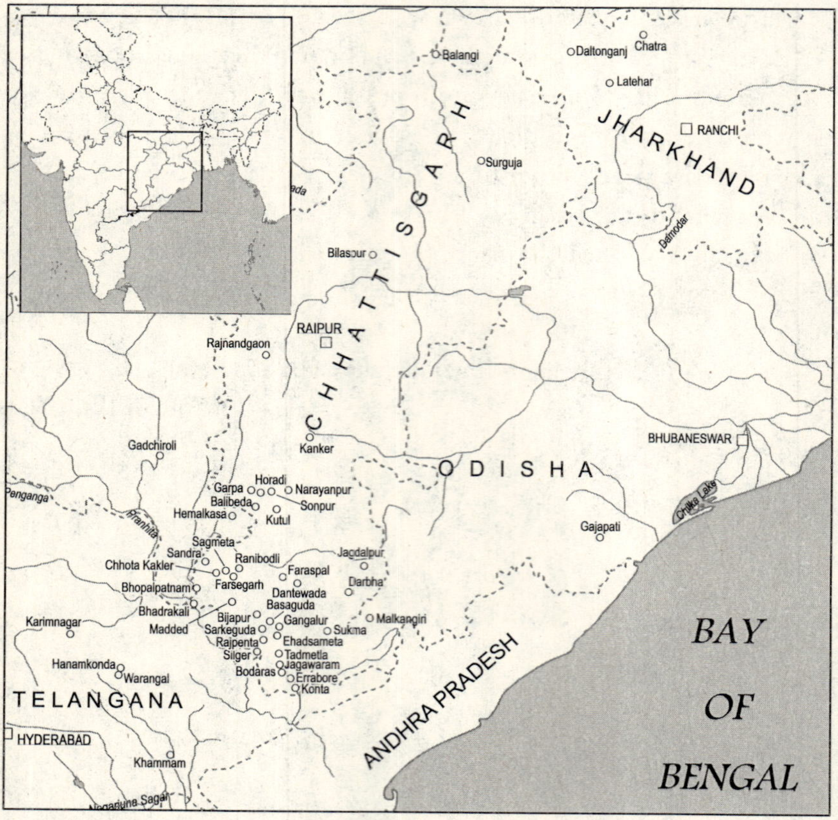

Contents

pre-text

In the beginning was a yearning. Before the beginning was a quest. You will come to realize only later that it was a quest that had brought you to the forest. Only later will you learn that the wilderness, stained with the endless bloodshed of war, was a medium to fulfil your impossible yearnings.

Some of you were guerrilla fighters, some were uniformed soldiers, some journalists and some novelists. Summoned by the forest from distant places, all of you shared one attribute – you had cast off your past before you set out, you had snapped all the threads that tied you to it. Some of you were naive and had arrived rather unmindfully, but soon enough you too realized that this wilderness would seize your past before it let you enter its maze.

Bizarre were the many lives of the Dandakaranya forest. Spread across several provinces, it had been transformed into a graveyard over the last four decades. A colossal pile of gunpowder lay dormant beneath its overgrown paths. The explosive also incubated your fledgling dreams – revolution, the annihilation of insurgents, news reports, a novel. Anything that would lend some meaning to your collapsing lives, give you some reason, however feeble, to stay alive.

All of you thought yourselves storytellers who had come there in search of the last tale of your lives. But could anybody ever possess a tale? You sought the meaning of your life in the eyes of a corpse – could there be a greater self-deception? You considered getting your hands on a girl's fake post-mortem report a colossal achievement – could there be a greater betrayal?

Living with the hubris of being narrators, you were the beguiled actors of *The Death Script* .

The arrogance made you overlook that, long before your arrival in the forest, long before the birth of history, this land had been teeming with the passions of its residents. They could not be your co-travellers, so they chose to become the silent spectators of your journey. The tales of your betrayals were going to be recorded on the leaves of the mahua tree, the eternal signpost of this forest. Dangling from its branches, the tales were going to hover over you forever, like an invincible Vetaal.

ONE

dream / i

My Madam. That's what I called her. I wanted to have a baby with her. I'm a dead man now. Whom will she have a baby with, I don't know. My name was Korsa Joga. It still is. Your name doesn't change after you've been murdered. The police register says: *Korsa Jogaram, alias Ranjit Madkam, alias Shivaji. Notorious Maoist. Age thirty-five years. Gond tribe.*

I was murdered fourteen days ago. The first day of the year 2015. In district Bijapur, division Bastar, Chhattisgarh state. The police people got my post-mortem done. On a piece of paper, they wrote about how I was murdered, how many wounds I received, and all the spots where daggers had pierced me. I had been in the Party for eleven years. I carried an AK-47, was deployed across Dandakaranya, ambushed and killed many policemen, and never received a single bruise. But my former comrades killed me within eighteen months of my joining the police. They attacked me when I was going to my village near Gangalur. One of them was a boy I had recruited three years ago. He lived near my village. I brought him to the Party, and he was the first to stab me. After killing me, they threw me on the road.

I knew they were planning to murder me. Additional Sahab – the additional police superintendent of Bijapur – had asked me to be cautious since I was on their hit-list, and advised me to live in the police barracks. Surrendered Naxalites live in the police lines and remain safe. But I thought that I could tackle my old friends easily. I did not leave the jungle to live with weapons and policemen. I wanted to live in my village with my Madam. I was getting a small home built for us. I was on my way to the construction site when I was attacked.

Sahab often called me for information on the jungle. Sahab gave me a new name: 'gopaniya sainik' or informer. I told Sahab many secrets about the Party. I had once stopped a passenger bus in Murkinar, ridden it with my comrades and ambushed a police post. I had also looted a godown of explosives at the National Mineral Development Corporation in Bailadila, Dantewada, on 9 February 2006. Nineteen tonnes of explosives, fourteen self-loading rifles and 2,430 cartridges. Us Naxalites had never looted such a large quantity of gunpowder earlier. We could now plant battery-operated landmines across Dandakaranya that would explode with the slightest pressure, even the unsuspecting tyre of a motorcycle. We could now blow up the dreaded anti-landmine vehicles of the police. Scared, the policemen stopped venturing out of their camps. Our authority was stamped upon the jungle.

I joined the Party in 2002. I lived in Silger village, in the district of Bijapur. East of Gangalur. Silger's neighbouring village Sarkeguda saw the murder of many adivasis by the police in June 2012, but I remember that year for a different reason. I was then a member of the South Bastar Division Committee of the Communist Party of India (Maoist). I headed a platoon and carried an AK-47. Once, I stopped at Penkram village with my boys. She was a teacher in a government school – I saw her and ... I was instantly struck ...

We left Penkram the next day. I wanted to go back, but I was a senior commander – I needed to have a reason to visit the village. So I devised a plan. Maoist commanders often call meetings of sarpanches, gurujis, health workers. I began calling meetings of the gurujis of that area. She would come ... and then ...

I cannot speak any more. The dead must not jabber on.

She had told me to stay back in Mysore. She did not want to return. But I could not grasp the significance of her words. Had we remained in Mysore, I would have gradually learnt some traits of the city. I would not have been murdered. I should have followed her. She was my teacher. My Madam.

displacement / i

What I'm going to tell you now, I have never shared with any outsider. It is not even recorded in the confidential files of my department.

Yes, I ensure the surrenders of innumerable Maoists in Bastar. I also recruit surrendered Maoists as auxiliary constables in the police force. I deploy some of them as gopaniya sainiks, some others I take with me to the jungle for operations. It is mandatory to record the surrenders on official files immediately and inform the Raipur police headquarters, which then submits a report to the Union home ministry in Delhi. But I do not follow either of these directives. In fact, I cannot.

Those who claim that I violate laws do not comprehend the law. Dantewada is not Delhi, nor is its policing the same. The Code of Criminal Procedure mandates that a person must be produced before a magistrate within twenty-four hours of the arrest. This is impossible in Bastar. Say my boys have gone for an operation towards Gompad or Kutul. If they catch anyone, it may take up to forty-eight hours to bring him to me, to the city. If I pick up somebody, will I first interrogate him, prise all the secrets out of him, or produce him before a goddamn magistrate?

If Ganapathy, the top boss of the Maoists, or Bhupathi, their politburo member, are caught, should I dutifully take them to a court, or keep them at a safe house for months and extract their entire history? Even if a divisional committee member is detained, I will not let anybody get wind of it, will grill him for weeks, and only when he has been completely drained, fit to be discarded, will I produce him before the media and the courts.

I follow a similar tactic with surrendered Naxals. How can I officially declare a surrender on the day the outlaw arrives at my door? I will keep him for weeks, months, squeeze all the juice out of him, and disclose him only after he is empty.

I am also aware that all those registered as surrendered Naxals on government papers are not Naxals. Many of them are villagers and Sangham members – ground-level, unarmed supporters. But who's complaining? Do I kill anybody? Lock them up in a police station? I merely bring some tribals from villages, declare them as surrendered Naxals, get their photographs clicked by the media, and return them with 2,000 rupees and a bottle of country liquor, thereby creating the possibility that they may feel obliged to me and rat out the Naxals, or that the insurgents will begin doubting them for visiting the police and bringing home money and a bottle in lieu of surrenders that were never there. I thus try to create friction between the villagers and the Naxals.

War is not fought on the battlefield. It takes place on the chessboard of your mind. If I have my way, I can eliminate every single Naxal from Bastar.

Some wise people concede me the right to script my tale, but wonder why I deploy the surrendered cadres in my force and send them for operations. What if a Naxal had surrendered only to deceive me, and he suddenly turned around in the middle of an operation in the jungle? My entire party would be gone in a second. Several surrendered Naxals have escaped with AK-47 rifles belonging to the police. Police barracks narrate stories of Naxal ambushes that annihilated my forces, ambushes in which surrendered Naxals who had accompanied the police for an operation suddenly switched sides in the jungle.

I admit the risk, but I have no other option. I will have to recruit surrendered Naxals. I am aware that the rehabilitation policy for surrendered cadres invalidates my acts, that it is indeed evil to hand over weapons to a surrendered Naxal and dispatch him to the forest with my encounter team, that I should give him training for jobs like that of a telephone mechanic, a carpenter or an electrician, that I should never keep him in the police barracks but ensure him a home and a livelihood instead. I am aware that the Naxals kill only those surrendered cadres who join the police. They never harm the ones who return to their villages or begin farming after their surrender.

But perhaps you are not aware that life is awfully cheap in Bastar. It is not guaranteed by a government document called the Constitution, but hinges on the bullet from a rifle. If it touches the right spot, a single bullet will swiftly make a corpse out of a man. A bullet is never cruel or unjust. The finger that presses the trigger of a rifle is erroneously taken to be merciless. In fact, it is merely exorcizing its fears. When a soldier caught in the jungle at night frenetically swirls around his rifle, releasing ten bullets per second and turning eight-, fourteen-, fifteen- and twenty-two-year-olds into corpses, he is merely foreclosing the possibility of becoming a corpse himself. A murder is recorded the moment he pierces the chest of a corpse with a knife and wipes the red beads gleaming on its edge with the dead body's clothes.

The difference between the dead and the living is a matter of chance in Bastar. In Bastar the hunt is for the dead, not for the living. My police force does not do it often, this corpse-hunting. But that's a different tale. For later.

A surrendered Naxal knows all the paths and secrets of the forest, the hideouts of Maoist commanders, the many ways to corner them. His worth as a soldier in the battle against Naxals is inestimable. Yes, it endangers his life, but my life also hinges on his continued loyalty in the jungle. A life in the jungle rests on the palm of a hand. He moved in the jungle for years with the looming threat of police attacks, where he could be killed at any time. He faces lesser danger with me than he did as a Naxal. I will ensure good medical care if he is injured by a bullet from his former comrades, and monetary compensation to his woman in the event of his death.

I have to take risks – for the liberation of Bastar, for the Indian Constitution. But they are well calculated. I never send him to operations immediately after his surrender. I keep him under observation for months: where he goes, who he meets, what he eats. I feed him chicken and mutton, and ply him with liberal doses of liquor so that his senses, hardened by years in the jungle, loosen up. I give him a mobile phone and keep his number on surveillance. I deploy him on the front line, my rifle pointed at his back, a fact he is not unaware of. He is also aware that his woman remains under police watch (she is always under my watch anyway) until he returns from the operation. We suspect each other, and this mutual distrust underwrites our lives.

I remember an incident. I was visiting a college friend in my hometown on a vacation. We were chatting in his bedroom, but my gaze was searching for something.

'Do you need anything?' he asked.

'How many doors does this room have?'

'The one you came from, why?'

'Only one?'

'How many doors do you need in a bedroom?'

'If somebody attacks us and barges in through this door, isn't there any secret door to escape from?'

Startled, he looked at me. 'Who will attack us here?'

Assaults can occur anywhere, any time. For the next eighty-three minutes that I was there, my eyes remained fixed firmly on the door, my ears alert, my fingers on the revolver tucked into the belt of my trousers.

I have police-officer friends in other provinces. They watch movies in multiplexes, go shopping in malls. Whenever I visit Raipur and go to a cinema hall with my wife and baby daughter – who live in the state capital as I don't want to imperil their lives by calling them to Bastar – my armed commandos stand guard at the gate until the show is over.

death / i

He was murdered within two years of my meeting him. Could I have saved him? Could I have prevented a marvellous love from reaching a bloodied end?

In March 2013, a couple caught my eye as I was whiling away my time in an office of the Intelligence Department of the Chhattisgarh police. They were sitting on a bench outside a room. The man had cropped, curly hair and wore a shirt and trousers with a half-sleeved sweater in an arresting shade of red. The woman was in a sari. I walked past the couple a few times, to observe them and also to get their attention and begin a conversation, but they completely overlooked this stranger who had passed by them and paced a few steps before turning and crossing them again. Not that they were immersed in an intense conversation which excluded me from their frame. They barely looked at each other, their gazes mostly fixed on their toes, only occasionally lifting their faces. Still, their silence radiated togetherness. It betrayed no anxiety or tension. A diaphanous silence. Submerged in lukewarm water.

Strangers often catch your eye, but the moment passes quickly and you are left with the imaginary tales you weave about them. An angular face. The translucent hues of a tunic. A lonely old man in a park.

I was once in an auto-rickshaw at ITO Crossing in Delhi. Vehicles were halted at the red light, when the window of an adjoining car rolled down and a hand stretched out. It was a man's hand. Its palm came to rest on the rear-view mirror. A thin ring of smoke wafted from a cigarette held between the fingers. Suddenly, the hand was pulled in, presumably for a drag, and the face of the girl seated next to the driver flashed in the mirror, before the palm returned to its place. But the placement of the fingers had now created some space for the girl's reflection.

Mirror. Cigarette. Smoke. And a reflection.

The lights turned green, the car sped off with a jolt and got lost in the ocean of vehicles.

But the tale of the couple in the police office would not limit itself to a fleeting gaze. Pacing up and down several times, I assumed that they wanted to either submit an application or register a complaint. A few policemen also passed by, oblivious to them.

After some time, the journalist in me reared his head and I decided to approach them. 'Are you waiting for somebody?'

The man suddenly stood up, almost at attention. 'Sahab asked us to be here.'

A sudden fumble in his voice, and I understood immediately.

'Where are you staying?'

'Here, with Sahab.' It meant that they were staying in the office barracks.

'Do you have a phone?'

He pulled out a Chinese model from his pocket. 'Sahab gave this, not working yet.' He held the phone out to me as if I could repair it. His face was enveloped in a cloud of innocence.

'When do you leave from here?'

He shook his head. I asked him to meet me at a nearby place after ninety minutes. 'You have a watch?' He pulled his sleeve up over his wrist to reveal the dial of an old HMT watch.

Thus began my bond with Korsa Joga and Varalakshmi, his Madam. He was a Gond adivasi, she was a Halbi. A mercurial love unfurled before me like the petals of a spring rose. Until a few months ago, Joga had swaggered across Bastar in the Maoist uniform, an AK-47 slung over his shoulder. He surreptitiously crossed the Godavari river with Varalakshmi, lived in the cities of Hyderabad, Bangalore and Mysore, before receiving an unexpected return ticket to Bastar.

He had met her when he was passing through a village in Bijapur district with his platoon. She taught at a local government school. 'I saw her ... and I was struck. Yes!'

Joga soon began looking for excuses to meet her. The easiest was to summon the teachers of the area. The two of them managed to carve out some moments for themselves. The wilderness of Dandakaranya can hold a cosmos within it, but it wasn't easy for Joga. He was a married man. His wife Savita Madkam, also a uniformed Naxal, was deployed in Gangalur. His bosses strongly disapproved of his bond with a government teacher.

The Maoist rulebook prescribes that if any cadre wants to marry a villager or an outsider, that person must first join the Party and work for a few years before the couple can approach senior leaders for permission to marry. Their marital life too must conform to the 'requirements of the revolution', with partners living strictly like 'comrades'. A couple is normally not deployed together in a squad.

Joga, a married man and a prominent rebel commander, could not have received permission for another marriage. In any case, he did not want a 'comrade' marriage. His relationship with Varalakshmi amounted to an act of gross indiscipline against the ideals of revolution. His bosses unrelenting, Joga soon decided to leave the Party he had been associated with for over a decade, to relinquish the dream of an armed revolution, the fight for 'jal, jungle aur jameen', that is, water, forest and land. He began dreaming of a life with his Madam in a distant city. 'It was over, it seemed to me,' he said.

Varalakshmi was apprehensive, but Joga persuaded her. As a top Naxal commander, he regularly extorted money from private contractors and deposited it in the Party treasury. He secretly collected ten lakh rupees and, without his Party getting wind of his plan, on 1 February 2013, he left Bastar, his uniform, his rifle – he cast his past aside and set out with her in search of a new life in the southern region of this nation which prides itself on being the guardian of diverse identities and dreams.

'We had ten lakhs. We believed it would be enough for us to begin a new life, to buy a home ... We were fools,' he laughed. He had never stepped out of Dandakaranya in his entire life, except for some clandestine visits to the neighbouring towns of Gadchiroli, Khammam and Warangal. He spoke only the adivasi language of Gondi, and bits of Telugu and Hindi. Varalakshmi had a little more experience of life outside, but the city was an alien entity for her too. And yet, the couple found themselves in the metropolises. They crossed Andhra Pradesh, got to Bangalore before ending up in Mysore, changing hotels along the way in this journey of over 1,200 kilometres. 'We wanted to settle down in the south, but city life seemed foreign to us. We didn't even know the language.' Joga was still smiling. A smile that resembled a forested stream.

With such passion for life, what caused them to return to Bastar in a police vehicle? Why did their romance get aborted midway?

They ran through their money rapidly. They could not find any work in Bangalore or Mysore. Apart from being daily labourers, what work could two adivasis have found in a metropolis in India? With their dream in danger of fizzling out quickly, Joga suggested that they shift to Andhra Pradesh. He had some contacts in Khammam and Bhadrachalam. It would be easier, he thought, to settle down in areas bordering Bastar which also had the presence of Gond adivasis. It was not, he knew, without grave risk as the Andhra police could have his dossier, but he persuaded himself into believing that it had been a long time now and that the police would have forgotten about him.

He could not recall exactly how he lost the plot. Soon after arriving in Hyderabad, he made a phone call to one of his acquaintances and found the police before him. Was the phone of that person being tapped? Or had he ratted Joga out? Or did some officers of the Andhra Intelligence Department posted at the Hyderabad bus stand find the couple suspicious?

All permutations and combinations notwithstanding, he was caught and taken back to Chhattisgarh. Since the police knew that he had already left the Party, he was not formally arrested or produced before the court. He was asked to declare himself a 'surrendered' cadre and become a gopaniya sainik. Joga was already tired of the life of the jungle and weapons. The last forty days had convinced him beyond any doubt that the city had no space for him either. 'Let's do the police thing now,' he thought.

Soon he was in Bijapur, the jungle he had left not long ago to live his love. From being a dreaded Naxal commander, he was now in the other camp – and on the hit-list of his former comrades with whom he had dreamt of revolution for a decade.

How does a Naxal rebel undergo this sudden change? The desire to leave the Party and begin a peaceful life is understandable, but what prompts a guerrilla to suddenly shun his ideology, to lead an armed battle against old friends, and to divulge their closely guarded secrets? You may dissociate yourself from your past, but can you also discard it so completely, betray it, given that the past was founded on ideals for which you had sacrificed your entire being?

Do arrested Naxals cave in before police excesses? I have met many Naxals who spent years in jail but resumed the fight immediately after their release. They did not reveal any secrets during their imprisonment. Rajnu Mandavi operates in Abujhmad with an INSAS rifle. He was lodged in Jagdalpur jail for a few years. 'The police thrashed me badly. I did not utter a word,' he told me once.

When a Maoist decides to surrender and come out, he is aware that the police interrogators will make him reveal the secrets of his Party. He mentally prepares himself for a long time before switching sides. But Joga was not a surrendered cadre. He left the jungle to begin a family, but was forced to join the police. In the entire history of Chhattisgarh, a province that has seen the greatest spread of Maoist insurgency, he was the most senior cadre ever to have 'surrendered'. He should have received several incentives, a home, a job, at least twenty-five lakh rupees under government schemes for rehabilitating surrendered Naxals. The Indian state promised him a peaceful life in a safe and secure place. But he was made a police informer and dispatched to the jungle.

I am left with only a photograph. Joga and Varalakshmi got it clicked at a photo studio. Varalakshmi is sitting on a chair. Joga stands behind her, his hand firmly but affectionately placed on her right shoulder. His middle finger has a glittering ring, perhaps gold-plated. She is wearing a purple sari. A fine line of vermilion flashes through her neatly parted hair, a long mangalsutra hangs upon the sari's pallu.

Having realized his desire for a new life with Varalakshmi, I suggested to him that he avoid Bijapur. If a job with the police was the only option, it would be better and safer in the capital city Raipur. He knew that his old friends were hunting for him, but he wanted to live in his village. His bosses in the police were aware of the threat, but he was their major asset in the jungle. They wanted to deploy him in a place where he offered maximum tactical advantage to the state's battle against the Maoists.

Minutes after he was murdered, the photographs of his corpse lying on a road in a puddle of blood reached me over WhatsApp. Minutes after he was murdered, a man deep inside me, who loves, who yearns for love, a part of that man was also murdered.

Varalakshmi resumed her teaching. She now lives in a village in the interior of Bijapur.

death script / i

> *I was looking for a quiet place to die. Someone recommended Brooklyn, and so the next morning I travelled down there from Westchester to scope out the terrain.*

Some novels enter your life without anticipation or notice, like the voice of forgotten ancestors, yet at a juncture when you need them the most. They then go on to define and shape your life, leaving you, an unsuspecting reader, stunned by the fact that this was a novel written by someone who lived several oceans away.

What made you a Death Reporter? What makes anyone a Death Reporter? When did *The Death Script* begin? On a dark morning of incessant rains, 15 August 2011? The morning of that Independence Day, when you were leaving Delhi? Or 17 August, the day you arrived in Raipur after driving through central India? Or the evening of 19 August, when you were still lodged in a hotel, yet to find a home, and learnt about the killing of ten policemen in a Naxal ambush in Bhadrakali? Death greeted a new resident to its province and, instantly embracing the residency, you began an eighteen-hour journey to the village.

The first chapter of *The Death Script* was, perhaps, written much earlier. In February 2011, you purchased a novel from a second-hand bookstore in Nehru Place but did not get the time to read it for months. It found its place on the passenger seat of the car, your co-traveller during the long journey in August, whose first sentence, as you began reading it at a dhaba near Jhansi, knocked you out.

It was the story of a man who had come to view his life as repulsive and hateful. With a cloud of gloom over him, he wanted to run away to a distant place. You quickly finished the novel and were astonished by its unexpected arrival in your life.

Nearly five years have passed following your return to the city after spending more than four years in the jungle. More than 3,000 days have passed since you first read that sentence. You have often dissected your life in the forest, asked yourself about what took you there, how you became witness to an incessant spell of death ... The answer you get each time is recorded in the first sentence of *The Brooklyn Follies*.

dream / ii

A few days ago, the Bijapur police had paraded a 'uniformed Naxal' and two young girls in front of the local media. The police said that they had unearthed a big racket which 'supplied minor girls to the Naxals'. The 'dreaded Naxal' Gujja, they said, was the chief supplier. A mere two days in the field were enough to puncture the police's claim.

But I would remember this trip for a different reason. I met Satyanarayan Masterji on my way to exploring Gujja's antecedents. He was not a native of Bastar, and had come to Bijapur to teach in a government school. He took me to his home in Madded village. It had a well with a large mouth. Several tortoises were lazing about, taking their afternoon nap in the water. He was sad because somebody had stolen a tortoise from the well. He was also surprised. How did the thief enter his home, scale down the well and steal the tortoise? And only one. The tortoise could not have jumped out and gifted itself to the thief. The well was reasonably deep; many giant tortoises were basking on the surface of the water. Masterji wanted to register a police complaint and declare a monetary reward for anybody who brought back the tortoise. But when he went to the police station, the policemen laughed him off. He now wanted me to write a story on the theft for my newspaper.

'I have just written a report countering a police claim, and I mostly do investigative journalism,' I told him.

'The theft of my tortoise is also a matter of investigation. The police are not helping me. At least you should.'

'It's a Delhi-based newspaper,' I said. 'In all of Chhattisgarh, it reaches only Raipur by the morning flight. It doesn't reach Bijapur, let alone your village. The news will have an impact if it's published in a local newspaper.'

'It would be good if word got around in Delhi. The Madded police would be taken to task,' he insisted and suggested that, as evidence, I take photographs of the well.

Looking at the well and the tortoises through the viewfinder of my camera, I recalled that in July or August, during the monsoons, a frog had mysteriously disappeared from my Raipur home after having made an equally baffling entry.

As I came home one evening and opened the door, I found the frog meditating in the centre of the living room. It sat like a monk in prayer. Its reflection motionless on the TV screen. We gazed at each other's images on the screen until I found myself turning into one of its cousins. I felt as if I was looking at a frog for the first time – now, with the eyes of a frog.

The threshold of my living room was several inches above the ground. It would not have been easy for the frog to jump in. The house also had a big lawn. The frog would have found itself happier in the soil, amid earthworms and insects. Why did it make the effort to place itself inside my home?

My house had three rooms. No furniture, except for a few chairs, a table, bookshelves and a TV cabinet. I slept on the floor; each room periodically found its turn. I earmarked a room for the new resident. I gave it breadcrumbs; sometimes I offered it soil from the lawn on a plate, hoping that it might find some nutritious food of insects and worms; a bowl of water too. I kept the door bolted to prevent its escape. I named it Tutuji.

Tutuji soon became my friend. We often stared at each other for long periods, playing a game of who-will-blink-first. I always lost. Tutuji sometimes let me fondle the flesh under its neck. I recalled the tale of the frog prince and the princess. I also felt sad remembering the biology class in school when, after laying it down in a tray and fixing its limbs with nails, I had slaughtered one of Tutuji's ancestors.

Then, Tutuji vanished. I opened the door after returning home one evening, and Tutuji was nowhere to be seen. Did it jump out of the window? But the window was firmly closed; it was far from the ground too. Tutuji could not have made such a massive leap. There was no way for a cat to enter the room. There was almost no gap between the door and the floor, making it impossible to squeeze through. Did Tutuji shrink itself and slip through the millimetre of space under the door? If it really wanted to, it could have done so on the very first day.

Tutuji's disappearance still remains a mystery.

Having photographed the well, remembering Tutuji, I suggested to Masterji that perhaps there was no thief, that it was possible for the tortoise to have jumped out of the well. 'What are you saying? It's such a deep well, how would it jump out? Why don't you write an article on this?'

During my return journey, and for several days after I had reached Raipur, I tried to figure out how the disappearance of a tortoise from the well of a village teacher could be given a national perspective and sold in Delhi. A week later, I had a dream that my story on Masterji's tortoise was published on the front page of my newspaper along with a photograph of the well that I had clicked. They had also given me the photo credit.

(Diwali, 13 November 2012. Rajasthani Bhojanalaya, Bijapur.)

death script / ii

A civilization, perhaps, finds its reflection in the bond it forms with its dead. Are they dead forever? Do they visit the living occasionally? Or are they perpetual co-travellers, cohabiting with them like eternal lovers? Wandering along the ghats of the Ganga in Benares – the city I spent the summer of 2014 in, covering a frenzied electoral contest between two aspirants for the post of prime minister – I found myself accosted by the shadows of the dead I had written about, shadows that had always trailed me, though I had conversed with them rarely, perhaps because of the fear that, if I gave them the slightest space, they would question and even reject my life as a journalist, prompting me to seek the easy, timid solution of shutting my being to their existence.

Varanasi was an escape for me from the central Indian forests. For nearly three years, I had been covering the Maoist insurgency, chasing corpses. Haunted by death, I left Bastar behind and came to Benares to drown my being in the furnace of election reporting.

Instead, I was in yet another zone of the dead, as their apparitions emerged from the flames of Manikarnika. Manikarnika, that eternal crematorium of Hindu mythology, which has never been quiet, never has respite, where the innumerable dead await salvation, while the entire city of Kashi celebrates their invincible appetite as they gobble up their kin's offerings of logs and dung cakes and ghee.

I was staying in a small lodge at Dashashwamedh Ghat – a site where Lord Brahma, the creator of the universe, was said to have sacrificed ten horses to invoke Lord Shiva, the supreme god of death. An inmate of the same lodge, Judith Mei, was visiting from Finland to shoot a documentary film on the meaning of death in various cultures. 'In Europe, death is often pushed aside, confined to hospitals or old-age homes. Bodies are kept in black caskets, buried in secrecy,' she said, wondering how 'in India, you are not afraid of death, you celebrate it in public'. The insatiable flame of Manikarnika took a gigantic leap and slashed the dark wind with its sharp golden edges, threatening to swallow the Ganga.

The question now stood inverted, turned inward: How do I carry my dead within me? In which casket of my being have they made their permanent domicile? Will I ever be able to count the corpses that have drawn new life from my own laboured breaths?

The question that hit me first in the Dandakaranya forest of mahua trees took a new form before the Ganga. The yaksha prashna found no resonance in the election campaign. Politics was completely oblivious to the pyres that formed Kashi's foundation.*

* * *

---

* It's believed to be a triad, three cities with an almost coterminous geography – Varanasi, Benares and Kashi. Many metropolises carry several cities within them. Delhi has seven, but with demarcated borders. Along the Ganga, Varanasi, Benares and Kashi flow into one another, and yet stand apart. Kashi is the city of light and wisdom, in Varanasi are absolved sins, while Benares (the Prakrit for the Sanskritized Varanasi) incorporates the crucial element of 'ras' – sweetness or joy.

There is another city within Varanasi – Sarnath – from where the first, and the greatest, philosophical challenge to the authority of Kashi was mounted. The Buddha attained wisdom in Gaya, but travelled around 250 kilometres to deliver his first sermon at the threshold of Kashi. The Buddha couldn't have anticipated that he would eventually be crowned as the ninth avatar of Vishnu and that the Ganga would assimilate Sarnath within its waters.

But Kashi is never short of grand ironies, and perhaps none is bigger than this – the mosque Aurangzeb built on the premises of the Kashi Vishwanath temple along the Ganga, which has been the centre of communal tension, is called the Gyanvapi mosque – the wisdom well. Possibly the only mosque in the world with a Sanskrit name.

You have collected a variety of dead in the last three years. They are carefully tucked away in your files. In the previous century, a novelist often embarked on road trips to collect butterflies. Butterflies of myriad hues and forms nourished his creative cosmos. A famous novel of his came out of one such trip.

The dead have replaced the butterflies. You are diagnosed to be diseased with the deceased. Your companions, escorts, doppelgängers, they are the milestones and signposts of your being. You have recorded some 200 deaths in Dandakaranya, a wilderness spread across several provinces and over 90,000 square kilometres. Teenage boys, rebel lovers, pregnant women, policemen, girls hit by bullets between their legs. The world believes them to be your subjects, embedded on your trophies for investigative journalism. You alone know that *you* are *their* subject. They write themselves through you. You are their chosen narrator.

You write their obituaries, their families cremate them. But they refuse to vanish. They will come to visit the Death Reporter on a frosty night and will find him defenceless. A girl will show him the bullet holes on her head that he had missed earlier. An aunt will complain that, although he wrote that her dead nephew was not a Maoist, he overlooked that the boy's body had not one but two dagger wounds.

Cornered and smothered, you will want to run away, but they will grab you by the collar and knock you down, reminding you of the German writer who wrote that 'no one ever masters anything in which he has not known impotence ... [and] this impotence comes not at the beginning of or before the struggle with the subject, but in the heart of it.'

* * *

The afternoon of 30 June 2012. A remote village called Sarkeguda in the womb of Dandakaranya. Fifteen corpses stare at you. Bloated, blackened corpses, resembling an organism that has undergone an awful taxidermy. The biggest 'encounter killing' of Maoists in Chhattisgarh, the state says.

You reach the village before the bodies are cremated. This is the first instance when you have seen more than one corpse at once. Several bodies have sharp dagger wounds. They were not killed by bullets fired from a distance during a shootout but were stabbed from up close. Their relatives scream, they lift the shroud to expose the naked bodies, urging you to take photographs as evidence that they were not killed in a gunfight but brutalized until their last breaths. You are unable to take the photographs but write about the deceased, one of whom – termed a 'notorious Maoist' by India's home minister – was a boy of fifteen.

The state refutes your reports in the absence of evidence, even claims that it had conducted a proper autopsy of the deceased. In the videotaped autopsy, the state says, none of the bodies showed dagger wounds, only bullet injuries. You obtain the confidential video within three days. The topmost authorities had lied through their teeth – several bodies in the video have clear knife marks.

Two years later, before an enquiry commission in July 2014, you state the reason for not being able to take the photographs. 'I was petrified by the sight of a heap of corpses,' you state under oath, 'and found it inhuman to store the naked bodies of children' – among the deceased was a twelve-year-old girl – 'in my laptop merely to secure some evidence and make the report appear more authentic.'

That was the first instance. Such doubts did not affect you in the future, and you never flinched before taking photographs of the corpses. Like the old protagonist of a novel who at first hesitates before assisting with the execution of old and diseased dogs, but is soon overpowered by the banality of death and learns to nonchalantly stuff their cadavers in a bag and consign them to the incinerator.

* * *

After a long day of reporting I am in a restaurant at Sigra Chowk. She is sitting at a table next to me. A little later, she leaves her table and occupies the chair across from me. This is my first visit to Varanasi.

I might be mistaken, but the impression I have of this city makes it hard for me to believe that a girl could come and sit across from a stranger at quarter to ten in the night. My meal has arrived. She orders her food to be packed. She has come here merely to carry food home. I am unable to understand her. She notices my unease and quietly says ... nothing as such.

She lives nearby, alone. She didn't want to cook today, so she came to this restaurant. The waiter brings her parcel of food. I am still having my dinner. She has guessed from my notebook and camera that I am not a resident of Varanasi. She is from Chandigarh and works here in a bank at Godowlia. She joined it a few months ago after clearing an exam for bank probationary officers. She also has a son who lives with her parents in Chandigarh. The son's father works in a bank in Himachal Pradesh.

'How old is your son?'

'Better ask how young he is.' She first smiles and then, without making any attempt to hide her sorrow, says, 'He is only six months old. I cannot keep him here. Who would take care of him? You are a journalist ... Don't you know someone who could help me with my transfer to Chandigarh?'

She has just started on the job. It may not be possible to get a transfer so soon.

A mother should be with her baby, isn't this a valid ground for a transfer?

She shows me photographs of her son on her mobile phone, plays his voice too. The laughter and cries of an infant echo in the restaurant.

I look at the baby's image on the screen, and then at her who is suddenly revealing her life to a stranger. At around quarter past ten, we move out. She hates Varanasi, sees only dust and heat everywhere. She has never been to Dashashwamedh. Rows of boats are anchored in the Ganga. It's election season, a contingent of policemen is patrolling along the bank of the Ganga. A lot of people are dozing off on the steps that descend to the water. It sometimes occurs to me that they are on a pilgrimage to the Ganga. Sometimes I believe that they are the residents of Kashi and have come to spend the night and sleep beside the Ganga. I also realize that I always want to call (and write) the Ganga by its name. If I use it ten times in a sentence, I'll still say 'the Ganga' and will never call it a mere river or any another word.

We stroll along the ghats. Her in-laws live in Lucknow, but her son lives with her parents. He would be ruined if he lived with his father's family. They are extremely conservative. It was a love marriage, only in its fourth year, but she is fed up. He lied to me before marriage, she says. She is fascinated by the Ganga glimmering at night. She couldn't believe that there was a ghat in Varanasi where boys would be playing cricket at this hour.

At around midnight, we take a rickshaw back home. I drop her at Sigra and turn towards my lodge at Assi. It's 7 May today, Wednesday. The city has big political rallies tomorrow and the day after. I will be insanely busy. The tenth is a second Saturday, her day off. She is taking a train to Chandigarh that morning. Monday is the day of voting, another holiday. By the time she returns, the elections will be over and I will be back in Raipur.

* * *

I often passed by a shop in Benares that said, 'Material to cremate corpses sold here.' Dung cakes, logs, ghee made from cow's milk. I always wondered whether it was pure ghee or some adulterated hydrogenated oil. Corpses would obviously not examine its purity, and even if they did, they would not tell others about it. I could not imagine somebody tasting the ghee to ascertain its quality before dabbing the corpse of their relative with it. Perhaps some truly devoted sons might do so...

I wanted to ask the shopkeeper how his customers purchase the material. Was there any standard quantity? Fifteen kilograms of wood, four kilos of ghee and five kilos of dung cakes per corpse, for instance? Or does it vary according to the size of the corpse? A son might need forty kilos of logs if his father was very fat. Do people feel a little embarrassed when they demand extra logs and ghee for bulky relatives? A scrawny woman might require a mere five kilos. Her relatives perhaps face a greater shame. The shopkeeper might stare at them reproachfully – heartless people, leaving their elderly mother to starve!

Numerous people arrive in Kashi every year to embrace their death. The Ganga is the reservoir of countless tales of salvation. The most revered hymns to the Ganga, the *Ganga Lahari*, were composed by Shah Jahan's court poet Jagannatha who was ostracized by his brahmin community for having a love affair with a Muslim woman. Jagannatha travelled to Kashi, the legend goes, and sat with his beloved atop the fifty-second step of Panchganga Ghat. With each of the fifty-two hymns he composed for the Ganga, it rose by one step until its waters touched the feet of the couple and carried them away in its eternal embrace.

But there is perhaps no salvation for those who find their only abode in the written word. Kashi answered the question that Bastar had raised. The Death Reporter can never bury his dead, he can never even deposit them in the Ganga. He will forever carry them on the nib of his pen.

On the train to Raipur, going back to Naxal country after spending over a month along the Ganga in 2014, I asked myself: 'Am I returning from Varanasi or Kashi? Did I live this summer in Kashi or Benares? Is there any traveller who comes to Varanasi, but returns from Kashi? Or who spends his days in Kashi, but his nights in Benares?'

The road from Bastar to Benares, I then realized, goes via Manikarnika.

There was also someone, I now recall, who rejected Kashi, who chose Maghar over Manikarnika, hell over salvation. He was a poet.

* * *

Both Assi and Dashashwamedh are ghats on the Ganga, situated at a distance of a few hundred yards, yet standing in profound contrast to one another.

The breeze of Dashashwamedh carries a nonchalant contemplativeness, a brooding melancholy that evokes an intimacy, one so mercurial that it completely eludes me, leaving me staring at the vertiginous steps of the ghat in the hope of finding clues that never emerge. The breeze gradually becomes alien as you move towards Assi. Eventually, only a slight familiarity remains to make you feel that this is now the last threshold of Benares. One more step, and the city will be left behind.

And the lane from Dashashwamedh to Manikarnika? It is the permanent abode of death on earth. At nights, the tangerine rays of street lamps merge with the yellowed flames of Manikarnika, obliterating the distinction between the dead and the living. In the long and sultry nights of May, I remember a man who plays a game of chess with Death, a wager where his defeat is preordained. As I stare at the ravenous apparitions of burning pyres floating over the Ganga, my sins come back to haunt me.

Life will not offer any opportunity for redemption, and if it does, the courage to confess will elude me, and I will quietly move towards death.

two

displacement / ii

23 August 2011. Bhadrakali village, Bijapur. A cab from Raipur to Bhopalpatnam, then a bike, and finally a boat across the river Chintavagu to reach a forest bordering Andhra Pradesh that saw the killings of ten policemen and a villager in a Maoist ambush on 19 August. The corpses lay in the rain and mud for eighteen hours because the police did not arrive to retrieve the bodies due to the fear of another ambush. Eventually, an old villager who had lost his son in the attack came the next morning with a bullock cart and carried back the bodies of his son and the others.

But this is the tale of a man who runs a small shop in Bhopalpatnam. Around fifty years of age, he presented himself as a police informer, took me to the Bhopalpatnam police station and introduced me to the policemen. The next day, however, the tone of his voice suddenly changed. His distrust, bordering on hatred, of those who wore the khaki uniform surfaced. He now seemed to be a local who had been tortured and forced by the police to become an informer.

No. His voice, like his gaze, was double-edged. At the police station, he was their close confidant and hated Naxals because 'they were against development', but when he took me to the jungle using a secret route, his heart began bleeding for his 'Naxal brothers'. His sympathies took a turn and he now seemed to be an informer for the Naxals.

He was not the sole representative of this tribe. An informer or a spy has obvious bonds with both camps. He is deeply embedded in both trenches, but his emotional and ideological affinity is certain. A native of one of the two camps, he betrays the other. But a distinct community has taken birth in Bastar that is loyal to neither, that stings both. One man with two tongues. A police attack on the Naxals or a Naxal ambush on the police is often a consequence of his tip-offs. Danger, thus, is two-fold for him. A confidant of two camps, he walks a tightrope, he thrives and pirouettes on a dagger's edge. Is he greedy? Cunning? Or just a reckless adventurer?

Caught between two enemies, Bastar adivasis know that they are often the only casualty of this war. Both sides forcefully extract information from them. The only way they can save their skin is by weaving tales of treachery.

The chiefs of the Red and Khaki brigades rarely want to acknowledge that their lives and deaths are often contingent upon this non-fighting adivasi. Few are aware that the cultural topography of an entire tribe has mutated in Bastar.

* * *

That was my first trip to Bastar, two days after I had arrived in Chhattisgarh. Seven years on, as I flip through my notes and prepare the final draft of *The Death Script*, I realize that in my very first encounter with the jungle I had already perceived one of its colossal truths – treachery has become an existential requirement for the adivasi.*

---

* The next entry in my diary:

> *26 August 2011*. Returning from Bijapur after reporting on a devastating Naxal attack the day before yesterday, I watched Bergman's *The Magic Flute* on my laptop in the cab. The actors performed Mozart's opera onstage. The screen only showed the audience's faces and their changing expressions for the first ten minutes. The imagery of Agyeya's poem 'Asadhya Veena' (The Invincible Instrument) flashed before me.

Years later, reading Michael Steen's book on the world's great operas, I learnt with surprise that the opera I had seen on my way back after learning about the double-faced character of the state–Maoist battle has a curious role reversal in the middle of the script. In the first half, evil appears to be personified in the high priest Sarastro, from whom the Queen of the Night wishes to rescue her daughter. In the second half, Sarastro comes to embody all that is good, whereas the Queen of the Night represents dark forces.

delusion / i

A morning in Balangi village, tucked away in a corner of Surguja district. A young woman, wearing a gold-plated watch, is grinding spices on a stone slab in a hut. This village was not on my itinerary. Flipping through the old files at the Balrampur police station, over 100 kilometres from here, one sentence caught my attention – *A Naxal commander killed by his comrades over the distribution of looted money.*

Naxals killing each other over a loot?

Such tussles, the Balrampur police said, are routine among the Naxals of Surguja. The residents of Balangi confirmed that Rengha Yadav, a Naxal commander, was running an extortion racket in the area. The thirty-five-year-old man had brought some two dozen youths from Jharkhand, had turned them into 'Naxals' and had been 'giving them training of Naxalism'. They lived in forests. A few months ago, they landed a big catch of six lakh rupees. He didn't give them their share and was consequently killed in June 2011.

Shanti, twenty-two, remembers her husband this morning in the courtyard of a hut, across from a well and a corn field. She is now dependent on her husband's poor agrarian family. The slender woman grinds spices on a stone slab, fries vegetables on an earthen stove, roasts corn. Amid the raindrops echoing through the courtyard, the gold-plated watch clinks against her colourful bangles. I've never seen a village woman wearing a watch here, and cannot recall any woman who wore one while grinding on a stone slab.

'He gifted it to you?'

'What?'

'He gave you the watch as a gift?'

Her eyes carry a look of surprise.

'He must have gifted it to you, that's why you wear it while working...'

'So? I am his wife. He brought me home after marriage. If I don't wear his gifts, who will?'

She was the second wife of the commander, the first was her elder sister. The in-charge of the nearest police station had said, and Shanti also told me, that the elder one only gave birth to girls, that's why he had married the younger sister. Shanti gave birth to two children in four years. The commander, she quietly added, had always liked her. In the police register, her name is recorded as the wife of the deceased. The elder sister lives in a hut outside the village. Shanti runs the marital home.

Closing the police register, the station in-charge had whispered, 'We were not surprised when he expelled his wife and married a girl fourteen years younger than him. You will find out when you see her.'

She tells me about her husband's life, moves from the stone slab to the stove. Her nephews and brothers-in-law, all adolescents, hover around her. They bring her corncobs, she roasts them over the fire.

'Once, a local moneylender implicated him in a false case and got him thrashed by the police. That's why he became a Naxal ... He lived in forests, visited home once every few months ... He also went to jail a couple of times, remained at home for a while after the release, but then became a Naxal.'

'Became a Naxal? How does that happen?'

'It happens.'

'Why did he rob people?'

'So? How would he have worked otherwise, guarded the forest?'

'Forest?'

'Yes, he guarded the forest.'

She holds out a roasted corncob to me. It's still drizzling. Across the courtyard, a man, seemingly her father-in-law, is weaving ropes with a wooden instrument.

'How will you manage in the future? You are so young, you have two children…'

Again, she doesn't seem to understand the question.

'So?'

She continues to nonchalantly nibble at the corn, then asks her nephews to pluck a few more corncobs from the field. The boys surround her, narrate tales of their uncle as if he was a wrestler or an archer who had demonstrated his skill in village fairs. For the boys, a Naxal is someone who covers his face with a scarf, brandishes an illegally procured twelve-bore gun, bullies people, kills a few policemen.

She is now on her fifth corncob. Her little daughter, nibbling at a guava, walks towards her. Her six-month-old son, too.

'Babu … babu…' She lifts the boy on to her lap.

The previous night, I had stayed at the Raghunath Nagar forest rest house, a little distance from the village. There was no electricity. The areas beyond Wadrafnagar had no power for the last two days. In such darkness, a wispy drizzle, so ethereal that it would escape notice unless one heard it falling on the leaves. A frog that had strayed into the rest house courtyard was croaking as if it was his last night. Its neck swelled as it croaked without letting up … As it halted to take a breath, its neck would deflate a bit, and then swell again. A cow tethered to a peg stood quietly under the rain. Her head bent towards the earth, not even the slightest twitch in her body. At first, I thought that she was motionless because she was tethered. But then I felt that she would stand like a statue anyway, getting drenched in the rain. Raindrops would fall over her body and trickle down quietly.

Fifteen days in this state. Almost every night on a new and alien bed, five nights in a moving car…

(3 September 2011. Surguja.)

displacement / iii

It's my eighth day in Sukma. We arrived here hours after the abduction. From all over the country. From Raipur, and as far as Odisha, Delhi and Andhra Pradesh. Around fifty journalists and camerapersons. There is little lodging space in this pocket-sized town, so we have all 'adjusted' in the guesthouse of the Public Works Department and the newly constructed Officers' Club. A couple of dhabas and a Rajasthani Bhojanalaya are the only eateries. Broadcasting vans of TV channels are anchored at the collector's residence. Every ten minutes, reporters regurgitate breaking news before the camera: the collector was spotted near the Andhra Pradesh border; 2,000 Naxals have surrounded the collector; an unmanned aerial vehicle pierced through the impregnable forest and located his coordinates. Some journalists laugh away the screaming news. We are aware of our frauds.

Carved out of Dantewada this January, Sukma is among the most densely forested districts of India. Its Konta tehsil has some of the thickest woods in a single administrative unit in the country. 2,200 square kilometres of Dandakaranya's wilderness lie here. More than the combined area of Bombay and Delhi. Konta made Dantewada notorious for Naxal violence. The blood of seventy-five Central Reserve Police Force personnel and one Chhattisgarh policeman was shed in Tadmetla in April 2010 – the most devastating Naxal attack in India, the highest casualties in a single day. The attack on the Errabore relief camp, with over two dozen people burnt alive. A passenger bus burnt to ashes in Chingawaram, with nearly thirty lives gone. Salwa Judum flourished in Konta – a constitutional government handed weapons to its citizenry and pushed them into its fight against the Naxals. It displaced residents of the forest and made them the enemy of their kin. The number of deaths per square kilometre is, perhaps, the highest in Konta. Bordering Andhra Pradesh and Odisha, 'Killing Capital Konta' now witnesses the abduction of the collector of Sukma.

We, the journalists, are stuck in the forest. A few enthusiasts have traversed Dandakaranya on motorbike. I spent two nights inside, scoured the dense forests. I could not trace the collector, but managed to meet the insurgents who had abducted him. They brandished AK-47s and asked, 'Did we have any other option?'

The Red soldiers are apathetic about the young and sensitive bureaucrat, Alex Paul Menon, who admires Che Guevara and has *The Motorcycle Diaries* on his bookshelf. He is also an asthma patient. His wife carries their baby within her. She keeps asking the journalists about her husband.

For many of us, this was our first assignment reporting an abduction. We struggled to stave off a sense of adventure. In the initial days, an unspeakable excitement followed us. It's the eighth day today. We are now in the grip of ennui. Nothing is moving. The news cycle is repeating itself: talks going on between the government and the Maoist negotiators in Raipur; medicines for the collector sent to the forest; a rally held in Sukma demanding his release.

'If he is not released soon, let's go back.'

This is the refrain of a lot of journalists. Many have already been replaced by another reporter sent by their publications. It is not physical fatigue – the mind has been made captive.

That's the tragedy of reporting. Plough a barren land daily, rewrite the same incident in new words. Invoke the ghosts of dying news to make it alive again for a while, and convert it into a seemingly fresh report. Find your byline with this corpse every morning. The unbearable depreciation of your voice. Have we also been abducted? Kites severed from their threads, suspended in the sky of Sukma.

'I have seen innumerable dead bodies in the last ten years ... charred bodies, limbs amputated, faces distorted ... You guys are new, so you attach great significance to a collector's abduction. Is there any account of the people who have gone missing in the jungle? How would it affect anyone if one more disappears?' a journalist from Dantewada, Suresh Mahapatra, asks. 'Earlier, I would rush to the spot. Now the news of an incident reaches me on the phone, and that is enough for me to draw its image.'

The detachment in his voice is scary. Are we sinking into the marshland this jungle has become? Should we run away before the blazing April sun dries up our veins?

The Maoists abducted the collector of the neighbouring Malkangiri district of Odisha last year. They released him after nine days. The ninth day is hours away, but the forest of Sukma offers no hope. There are few homes in the villages of Bastar that have not seen a killing, or a relative joining either the insurgents or the police in the last thirty years. The insurgents have announced that they will treat the collector as a prisoner of war. Forest dwellers are not so privileged. Maoists often kill them after taking them hostage. The Indian state still doesn't call it a war, but a mere conflict. Let them indulge in the politics of lexicography. It *is* a war.

Along with the collector, many of us are also waiting for our release from this wilderness, aware of the tormenting possibility that after returning to the comfort of our cities we will quietly bury the memory of these April nights – sunburnt skin, thirst and mosquitoes, anti-landmine vehicles, soldiers armed with mortars and grenade launchers. We will eventually return to the city, but the bullets will continue to find new targets in the jungle of Sukma.

(28 April 2012. Sukma.)

death / ii

On the afternoon of 30 June 2012, fifteen corpses, bloated, darkened and stiffened, resembling organisms that have undergone an awful taxidermy, are waiting to be cremated in the three neighbouring villages of Kottaguda, Sarkeguda and Rajpenta in Bijapur district. Some are covered with a fresh white cloth, others have to make do with an old green sari as their shroud. A dholak is kept beside one corpse. Nineteen people were killed two nights ago, fifteen of them will be cremated this evening. The villagers are searching for logs. It is drizzling, making it difficult to find dry wood.

The state has termed it the 'biggest Maoist encounter' in Chhattisgarh. Among those killed, said Union Home Minister P. Chidambaram, were three important Maoists – Mahesh, Nagesh and Somulu. But there is no Mahesh among the deceased. There are two Nageshes, and one Ramvilas.

Sandip Irpa, one of the survivors, says, 'The three of us from Kottaguda village made our first trip outside the state this January. Our school had taken us to Visakhapatnam. We were the first from the south of the Talperu river to make such a journey – Kaka Nagesh who was fondly called Rahul, Madkam Ramvilas, and I. We studied in class ten in a residential government school adjoining the Basaguda police station. We saw the sea for the first time in Visakhapatnam. You ask any teacher – they were very good at studies, among the brightest in our school. Always got first division. We were visiting the village during our vacations. The villagers had assembled for the festival of Beej Pundum that night. I was also required to be in the gathering, but I had gone to sleep early ... so I was saved. I was well behind them in studies ... I still cannot believe that my friends are no longer alive.'

Their school notebooks confirm what the villagers say about the two boys, particularly Ramvilas's command over English. The second page of his Sanskrit notebook has a marvellous sentence about the language: 'Thee, thou, thy and thine are not used in modern English. These words can be used in poems, or for god.' How did this village boy learn that poetry had a different language? Why did he write this sentence about English in his Sanskrit notebook? If the sentence was in his English textbook or dictated by the English teacher in class, wouldn't it be in his English notebook? His classmates are unaware of this sentence. How did it reach him? Did he write poems? The virginal poems of one's early teens? His other notebooks are silent about this. His parents know nothing either. Is there anything elsewhere? Any diary or journal? But there is nothing to be found. That lone sentence remains suspended in the sky of death.

Another notebook in his schoolbag has a 'no objection certificate' that he had written on behalf of his mother before leaving for Visakhapatnam: 'I do not have any objection in sending my son. The school will not be responsible for any untoward incident during the journey.' His sister Ratna has carefully kept his books and notebooks.

And Kaka Nagesh? The boy of fifteen was good at maths. His expertise in the subject brought about his death. The villagers often asked him to do their accounts and calculations. He had been especially called for the Beej Pundum assembly on the night of the killings to calculate the possible expenditure the local festival would entail.

Another Nagesh – Madkam Nagesh – was a dholak player of thirty-two years who visited nearby villages to play the dholak on various occasions. He had two little children, his wife Shammi was pregnant with a third. 'Do you know of any Naxal who plays the dholak? If he were a Naxal, would he have played the dholak at weddings?' his sister Sushila asks.

There is no Irpa Somulu in the villages. The man whom the police have called Irpa Somulu, villagers say, is a thirty-five-year-old man named Irpa Dinesh, who is survived by his wife Janaki and three children. The police didn't hand over his body to the villagers, but buried it in the backyard of the Basaguda police station.

But not every corpse receives a quiet burial in police stations, especially bodies that have dagger wounds. Kaka Nagesh's aunt Kamala uncovers the wound on her dead nephew's chest and screams: 'First they fired at him, then they struck him with axes ... Please take this photograph.'

Their relatives wail and bellow, show their naked bodies. They want photographs to be taken as evidence. And since the photographs can't be taken because you are petrified by the sight of the dead, and also find it inhuman to store pictures of naked corpses on your laptop for the sake of what they call evidence – because can there be bigger evidence than what your eye has already recorded? – the state refutes your news reports, citing absence of proof. 'We conducted,' the state asserts, 'a proper autopsy of the deceased, the autopsy was videotaped too. None of the bodies had a dagger wound, everyone died of bullet injuries.' The state also refuses to show the video or make it public.

But you obtain the video within forty-eight hours, and the video doesn't lie. The bodies are indeed pierced by dagger-like instruments. The video also shows that the post-mortem was conducted inside the Basaguda police station. Sixteen corpses lying on the ground, covered by khaki tarpaulin. Many policemen surrounding them. A villager lifts the tarpaulin to uncover the bodies smeared with fresh blood. One by one, all the corpses will be upturned. Some have large exit wounds – the bullet of a rifle makes a small ring-like hole as it enters the body, but it tears apart the innards and skin as it comes out. Several bodies have dagger wounds, but the government doctor records only the bullet wounds in his official report.

The hope of salvation after death, however irrational, may surface if one dies of old age, or of diseases like malaria and cancer, or in an accident. That is, if something still survives after death. Funeral rites, the immersion of ashes in a holy river and the rituals of paying homage to the departed are the offspring of this hope. But being killed by the blow of an axe shatters all hopes. When a body is cut into pieces, its innards mingling with the mud, the Garuda Purana brings no consolation. But does the Garuda Purana ever offer any solace to those who have been left behind?

The living dies in the city. The corpse awaits its death in the jungle.*

The sea left Kaka Nagesh and Ramvilas amazed. The life of a mariner instantly fascinated them. Their only memory of a water body was the

---

* A year later, in May 2013, the neighbouring village of Ehadsameta in Bijapur saw a near repeat of the Sarkeguda killings when eight villagers were killed after the CRPF opened fire at a Beej Pundum gathering. (This is described in detail later in the book.)

The ghosts of Sarkeguda and Ehadsameta soon returned when, citing unprovoked firing by the 'new [CRPF] troops' that caused the killings of tribals in his district and sullied the 'public image' of the police, the Bijapur police superintendent Prashant Agarwal shot down a 'massive anti-Naxal operation' planned by the CRPF in February 2014. The CRPF men had already left their camps for a forty-day operation involving 3,000 troops across Bastar when the state police asked them to cancel it at the last moment. The CRPF, as per the rules, cannot take up any operation on its own and needs prior approval from the state police. On 8 February, Agarwal wrote to his bosses in the state, cautioning against military adventurism and termed the CRPF's plan 'very risky'.

Both the killings were probed by a retired high-court judge. The court hearing took place at Jagdalpur – a daylong journey of over 200 kilometres from the villages, which made it very difficult for the witnesses to depose. And after more than seven years, his report on the June 2012 Sarkeguda killings came out in December 2019. It ratified my investigation and noted that innocent adivasis were indeed killed in the CRPF firing, several wounds were not by bullets, confirming my observation that it was not an encounter as the security forces had killed them with daggers. The judge submitted the Ehadsameta report in September 2021 and confirmed my findings that those who were killed were adivasis, not Naxals. The victims' relatives now await the prosecution of the CRPF men.

river Talperu in their village. A languid forest spreads out on both sides of the river. The seventeen-kilometre path from Basaguda to Avapalli flaps like a butterfly in the rains. It connects the river to a highway. The path is dotted by CRPF camps, ruins of vehicles blown up by landmines, and memorials for killed soldiers, but the mahua forest continues to bloom. Until 2006, the villages to the south of the Talperu were among the most prosperous ones in Bastar. Forest produce, like tendu patta and chironji, was harvested in good quantities. As villagers migrated during the Salwa Judum years, the Talperu became the 'Line of Control'. The police on this side, the Maoists on the other. Bullets on both sides. The area became a battlefield. Around 2009, some villagers returned home. A school and a ration shop also came up near the police station as a symbol of hope. Rahul and Ramvilas were the offspring of this hope. So was Kaka Sarita, a girl of twenty, the first girl in the area to clear her class-twelve exams. She took admission in BSc (Nursing) in Jagdalpur. She was in her hostel when she learnt that her elder brother Kaka Samaiyya was among the villagers killed on 28 June.

It is raining. The rains of Bastar are intoxicating. Kids with feet of koels hop over the river's surface. Uniformed soldiers deployed on the bridge steal moments from their sentry duty to watch the children play in the water. The bridge links Basaguda to Sarkeguda. Soldiers, a river, a bridge and the jungle. Several movies come to mind. The Talperu weaves a language of myth and dream. The Bridge on the River Talperu. Around 250 troopers crossed this bridge on the night of 28 June and moved towards Silger village where, according to their information, Maoists from Odisha were holding out. They unexpectedly came upon a Beej Pundum gathering, and the frightened soldiers, who had been moving in the dark in anticipation of a massive face-off with the Maoists, couldn't think of anything else and took the villagers to be the insurgents. The night was soon devoured by bullets and daggers.

Pyres smoulder on the evening of 30 June. A bitter humidity pervades the jungle. It will rain heavily tomorrow and the day after.

The embers will be doused. Not a single mark will remain on the soil. At the site of the killings, a dead pig is rotting, getting drenched in the rain. One bullet hit its jaw, two hit its back. Its corpse has entry wounds, but no exit wounds. The brass is still embedded in its body. Is it also a Naxal? The spraying bullets and the deafening screams of that night are imprinted on its half-open eyes. Its eyes, the final witnesses of that night. The CRPF lugged back all the bodies after the killings but left this behind. Perhaps it isn't a Naxal, then. At least there is someone who isn't a Naxal.

The villagers have returned to their homes, leaving the pyres burning. One task is still incomplete. In some adivasi communities, it is believed that a dead man takes two distinct forms – a ghost and a soul. Both of them visit their homes and are required to be addressed differently by the relatives. The village priest draws some figures on the earth. The villagers have brought back a handful of the blood-smeared soil, which they now place before him. They surround him. He is chanting mantras to ward off evil. The ritual will continue late into the night. The soil will be deposited along with the ashes of the dead. It will exorcize their ghosts. The jungle will be purified and consecrated once again.

death script / iii

Darbha is the site of the deadliest-ever Maoist attack on a political party – one that killed twenty-seven people, including the state Congress president Nand Kumar Patel and the adivasi leader Mahendra Karma. In the Valmiki Ramayana, the first sight that catches Rama's eye as he enters Dandakaranya with Sita and Lakshmana during his exile is a marvellous landscape covered with darbha, considered the most sacred grass in Vedic literature. Millennia later, the Ramayana's Dandakaranya, the seat of revered sages, has transformed into a treacherous battlefield, as the sacred grass now nourishes the mightiest insurgency of independent India.

Sita, it seems, had anticipated the turmoil when she gave Rama a lecture on kshatriya dharma, that is, a warrior's ethics, soon after they entered the wilderness. A rare instance in the epic when Sita advises her husband to be cautious. He has decided to eliminate the demons living there, but Sita warns him that his use of force may damage the forest and his own reputation. Of the three grave evils, she notes, two – 'telling lies' and 'lusting after another man's wife' – are absent in him. However, he should be particularly careful about the third, 'cruelty without a justified cause'. Sita says, 'The third weakness which men succumb to because of their passions, the inflicting of violence and cruelty upon other beings without reason or enmity, that weakness appears to be present in you now' – a clear warning against collateral damage. She fears that in his fight against the demons, Rama may inflict injury on innocent beings living in the forest. She goes on to say, 'Our journey into the Dandaka forest makes me anxious and I am not comfortable … Now that you are here with your brother and both of you are armed, you shall see many forest creatures. Inevitably, you will be tempted to use your arrows.'

Sita is outlining the rules of war – if it's not just, if it hurts innocents, it is evil.

She doesn't stop here, and goes on to talk about how making weapons one's constant companion may destroy a person. She tells Rama the tale of a sage who was once given a mighty sword for safekeeping by Indra. The sage began to carry the sword wherever he went, and soon came a time when he 'even took it with him when he wandered through the forest searching for roots and fruits'. The 'proximity to a weapon' soon turned his mind to cruelty. 'He began to relish brutality and he fell into unrighteous ways. Eventually, that holy man went to hell …' Warning Rama against such an association with weapons, Sita says: 'May it never happen that you attack the rakshasas of the forest without reason, simply because you carry a weapon. I cannot bear the thought of innocents being killed, O hero!'

She, in other words, says that even those whom the state considers its enemy have the right to a dignified life, and he cannot harm them or intrude upon their forests unless they commit an offence. Located in an ancient text, Sita articulates a wisdom that could be the foundational feature of any modern Constitution. Cautioning him that 'the mind is perverted by extreme proximity to weapons,' she advises him to 'learn to respect the code of behaviour of the world we now inhabit' and to 'enjoy the beauties of the forest with a pure mind'.

In effect, just when Rama is about to begin his greatest adventure, Sita questions the entire campaign by listing the grave faults inherent in it. Rama, of course, goes ahead, arguing that he has already promised the sages that he would clear the forest: 'I could more easily give up my life or renounce you or Lakshmana than break a promise, especially one that I have made to brahmins! It is my duty to protect holy men under any circumstances.' A kshatriya's promise overruled sane advice. But by then, Sita had already predicted the future of Dandakaranya.*

---

* I am reminded of the Diwali of 2016, which I spent in Ayodhya on a reporting assignment. I was surprised to find that the festival was bereft of the lights one associates with it in other parts of northern India. Diwali in Ayodhya, locals said, has often been 'flavourless'. Compared to the other famous temple cities like Mathura and Kashi, Ayodhya looked desolate and melancholic.

They called it the curse of Sita. 'When Sita was wrongfully accused and banished from Ayodhya on account of a washerman, the inhabitants of this city were cursed that they would never prosper. Ayodhya carries the burden of that curse,' said Shubhangie Mishra, one of the youngest members of Ayodhya's erstwhile royal family. Mahant Satyendra Das, the head priest of the makeshift Rama temple, agreed. 'If you cause injustice to a true saint, even if she doesn't say anything, you will inevitably be affected ... Santan ki kshama shaap se bhaari (a sage's forgiveness is more severe than her curse). Ayodhya has been in ruins ever since,' he said, insisting that the curse is felt periodically.

The violent Ram temple movement was, perhaps, one of its manifestations. Ayodhya may have forgotten that, long ago, Sita had warned against the use of force on innocents ...

delusion / ii

'Let's meet at leisure ... This court is not the best place to chat.'

'Are you free in the evening?'

'Around nine?'

'That late?'

'It's fine ... Come to my office.'

It is September 2011. She is investigating the famous Essar case. The Dantewada police have accused the Essar Group, a company owned by one of India's richest people, of giving protection money to the Maoists. It has caused quite a stir within India Inc. Dantewada has India's richest iron ore mines. Essar has built a mammoth plant right under the watch of the Maoists who spare no opportunity to spew hatred against private companies, especially those who are 'looting the mineral wealth of Bastar'.*

The company has laid an underground pipeline to carry iron ore fines or slurry from Dantewada to the nearest port of Visakhapatnam. Over 270 kilometres long, it is among the world's longest such conduits. A pipeline that passes through the Maoist heartland of India. The company, the Dantewada police claim, has paid the Maoists to secure the safe operation of the pipeline, and Pawan Dubey, the

---

* The water resources minister of the Chhattisgarh government, Ramvichar Netam, informed the state assembly on 23 March 2012 about the illegalities associated with Essar's operations. The company had overdrawn 28.5 lakh cubic metres of water without permission from a natural stream near Kirandul, Dantewada, between October 2006 and October 2011.

chairman of a nondescript Bastar-based NGO Jai Johar Seva Sansthan, is their middleman.*

Even before I met Deputy Superintendent of Police Pratibha Pandey in the Dantewada court, her reputation as a tough cop had reached me. She had gathered crucial leads about the case. She would interrogate the accused in the police station through the night. With such an image in mind, I was startled to find a petite woman in her early twenties entering the court complex, surrounded by security personnel carrying AK-47 rifles.

An even bigger surprise awaited me in her office. As I entered her cabin, I found a man sitting across from her at the table. He wore a decent shirt and trousers and looked like a corporate executive. I knew that she was interrogating several Essar officials. For some inexplicable reason, I felt that he was one of them – the general manager of Essar, to be precise. I don't know why I thought so – I had never met him, and had only talked to him briefly over the phone once. But the possibility that this was the same person made me slightly uncomfortable. Another reason for my discomfort was that I had looked forward to having a relaxed conversation about the case with Pratibha, but that wouldn't be possible in his presence.

'Please have a seat ... You were saying something in the court?'

---

* On 17 January 2011, Dubey wrote to the Ruias, the owners of the Essar Group, submitting a proposal to manage the company's activities under the corporate social responsibility fund in Bastar, for which he sought one crore rupees. Three days later, Malay Mukherjee, the CEO of Essar Steel Business Group, sent an email to Essar Steel India CEO Dilip Oommen asking him to release the money immediately to the NGO as 'it has become essential to maintain the operation of Kirandul pipeline ... [that] such activities be undertaken.' On 21 January, Dubey again wrote to the Ruias, reminding them of a meeting in Mumbai and saying, 'Rakam dene ka kasht karein (please provide the amount).' A day later, one crore rupees reached Jai Johar Seva Sansthan's bank account.

I signalled towards the man on the chair next to me. She instantly understood my hesitation and initiated a conversation about the case, which meant that I need not worry about him. We gradually opened up. She spoke about the Naxal threat, the perpetual fear the police were living under – a slight slip and they would be butchered. We also talked about the interrogation of the Essar general manager, whom I had earlier thought to be the man next to me. Pratibha spoke in detail about the investigation, what the police had extracted from him and what still remained. The recoveries and seizures, and the documents the police were still searching for. She also spoke about herself. She had recently joined the police force, and this was her first case. She was determined to ensure conviction and punishment. She betrayed little trace of being a tough cop. Her face and voice seemed very familiar, like that of a girl from my neighbourhood.

A chart of the crime data under the jurisdiction of the police station hung on the wall next to a big map of Dantewada that had several marks in red and green upon it, indicating the deployment of the police and the CRPF in Naxal areas. Pratibha's fingers often toyed with the pen, sometimes she tapped the glass table-top with it. I almost forgot that a stranger was sitting next to me. Whenever the conversation touched upon a confidential issue, I would feel a bit uneasy about his presence, but I would soon shrug it off – if she, the investigating officer, was not concerned, why should I be? I also thought that he could be a policeman who was visiting from another city to assist with the case.

After half an hour, her peon knocked at the door. Somebody had sent for her. 'You stay here, I'll be back soon.' Now only I and the man were in the office. His gaze was pointed downwards, probing his shoe's edge. I suddenly noticed a Blackberry on the table. This was 2011. Almost all of us used Nokia phones. Who could afford a Blackberry in Dantewada? The worm twisted inside me once more. Was he indeed the general manager? I had his number stored in my phone. Slyly, I dialled it. The Blackberry began vibrating.

Police officers employ many methods to put psychological pressure on the accused, but mostly those policemen who are hardened after long stints in the field. Her short hair loosely tied with a rubber band, this young woman had humiliated a senior executive for thirty minutes, while I, absolutely unaware, had joined her in cursing the man sitting next to me. And this was her first case!

The transformation of a young woman, all of sixty-two inches tall, whose voice carries the fragility of dewdrops, into the protagonist of a noir movie is perhaps possible only in a Bastar police station.

death / iii

They were my children, I named them all: Sukhini, Sukta, Surila, Bhootni, Ladgudni. As I cleared the class-five exam, I told my parents – no more school, I will play with my kids along the river Kanhar. The hills of Chunchuna and a vast forest surround our hut.

I don't exist now. The five of them stare at my younger sister. She is unsure about her elder sister's kids becoming hers. This season sees incessant rains. Our thatched hut is totally drenched. They are hungry. My sister picks up a broken umbrella lying near a cot, and takes them out to graze near the Kanhar that has now become my permanent abode.

All my belongings – my old clothes, broken toys, school notebooks – have been buried along with me. Just an old photograph of mine remains with Ma and Baba. I am wearing my school uniform, a blue tunic. It was taken several years ago at a village fair, or perhaps elsewhere, I cannot recall.

Many people from distant places visit our home these days. Baba goes inside the hut, takes that faded photograph, which has been neatly placed between the pages of our ration card, out of a tin box and shows it to them. They ask Baba to hold it in his hand, to place it near his chest, and look straight into the camera. Then they click a photograph of my photograph.

'First they killed her, then they said she was a Naxalite, now they call her a whore,' Baba tells everybody. He once stood five and a half feet tall. Now he is losing an inch every year. Ma has always lived like a crumpled and frayed sack of rice whose threads could come apart at any time. The mud walls of our hut had a red stamp that has turned pink in rains. The huts in my village have stamps of several colours, colours allotted as per their ration cards. Red is for the poorest families. I could never understand what free rice had to do with the colour of blood.

The hut next to mine is 500 steps away. Our village is yet to get electricity. Two months ago, around four kilometres away in Chando, two police bullets hit me – one in the chest, the other below the waist. A police team had come out to confront a 'platoon of thirty-five Naxals', but their bullets found only me in the 'encounter' which, they say, took place in the dark. To eliminate thirty-five Naxals, some thirty policemen fired only three bullets, two of which entered my body. I cannot recall the time, but they say it was 3 a.m.

My body and clothes, the doctor who dissected me recorded, have the fresh marks of men. But he also wrote a lot more about me on government paper.

I cannot say any more. Baba becomes nervous when he hears. 'It's good,' Ma says, 'that you found a home beneath the ground. We should also have accompanied you.' But my children, the goats? They need somebody. They sniff at the earth under which I lie. My sister will take them out now. But how long can she? She's also a resident of the forest…

(1 September 2011. Karcha village, Surguja.)

death script / iv

Death Reporter. Nine months. Can a man's link with a colossal truth of life change so suddenly and drastically?

You left Delhi one dark and rainy morning last August. A few books, a laptop and your editor's advice: *No report is greater than life.* Some 275 nights since then. Nearly half of these spent in a car, or in the forests of Bastar and Surguja. You became friends with a variety of rifles, witnessed the might of the bullet. Empty cartridges scattered at ambush sites. The vapours of freshly spilled blood rising from the earth. Video clippings of corpses being sliced open – an act known as a post-mortem – flash on your Nokia 5130. A doctor cuts open a chest, inserts his gloved hand, rummages through the innards and fishes out a bullet. This is not a hospital. The corpse is sliced up in front of relatives and neighbours.

Nine months of death. You can count the deaths of your relatives and acquaintances on the fingers of your hands. Just one of these occurred before you, survives in your memory. In the last nine months, some sixty corpses have already been recorded on your laptop, with many of whom your conversation began after their deaths. Not the conversation that a journalist has in a murder investigation, rather an affinity that evolves as one delves deep into the past of the deceased. As you unravel a killing, you realize that you are perhaps kin to the dead, a long-lost cousin who has now arrived to invoke his ghost.

The pasts of the deceased explode in your consciousness. A young police officer who placed a revolver on his forehead and – bang. He was so calm, his wife said, when she had spoken to him a few hours before his death. The previous night, out for a stroll in the park, the couple had drawn up the guest list and menu for their son's upcoming birthday party. He had called her from office in the morning, and when she told him she had cooked rajma, his favourite dish, he had said: 'Don't send the tiffin, then. I will come home for lunch.'

His body arrived minutes later.

He had got himself transferred from Raigarh just three months ago, to live with his wife who was posted in Bilaspur. What had tormented him before he pressed the trigger?

In a similar moment, someone remarked that there should be a designation like Death Reporter. Death Bureau Chief. Death Copy Editor. Death News Editor. Death Editor-in-Chief.

A mere number in a news report, death becomes your companion in the pages of your diary. A person may live unnoticed, but a corpse unveils itself in myriads of forms and plays bewitching games with the spectator.

Among all the corpses, one has hovered over you like a carrion bird, pecking at your flesh. Not even the corpse – the post-mortem report with the doctor's comment: *Having dilated vagina. Habitual about sexual intercourse.*

Only seven words.

A rare post-mortem report that had a doctor first emphasize the 'sexual behaviour' of a girl, and then give 'evidence' for it. The girl belonged to the poverty-stricken Oraon adivasi community. She was often seen playing with her five goats in a village in northern Chhattisgarh. One night in July 2011, around forty-five days before your arrival in the province, she was killed by police bullets. When you reached her village Karcha, the residents of neighbouring villages took an oath upon the forest and said, 'She was not a Naxal. It was a rape and murder.'

The home minister of the province, Nanki Ram Kanwar, also an adivasi, makes an 'on-record' statement: 'Doesn't the post-mortem report say that she was habitual? If so many policemen had done something to her, wouldn't there be swelling? Where was she returning from at 3 a.m.?'

The duty of a doctor who conducts a post-mortem is merely to record the nature and cause of injuries and their relation to death. At the bottom of the injury column, the seven words were added with an asterisk, ostensibly inserted as an afterthought. The report admits to the tearing of the uterus. The adivasi doctor quietly discloses that the entire post-mortem was videotaped, and that he can provide a CD.

Did all of this actually take place?

The report also says she was only fifteen years old.

1 September 2011. It is raining, but the five of them stand quietly in a pen near a hut with a pink stamp. Five kids, their mother has gone out for work, asking them to stay well-behaved in her absence and not bother anybody. She seems to be working late. They are anxious, but since their mother has left them by themselves for the first time, they want to honour her absence. They stand in silence beneath the dripping sky. What one often believes to be one's life is perhaps a quiet drizzle of death.

You come to the pen and join them under the rain. It's your fifteenth day in the forest and the thirteenth death.

This is just the beginning. You cannot even anticipate that, in the coming months, this rain will burn down the sparrows nesting inside you and stamp you with their charred feathers. Not the stamp the state embosses on the homes of its subjects as a perpetual reminder of their servitude, but the stamp death engraves on a human being to make him a permanent member of its tribe.

(17 May 2012. Dantewada.)

THREE

delusion / iii

16 February 2013. Chhota Kakler village, Bijapur. Morning, quarter past seven. How long will I remain captive in this desolate village with a few scattered huts? The cot they have given me, was anyone ever ferried on it to Bhopalpatnam? If someone was, there would also be a goat that was dragged along. Only one of the two would have survived – the man on the cot, or the goat. Or neither of them.

Plucking at the cot's twine, I look around. There is no goat, but some wild hens are hopping about. Who will survive today? The hens? Or me?

I was crossing this village yesterday when several young men blocked my way at around 4 p.m., suspecting me of being a police informer. I showed them my identity card, but it didn't convince them. I carry clippings of my newspaper reports just for occasions like these, but they couldn't understand them because they were in English.* Perhaps they wouldn't have understood Hindi either. Around ten men surrounded me, asked me to park my motorbike close by, inspected my bag which was tied to the bike. It had clothes, biscuits, medicines. Soon, many more villagers arrived. They had weapons like bows, axes and bharmaar or muzzle-loaded country-made guns (bhar+maar, meaning fill+shoot).

'You can ask your seniors, they know me.' I gave them the names of Naxal leaders I had met earlier. But they operated in other zones of Bastar, and the residents of this area were not aware of them.

---

* The English newspaper has an amusing place in Naxal lore. In the 1970s, a Naxalite fled from a guerrilla zone, came to Calcutta and began working at a small hotel. The unassuming man escaped everyone's gaze until someone found him reading an English newspaper a customer had left behind. A low-level hotel employee reading an English newspaper was enough to raise suspicion. The Intelligence Department was alerted, and soon he was in jail.

Taken to be a police informer, I had been forced to stop in the wilderness earlier too, and on each occasion, after a safe escape, I had resolved to not let even the shadow of fear cloud my face if I found myself in a similar situation again. Yet, as on each of those previous occasions, even though I tried hard to conceal it, my voice was not free from nervous twitches.

They examined my bike. It didn't have a number plate. Would it make them suspicious? It's usually policemen who drive bikes without number plates in Bastar. Should I have used a bike with a number plate? Does this bike have any markings of the police? It was my fault. I should have carefully inspected it before leaving.

'Who are the Naxal leaders in this area nowadays?' I asked the villagers. 'Please give them my letter.' I wrote a letter telling them about myself, and attached my news clippings. They agreed to be my messengers, but I was required to stay in the village until I got the green signal from the people who mattered.

I was taken to a hut. Initially, they were rude and harsh, or perhaps I had imposed my fear upon them, but they became comfortable with me by late evening. Someone brought me a cot. 'Otherwise you'll say we made you sleep on the floor.'

The journey to this captivity had been long and winding, solely because of my foolhardiness. It began on the morning of the thirteenth, when I had started from Dantewada, scouring through the forest to reach Bijapur in the evening.* I meant to go further south towards Pamed. But I learnt in Bijapur that a major gathering of Maoists was

---

* Exactly a year later, on 13 February 2014, I started from Raipur for a three-week stay with the Maoists in Abujhmad. I was required to make a night halt in Kanker on the thirteenth, and left for Narayanpur on the afternoon of the fourteenth – Friday, Valentine's Day. But not before I had watched the 'first-day first-show' of the movie *Gunday* in Purwa Cinema Hall. Thirty minutes in, I wanted to leave. But the man at whose insistence I had come was enjoying it. Finally, I persuaded him to exit at the interval.

scheduled at Sandra along the Gadchiroli border. So I changed my plans, and left Bijapur on the morning of 14 February and drove all day to reach Farsegarh in the evening. But I was advised at Farsegarh that the bike might not go any further, that a thick wilderness lay between there and Sandra, that I wouldn't find even muddy paths. But who listens to such childish advice? There was still time before dark.

After riding the bike, which neighed and whined in turn, for several kilometres, I came across a river of sand tucked away in a small valley, a bald stream whose head had been tonsured in its childhood. The bike glided down the valley, but on the way up it was paralysed by the sand. First gear, full speed. But so steep and sandy was the slope that the bike didn't move an inch. At best, it would go up a yard before sliding down again.

It was winter, the month of February, but my shirt was dripping in no time. I cursed myself – when would I learn that the right vehicle for the forest is not the motorcycle, but the bicycle.

It was gradually turning dark. I decided to find shelter for the night. But someone might make away with the bike ... What would I tell the person from whom I had borrowed it? To guard the bike, I lay down under a nearby tree. With the fear of wild animals looming, it wasn't easy to sleep. Around two hours later, at 8.30 p.m., I finally admitted to myself that it had been epic foolishness on my part to spend the night here. At a place where there was no human life for miles, who would come to steal this cursed machine? Leaving the monster in the jungle, with my rucksack on my back, I set out in search of shelter.

Hopelessly lost in the wilderness, walking in the dark, I formulated two rules mandatory for travelling in Dandakaranya – one of which I broke the very next morning, thus landing myself in captivity.

First: Don't take a motorbike into a jungle which does not have any pathways, a wilderness that is criss-crossed by streams and hillocks, where boulders and monstrous roots of trees mark the earth. It's not about your bones breaking if the bike skids, or even the agony of pushing the bike through such terrain if it gets a flat tyre, as I have on many occasions. The worry is about the bike getting damaged beyond repair, in which case it will have to be abandoned in the forest, creating a new set of complications.

Second: Don't spend the night in the open. Walk for as many hours as you need to, but reach a shelter, whether it is a thatched hut or a ruined school building.

After losing and finding many a path for over two hours, I reached the government school in Farsegarh. The following morning, I came to the bald river with the school's watchman Manoj Mandavi and two students, and pulled the bike out with their help. I had taken the wrong path, Manoj told me. On our way back to the school he showed me the forested trail towards Sandra.

I should have returned then, this jungle was not for the bike. But what excitement would there be in life if the lessons of the night were not discarded the next morning?

I went to Sandra, but couldn't get access to the Maoist meeting. I am now awaiting my release in Chhota Kakler, a nearby village. There will be many people worrying about me. My friend, who is getting married in Raipur tomorrow. The Dantewada policeman whose bike I had borrowed, promising to return it within a day. And the caretaker of Dantewada's circuit house – my room has been locked for the last three days, the keys are with me, and my laptop is in there.

But the secure life of the city seems enervated and timid before the unanticipated perils of the forest. The forest a leaping tiger, the city a crawling earthworm.

Four nights, four different places – Dantewada, Bijapur, Farsegarh and Chhota Kakler. The last three were unexpected. The last two were decided just before night fell. When I reached the school in Farsegarh, Manoj was high on mahua, his eyes burning. Yet he had enough wits about him to say, when I showed him my identity card and sought shelter: 'I have one condition. You must have connections in Raipur. This school has a hundred children, but not a single bathroom. You will have to get a bathroom built here.' He spoke only about the bathroom. All the classes ran under a tin shed. The 'school' did not have any rooms.

Chhota Kakler is some twenty kilometres into the forest from Farsegarh, which has the last police station and CRPF post near Sandra. Sandra is a 'liberated zone' today, but T. Kantaiyya, a teacher at the Farsegarh school, says, 'Sandra was once like a city.' The government documents showed a forest rest house in Sandra. However, these are mere symbols of the British Raj and the Madhya Pradesh government. I found no rest house. The Chhattisgarh state has not reached here yet. It has been nearly two decades since the formation of Chhattisgarh, but the rusted government boards still say 'Madhya Pradesh'. The board of Indravati National Park near the neighbouring Sagmeta village says 'Madhya Pradesh Forest Department'.

'We'll go to distant cities in Andhra Pradesh, but we avoid the nearby areas of Chhattisgarh,' says Durgam Mallaya, a resident of Sagmeta. Such a distrust of their home state among people is rare. Mallaya is a Mahar, the same caste as B.R. Ambedkar, and among the few scheduled castes in this adivasi zone. He cannot recall when his ancestors came here from Maharashtra.

The young men of Chhota Kakler who made me stop are almost illiterate. Let alone the Mahatma Gandhi Rural Employment Guarantee scheme for unskilled labourers, even the bonus that the state government provides for plucking tendu patta has not reached the area. The arrival of the police with the Salwa Judum in 2005 forms their only recent memory of the state.

Traders from Warangal arrive in the months of March and April to purchase tendu patta. A bundle goes for 120 rupees. The yearly income of an average family selling tendu patta and mahua flowers comes to a few thousand rupees. Some men go to Andhra Pradesh twice a year and work as daily labourers – 6,000 rupees per month, basic food and a tiny room in which they live with several others. Chicken once a week.

The men have now opened up to me. Satyam Khurram narrates a tale in response to my question: 'What do you do if someone needs urgent medical attention?'

'Usually, we accept that their time is up and let the person die here. But sometimes, if we feel that it is important to save them, we arrange for a cot and a healthy goat.'

'A goat? On a cot?'

'No. We lay the patient down on the cot and tug the goat along. We reach Bhopalpatnam after walking for a day. A healthy goat fetches around 5,000 rupees. It pays for the treatment.'

'And if the patient's condition is very serious, and something happens on the way? Or if he collapses in the decaying government health centre of Bhopalpatnam?'

'So what?' another man replies. 'The goat will still be sold. It will pay for a lot of liquor.'

I came across a similar narrative in the jungle of Sukma in April 2012. A teenaged girl, Podiyami Irre, fell off a tree in Jagawaram village. The health centre nearest her home was more than twenty kilometres away in Dornapal, with a thick forest in between. Her relatives managed to arrange for a bicycle, but the girl could not survive the distance. 'We try to take critically ill people to Dornapal, but they often succumb on the way,' her neighbour Balram said. The relatives could bring her body back home because she had died at a manageable distance. For many villages, the nearest road is a day away, and if patients die close to the town, they often do not get a burial near their homes.

'No point in carrying them back. We bury them somewhere in the forest,' Balram says.

'And those who are not critically ill?'

'They live and die in the villages.'

'And the goat?'

death script / v

Bastar is a museum of death. The police, the Maoists, the villagers, the Salwa Judum leaders – everyone records their deaths in brick and stone. I was captured in Chhota Kakler because death had halted my steps. Two red memorials gleaming under the sun in a grove caught my attention as I was returning from Sandra. A row of bricks, freshly painted red, around them, indicating a recent Maoist gathering of considerable size. Whose memorials were these? I drove closer and parked the bike.

One was for the CPI (Maoist) politburo member Mallojula Koteshwara Rao, alias Kishenji, killed in an encounter in November 2011. The second was in the memory of the Indravati National Park Area Committee member Kawasi Govind, killed in March 2012. I took many photographs from all sorts of angles, climbed up the platforms. The monuments stood at around fifteen feet high. Someone, in the meantime, spotted me and soon many villagers had surrounded me.

On the way to Chhota Kakler, a little before Farsegarh, is Kutru – where some of the earliest Judum violence was recorded. Right across the Kutru police station is perhaps the first Judum monument. 'Salwa Judum Shahid Smarak. Many Salutes to the Martyrs. Established – June 4, 2005.'

I recalled that Gota Chinna, one of the earliest Judum leaders of the area, was killed by the Maoists last December. Villagers have no love for the guerrillas, but they celebrated the killing.

A small grocery store near the memorial has a poster of Baba Ramdev. 'Patanjali products are sold here,' it says, and further urges: 'A free yoga camp from 22 to 24 February in Jagdalpur.' This is February 2013. His favourite political party will not form a government at the

Centre for a year still, but the businessman Baba has already reached areas of Bastar that see little presence of outsiders. His rapid ascension in such a short time is a sociological phenomenon that is yet to be fully decoded.

A little before Kutru is Rani Bodli which witnessed the second most devastating Maoist attack in Indian history. Fifty-five policemen were killed in 2007. Old photographs swarm up in my memory – charred corpses lying on the ground, two policemen, with notebooks in hand, trying to recognize them. 'I came here,' Suresh Mahapatra, a Dantewada journalist, once told me, 'to report on the attack. This incident was the defining point of my life. When I took photographs of half-burnt and beheaded bodies, it occurred to me that this war had no rules now, that I had seen in life all there ever was to see.'

I stare at the soil of Rani Bodli for a long time. The Maoist documents vividly describe this attack. I had not even begun journalism in 2007. Where was I then? I couldn't recall reading about the Rani Bodli incident in newspapers. Could I have ever anticipated that, years later, death would call me, and I would pay a visit to her milestones?

The state also glorifies its sacrifices. Chhattisgarh is gearing up for the assembly elections in November. Congress banners flutter in a Bijapur rally – 'Indira, Rajiv ka balidan, yaad rakhega Hindustan' (India will remember the martyrdom of Indira and Rajiv). Bastar recognizes neither the names, nor the 'martyrdom'. The divorce of the state from the forest is almost absolute.

The largest Maoist memorial is in the forest of Sukma. I was riding a bicycle beyond Chintalnar in January 2012, when a red Qutub Minar suddenly emerged out of nowhere in the jungle. Tadmetla, a few kilometres from that red tower, had seen seventy-six personnel fall in April 2010, the biggest single-day casualty of Indian paramilitary forces. The memorial had the names of eight guerrillas killed in the attack – Rukmati, Vaga, Vija, Hinga, Rama, Raju, Mangu, Ratan.

Twenty-one AK-47s, forty-two INSAS rifles, six light machine guns, seven SLR rifles, one 9mm Sten gun, 3,122 rounds and thirty-nine grenades were among the weapons and ammunitions the guerrillas had snatched from the police personnel in the Tadmetla assault.

A bureaucrat later told me that, while conducting a survey of the area in a helicopter, the imposing tower had taken him by surprise. The nearest ration shop is several hours away. It would have taken several days to get the bricks and cement. And given the massive deployment of forces all around, which road had the Maoists taken to bring the material? Or was the material provided by a government contractor?

The police have erected no fewer memorials for their deceased. Around a dozen statues of uniformed policemen stand in line near Errabore police station in Sukma. Each of them is holding a rifle. The statues gleam in the sun. Their faces are alike. Does death occur only once, merely repeating itself subsequently? All the statues have watches on their wrists. The needles of all the watches are stationed at an identical hour. Is it the hour of death? Or does death not discriminate in choosing its hour?

To preserve death is a tradition, perhaps an addiction, in Bastar. Bastar is strewn with memorials of stone and wood. The adivasis erect these stones in memory of their dead, draw artistic figures on them, colourful pictures that depict the life of the deceased. The faces of these drawings often look alike. Narsu Mandavi and Lachhu Kashyap were buried at a distance of 250 kilometres, but their faces drawn on the memory stones make them near-twins. Can the Death Painter of Bastar draw only one face? Does he find every face alike? Or does death have only one face, which is merely repeated and reproduced elsewhere?

Such memory stones are seen everywhere in Bastar, but I have never seen any relatives sitting by the graves, remembering the dead, visiting them on their death anniversaries, offering flowers. Having ornamented and consecrated death, the painter has moved elsewhere. Death sustains and nourishes itself on its own.

* * *

A large number of memory stones line the approach to Faraspal, Mahendra Karma's native village, casting their shadow over it. A big statue of his, nearly fifteen feet tall, stands right outside his home. A garland of shrivelled flowers hangs around its neck. A little further, on both sides of the road, dozens of memory stones have been erected for the Karma family. I tried, but couldn't count them all.

The history of the Naxal movement in Bastar, that museum of death, can be viewed through the lens of Mahendra Karma's life. Karma, who wanted to free Bastar from the Naxals, eventually ended up accelerating their spread. He launched the Jan Jagran Abhiyan to flush out the Naxals in the 1990s, which led to a sudden spurt in guerrilla activities. In 2005, he spearheaded the Salwa Judum, and soon the suppressed forest dwellers joined the Maoist ranks, helping the insurgents assume an invincible air.

He was an out-and-out adivasi leader, a man of the forest. He had little reach beyond Bastar, nor did he ever aspire to it. But wherever one looks at the skies over Bastar, he hovers like a character from an epic. Once a staunch communist, he began his political career as a CPI legislator. He lost the next elections against his elder brother Laxman Karma, a Congress leader. Later, he joined the Congress, but curiously left the party over an issue that could have made the adivasi zone of Bastar autonomous, substantially reducing the interference of external forces like the government and the market. When Digvijay Singh's Congress government in the undivided Madhya Pradesh proposed to bring Bastar under the Sixth Schedule of the Constitution – a provision that would have given the same rights to its residents as are available to several Northeast states – Karma left the Congress and fought and won the 1996 Lok Sabha elections as an independent candidate by making the argument that the Sixth Schedule would make private industry difficult in the region and, thus, end up helping the Naxals. Later, he re-joined the Congress. Bastar, meanwhile, is still struggling to get Sixth Schedule status.

Dantewada and Sukma were once Mahendra Karma's strongholds, but the areas soon became insurgent outposts. The dialectic of history plays a bewitching game with its subjects. To defeat Karma, the Bharatiya Janata Party sought the support of local guerrillas in the elections – who saw no contradiction in helping their ideological enemy, the BJP, which won eleven of the twelve seats in the Bastar zone in the 2008 assembly elections, at a time when the guerrillas were scaling new heights, when they seemed invincible and were capable of attacking the police at will.

As Karma became weaker, the Maoists gained in strength. An area whose politics was limited to the Congress and the Communist Party of India, now saw the BJP and the Rashtriya Swayamsevak Sangh flourishing. Bastar thus became a rare zone which witnessed the simultaneous surge of ultra-Left revolutionaries and the right wing.

Karma was trounced in the 2008 elections in his home seat of Dantewada, standing third behind the BJP and the CPI. The election was fought in the aftermath of the Salwa Judum violence, during which the BJP government had supported the Congressman Karma to the hilt, with both money and weapons. But when the Judum drew all-round criticism, the BJP conveniently dissociated itself from him.

'Raman Singh betrayed our father. It was Papa's mistake to take the support of the BJP government during Salwa Judum. Raman Singh withdrew later, and left us in the lurch. The BJP used Papa,' Karma's eldest son Deepak told me later.

The 2008 Dantewada election maps the treachery of the Maoist movement. A Maoist, Podiyam Linga, was arrested just before the 2013 November elections for the murder of Dantewada's BJP vice president, Shiv Dayal Singh Tomar.

In the presence of the Dantewada police superintendent Narendra Khare and CRPF officers, Linga told the media that he had helped his uncle, the BJP candidate Bhima Mandavi, during the 2008 elections. Speaking to me later, Mandavi did not admit to taking Linga's help, but admitted that he had known Linga well, and that he was a resident of his village Toylanka and was closely associated with Tomar. He had even worked for the BJP in another election. 'Tomarji assigned him some work during the Bastar Lok Sabha by-elections in 2011. They also had lunch together,' Mandavi said. BJP's Dinesh Kashyap won the Bastar Lok Sabha seat then.

Elaborating upon the links of the Maoists with the BJP, Linga also told the police that he and other cadres had visited the Dantewada district headquarters and met Tomar and other BJP men. The meetings, he said, often took place in the circuit house, less than 500 metres from the SP's office.

Tomar was an influential contractor who carried out construction projects for the government. Tomar, Linga continued, was murdered because he did not pay them a commission. Linga, Khare said, had asked Tomar for 60,000 rupees in lieu of a construction project the Maoists had allowed them to complete the previous year. But Tomar refused to pay, saying, 'Do whatever you want to.'

The BJP's politics in Dantewada came full circle when Mandavi was killed by the Maoists on 9 April 2019, two days before the Lok Sabha elections in Bastar.

The line between revolution and politics, the left and the right, often becomes hazy in Bastar. A battle, the Mahabharata noted long ago, is fought on the foundation of betrayals.

* * *

One can only imagine what the trajectory of the Maoist movement in Bastar might have been in Karma's absence. During my long conversations with him, whenever the topic turned to the excesses of the Salwa Judum, he would retort, 'Bastar belongs to us – us adivasis. Why did the Naxals occupy our land? They talk of justice. What have they given us? They destroyed our customs, our culture.'

His wife Devti Karma, who spoke only Gondi, made an unexpected, perhaps foretold, entry on the theatre of Dantewada. For years, she had led the life of an ordinary adivasi woman, taking care of her home while her husband led a ragtag army against the Maoists. 'Once, I joked that when Papa moves to central politics, she should contest this seat [Dantewada], and she ran after me to thrash me,' their son Chhavindra Karma told me, smiling.

Mahendra Karma could not have anticipated that, soon after his assassination, she would stake claim to his legacy from his constituency Dantewada, against Mandavi.

Devti and her four sons – Deepak, Chhavindra, Ashish and Divyaraj – received Z-plus security after Karma's death. They all are on the Naxals' hit-list. Perhaps the only family in India that has five members with Z-plus security.

* * *

On a November afternoon during the 2013 election campaign, flanked by a pilot car in front and a vehicle behind, a beige Scorpio moves upon a forest road in Dantewada. There are around twenty AK-47-wielding policemen in the three vehicles. Policemen have been deployed along the road at every 300 metres. 'Turn right,' the man in the Scorpio suddenly says. A muddy path trails off into the forest. It is not part of the itinerary. The man has been strictly advised to follow the pre-determined routes, where road-opening teams have been deployed. Wiping the sweat on his forehead, his personal security officer seeks confirmation. 'Turn right,' he repeats. The boss will have to be obeyed. The three vehicles are now in unknown woods.

The policemen are suddenly on high alert. One doesn't know what one might come across. Police vehicles often become target of Naxal attacks when they suddenly take a new route. The route for Deepak Karma's election campaign has been cleared in advance. Policemen often complain that Karma's sons change the route without any reason, that if any incident occurs the police will be blamed. But Deepak is nonchalant. He wants to show me an orchard from his childhood. The Naxal threat cannot curb his steps. Politics in Bastar is not for the lily-livered.

A year and half later, in the summer of 2015, Bastar is anticipating a Judum Part Two. Exactly ten years ago, on 4 June 2005, the Chhattisgarh government had signed a highly publicized MoU with the Tatas for an ultra mega steel plant in Bastar. A day later, the Salwa Judum was formally launched to evict the Maoists from the region – a move that defined the insurgency for the next ten years.

In 2005, Mahendra Karma led the battle. Now, his second son Chhavindra is taking over. On the previous occasion, Tata's proposed steel plant was in the works. Now, Prime Minister Narendra Modi has arrived to inaugurate a new steel plant.

Mahendra Karma had three chief lieutenants heading each district where the Judum was operational – Soyam Muka in Sukma, Chaitram Attami in Dantewada and Mahadev Rana in Bijapur. Rana was killed long ago. Muka and Attami were uprooted from their villages during the Judum a decade ago. Attami still lives in a camp for Judum refugees.

* * *

A May 2015 afternoon in Jagdalpur. Muka and Chhavindra are arguing over who has lost more relatives in the battle. Death is a medal, corpses an addiction in Dandakaranya. 'You will find maximum Soyams in the list of the deceased,' Muka insists, his voice fumbling as he remembers his elder brother Soyam Mukesh. 'Check the papers in the tehsil office if you don't trust me.'

Muka was a primary school teacher. He had been living a peaceful life when he picked up the rifle at the prompting of his uncle, Mahendra

Karma. A decade later, Karma's son is urging him to join the second edition of the Judum, but his rifle has now turned cold.

'After his [Karma's] death, I lost faith. When he was alive, I thought we could defeat death. To remain alive, Karma often said, it is important to know your enemy as well as to maintain a distance from them,' says Muka. Chhavindra winks at Muka, who is married to a distant cousin. 'When will you make your exit? It's enough now ... He's so shameless, he continues to hold on to his wicket,' Chhavindra teases his brother-in-law, not at all bothered about his sister becoming a widow. Muka can only smile wryly.

The Judum once had nearly a hundred major leaders. Only around fifteen survive today. Another Judum leader, Sattar Ali, has lost almost a hundred friends. The Maoists once attacked his home. A bullet pierced through his shoulder before penetrating the body of his brother. 'If you don't trust me, I can take off my shirt and show you the bullet wound.' Then, immediately, he adds, 'But I am not deterred by attacks or deaths.'

Sattar was in the vehicle with Mahendra Karma when the Maoists attacked the Congress convoy in May 2013. I was scheduled to be part of the convoy as well, but another assignment took me elsewhere a day before.

When I ask Attami about the Judum excesses against the adivasis, he gets agitated: 'You talk about police atrocities, but do you know what the Naxals did? If they wanted to kill a person, they forced his parents to throw stones at him ... If someone kills your father, what would you do? This is my land. I don't want the Maoists here.'

Police vehicles are parked and armed guards stationed outside his home. Large framed photographs of the first two RSS chiefs, K.B. Hedgewar and M.S. Golwalkar, hang on the wall inside. Attami is not an RSS member. I wonder why the photographs are here. Attami was among the earliest Judum members to be given the rank of Special Police Officer. The Supreme Court declared the SPOs unconstitutional in July 2011, but the Chhattisgarh government immediately provided them a back-door entry by renaming and re-employing them as auxiliary constables.

In the initial years, the Maoists helped the adivasis a lot, Attami admits, but then came the pressure to join their ranks. 'Why did they have to punish us in jan adalats, forcefully collect chicken and mutton from us?' A lot of villagers in his Judum camp earlier worked for the Maoists before they quit. Accusing the Maoists of dragging tribals into their battle, Attami goes on, 'If they had a grudge against capitalists, why didn't they kill them on their own? Why did they make us their medium? We adivasis knew nothing about the world, but they made us fight their battles. Is this New Democracy?'

Ask about Karma's role in enabling the entry of the mining industry in Dantewada, and the Judum leaders get furious. They admit that some vested interests entered the Judum campaign, but quickly say that the Judum leaders continue to live with limited means. 'Which industry? What benefit?' they say. 'We fought only to secure our land, and gained nothing out of it except death.'

In the thirty months of the Judum campaign, Chhattisgarh saw the deaths of 325 security personnel, 609 civilians and 165 suspected Maoists. That's 1,099 deaths – or one death every day. And these are the official figures, the Judum leaders and the local police place this number far higher.

Come evening, the shadow of the Judum descends upon Karma's gigantic statue – bespectacled eyes peering over the horizon and folded hands, a gesture the aggressive man rarely adopted. It has gone mostly unnoticed that Karma's stance had changed in the months preceding his death. 'The violence must end now' had become his refrain. Was he exhausted? Or had he realized the futility of the gun? Just a fortnight before his death, he had made a stunning statement after eight adivasis were killed in CRPF firing in Ehadsameta village. 'Let the Maoists grow, but not a single adivasi should be killed in police firing.'

Days later, he joined his adivasi brethren.

'Including my father, ninety-five people of the family have been killed in this battle. They say I am doing politics by launching this movement. I'm merely carrying the family responsibility of freeing this area from Naxals,' says Chhavindra, aged thirty-four. 'Yes, when we go inside, they [the Maoists] will attack us. But this war can't be won without sacrifices. Let the first bullet hit my chest,' he adds.

The Karmas have seen too much blood to be guided by sanity or rationality. Many women of the family have been killed who had absolutely no link with the Judum. 'If you have Karma attached to your name, you are gone,' Deepak says.

Deepak is cautious about Judum Two, and advises that 'we must learn from earlier mistakes', but his aide wants him to emphasize that 'Judum is beyond politics'. Deepak smiles – 'Why are you trying to make me a martyr?' – but cannot avoid adding that 'it is our family responsibility'.

In this battle, like any other, the distinction between right and wrong cannot be easily made. Karma wanted to free Dantewada from the Maoists, but he also hobnobbed with mining companies and crushed a large number of his adivasi brethren during the Judum. Yet, when one looks at the memory stones of the Karma family, stones that cloud the sky of Faraspal, it appears almost like the battle of a chieftain with outsiders over control of the jungle. Bastar, he was convinced, belonged to him and his community. He would nourish it or destroy it, but he wouldn't tolerate the hegemony of educated comrades from Andhra Pradesh. This was a battle of pride, though like many other battles, it was coloured by cruelty and treachery. After all, who would stake his life, and the lives of his entire family, on this? Not a businessman or a politician. A man with commercial or political ambitions cannot possibly lead a life that entails the prospect of witnessing his entire clan meeting a gory death, one by one.

Deepak had father's phone number saved as 'Big Boss' on his cellphone. It is still there. After the death of his father, the number is now his mother's. Whenever she calls her son, his phone screen gleams 'Big Boss calling' and he often gets a shock. Is it his father calling? At times, he even answers the phone with 'Yes, Papa?'

* * *

Elsewhere, this book records the love of daughters for their rebel fathers. Here's the account of Mahendra Karma's youngest daughter, Aanchal. Now in her early twenties, she is studying law.

> I had realized early in my childhood that my surroundings and my family weren't normal. I saw gunmen follow my father twenty-four seven. I was sent to a boarding school in Raipur along with my youngest brother Divyaraj. We knew that Papa wouldn't turn up for the parent–teacher meetings or annual functions, but he regularly wrote letters describing his travels in Bastar, and called us home every month. I spent my childhood travelling with him to many dangerous places. It was pretty exciting. I have a haunting memory of attending the funeral of a policeman in Mirtur. During our travels, Papa would indicate the spots where the Maoists had planted tiffin bombs and landmines. He taught me to never panic in case of an attack, and instructed me to always inspect the road I was taking. Once, the Karma family visited Bedma village for a wedding. Chhavindra bhaiya and I danced to Gondi songs. Only later, we learnt that a large number of Naxals had been present in the crowd. I sometimes wonder whether I had danced with the Maoists.
>
> Papa was mostly away during the Judum. Only he could have handled it. We were always worried and praying for him. But we knew that he had prepared us for what was coming. We could see it clearly, and that is why we all could pick ourselves up and come back on track.

Ours is the first family on the front against Naxalism. Even after so many attacks and deaths in the family, we are holding up like a wall for Bastar. Once, he asked me about my ambition in life. 'I want to become the youngest woman chief minister and a leader like you,' I replied. He laughed.

My mother ... Papa often told us about the time when I was not born and we had hardly any police protection. She held guard with a gun while Papa had his dinner, and vice versa. Soon after his death, we started receiving death threats, but my mother did not give in. She held her ground and collected the broken pieces.

I am in Bombay now, but my Faraspal memories have not faded away. I will never forget how he was killed by the Maoists. When I saw his mutilated body, my fear vanished and I promised myself that I would fight against the Maoists until my last breath and carry his legacy forward.

* * *

On 25 May 2013, around 150 Naxals had surrounded and killed the unarmed Mahendra Karma before they trampled upon his corpse and celebrated over his dead body. His body had seventy-two wounds, caused by both bullets and daggers, the maximum number of injuries I have ever seen in any post-mortem report. Except for a wound on the knees and one on the left ankle, the remaining seventy were on his torso, face and head. Of these, fourteen were on the face and neck, thirty-three on the chest and stomach, and twenty-three on the back. The diagram of injuries on his body looked like a cardboard target for young recruits to practise firing on.

The fractures suggested that Karma had also been beaten up with sticks. 'Multiple chop wounds present over scalp, with fractures of skull bones into pieces. Cranial cavity exposed to exterior & brain matter partially missing and oozing out ... Features distorted due to fracture of facial bones ... Stab injuries over various body parts. Depth varying from muscles to cavity deep.' That's how the doctors reported it. The injuries were both ante- and post-mortem, indicating that his body continued to receive wounds even hours after his death.

On the same day, 25 May, in 1967, eleven people were killed after the police fired at villagers who had been demanding land for tilling. That village was Naxalbari. Between these two dates, separated by forty-six years, lies Karma. The most prominent target of the Naxals was killed on the day the Naxal movement had taken birth. His post-mortem report is a map of the Maoist movement in Dandakaranya.

How does his daughter Aanchal remember that day?

> On 24 May, Papa, my three brothers and I were in Jagdalpur. His party workers visited him in the evening, discussed politics and asked him to dress up for a dinner hosted by the Congress in a hotel. He went inside and called me, 'Beta Dimpy, how do I look?'
>
> He was in his three-fourth shorts, hands in pockets. 'You look great Papa,' I said, and gave him his handkerchief and his asthma inhaler.
>
> On the morning of the twenty-fifth, I woke up at 7.30 a.m. Deepak bhaiya was sleeping in the hall. Papa and Chhavi bhaiya were reading the newspaper in the veranda. Divyaraj had already left to play football. Papa asked me why I woke up so early. I wanted to go to Sukma with him. I thought I would get ready soon and sit in the car before him so that he couldn't say no to me. He finished his breakfast, gave me 500 rupees asking me to have a good dinner, and stepped out. I rushed inside to get my bag, but the car had sounded its horn and was moving out of the gate. I cursed myself for not being able to sneak into his vehicle.
>
> My brother and I visited my sister Tulika in the afternoon. I was playing with her five-month-old baby in the veranda, when she screamed, 'Aanchal, come upstairs.' I rushed up and saw the

news of the attack on the Congress convoy on TV channels. We were accustomed to such news, it didn't affect us.

Yet, we cancelled our evening plans and went back to the Karma bungalow. The situation seemed to be getting worse. We still hoped that Papa was safe, that he would return to tell us the entire story as he had often done in the past. The police assured us, but we could sense the growing darkness. We left for the spot, nearly forty kilometres from Jagdalpur – Tulika di, her baby, her friend who drove the car, Divyaraj and I.

On the way, we got the news that Papa was no more. We held each other tight, told each other that we would not believe this until we saw his body. The sky was getting dusky. This evening wasn't like any other. A strong wind was blowing. It carried a different sort of chill. We drove at 140 kilometres per hour before we came to a screeching halt. A familiar car was parked along the road with its indicators on. It was Deepak bhaiya, crying. We all hugged each other. I still couldn't believe it. We drove on, but the road beyond the Darbha police station was barricaded.

We banged at the iron gates of the police station, but no one responded. I couldn't find a single policeman inside. The lights were switched off. Petrified, some survivors were rushing in from the spot. Among them were the drivers of my father's convoy. Finally, it was confirmed.

But we still hadn't seen the body. We requested the ambulance staff to get the body but, sensing danger, the driver returned midway. Then, one of Papa's supporters drove the ambulance and brought his body.

After he was captured, the Maoists asked what his last wish was – whether he wanted to wear new clothes or eat food. But he remained silent. The next moment, a bullet went through his stomach. One of them hit him with an axe on the back of his legs, he fell on his knees. Another bullet pierced his head.

Their revenge was not complete yet. They surrounded his body and jumped upon him, celebrating their success, stabbing his body many times.

I still have the 500 rupee note. I got it laminated.

Karma was not an exception. Brutalizing the body of the enemy, the Maoists say, is a psychological requirement. Comrades stomp upon the corpse, make a video of the scene, and then watch it repeatedly for years. It inspires several generations of guerrillas to no longer fear the enemy. I have seen young guerrillas in Maoist camps watching ambush videos. Their eyes gleam with an animal thrill as they watch their comrades humbling the corpses of policemen onscreen.

They justified the barbaric treatment of corpses in the Rani Bodli ambush with these words: 'The families of the local comrades were shattered due to the SJ [Salwa Judum]. Their sisters were raped and they lost their parents and brothers. So the hatred was boundless. Due to this hatred, the comrades could fight courageously. Hacking down the Judum goons is an expression of this hatred.'

Is the Maoist-versus-state battle the Mahabharata of independent India and Dandakaranya its Kurukshetra?

More than eight decades ago, Ernest Hemingway wrote: 'Certainly there is no hunting like the hunting of man and those who have hunted armed men long enough and liked it, never really care for anything else thereafter. You will meet them doing various things with resolve, but their interest rarely holds because after the other thing ordinary life is as flat as the taste of wine when the taste buds have been burned off your tongue.'

Bastar inverts the proposition by replacing 'man' with 'corpse'.

delusion / iv

Of all the Maoist videos I have seen, one stands out for capturing a moment that is in unashamed contrast to the assault it was meant to record. The video shows the rebels' attack on the police, on 28 May 2007 in Kudur, Bastar.

It begins with the sound of birds chirping in the forest. One can see a forested path that has a landmine underneath. Armed and uniformed Maoists are inspecting the earth, covering the landmine with dry leaves, and taking their positions. Another Maoist points out that they have planted quite a few landmines in a small stretch. All this while the chirping continues in the background. The videographer seems keen to capture the sound. They are expecting a police vehicle any time. It's obvious that they know about the police's movements.

The chirping sound increases as the camera zooms in. It is a long and aesthetic shot of a lone bird, perched upon a leafless branch of a tall tree. One can now clearly hear the sound that reverberates through the forest. It is a common hawk cuckoo, also called the brain-fever bird, known for its restlessly melancholic chirping. The sound becomes more prominent, its edges finer. When I first watched it, I wondered whether it was an ambush video or a National Geographic clip, or a Tarkovskian frame.

Suddenly, a jump cut and a blast.

In the next scene, bodies of policemen are strewn upon the road. Three uniformed policemen are sitting on the ground, two on their haunches, all of them with their hands tied behind their backs. Some twenty-five Maoists, including ten women cadres, are visible in the video.

One Maoist pours water into a policeman's mouth. 'Don't worry. We won't harm you,' he says. Another Maoist shouts, 'Number three, number four, surrender or we will kill you.' Two policemen lower their heads, one seems to utter something, and immediately a third Maoist interrupts, 'Hey, what are you guys signalling?'

One policeman, visibly the youngest one, wets his trousers. The camera repeatedly focuses on the damp patch. A voice asks him to look into the camera.

The policemen can hardly be heard, only their lips move. One distinct word they use to address the Maoists is 'sir'.

A Maoist asks, 'Which battalion do you belong to?' Two policeman reply, almost together, 'Not battalion, DF [District Force].' Suddenly, the Maoist's tone changes. 'Oh, he's from the DF. Let's leave them.' Their sympathy for the local Chhattisgarh police betrays the Maoists' deep resentment for the central paramilitary force, the CRPF. Another Maoist says, 'Are you from the DF? No problem, we'll let you go. You people are not our enemy. No one in Chhattisgarh is our enemy.' 'We are also not your enemy, sir. We are in this job out of compulsion,' the youngest policeman says.*

---

* The helplessness of the police in the face of a Maoist assault is perhaps best reflected in a video which captures the 24 March 2006 attack in Odisha's Gajapati district.

This video, recorded shortly after sunrise, is of a simultaneous attack by the Maoists on an Odisha State Armed Police camp, a police station, a sub-jail, and communication towers in the R. Udayagiri block of Gajapati district. Three policemen died and three were injured in this attack. The Maoists seized thirty-four weapons, including one AK-47, one light machine gun, twenty-four SLRs, besides one grenade launcher, ten grenades and 4,000 rounds of ammunition. They also freed their cadres and other inmates of the jail, while abducting two policemen – Station House Officer Ranjan Mallik and Sub-jail Superintendent Rabi Narayan Sethi. The attack, a Maoist document noted, 'gave us a better experience in successfully raiding a camp with sufficient fortifications'.

In the video, scores of local residents can be seen, seemingly gathered by the Maoists to witness the assault. The Maoists first overrun the police station premises, and then hold a meeting of locals outside the jail where they talk about their ideology. Right in front of the jail, over two dozen policemen lay

In this attack, the Maoists killed ten policemen, seized three AK-47s, seven SLRs, one INSAS, one 9mm pistol and one two-inch mortar, besides 611 rounds.

'Sir, his arm is paining a lot,' the youngest policeman points to his colleague.

'No problem. We're doctors. We'll treat you,' a Maoist says, his voice suddenly reflects some compassion. This man is not visible onscreen, but he talks the most and seems to be the leader of the group. The rebels who gave me this video said he was Mallojula Venugopal Rao, alias Sonu, alias Bhupathi.

The camera then shows the policemen's motorcycles burning, charred bodies lying on the ground, as the Maoists gather in a circle and shout 'PLGA zindabad!' (The PLGA is the People's Liberation Guerrilla Army.) One of the armed uniformed guerrillas seems to be a teenage girl. She giggles as she lifts her arm for the slogan. This fair-complexioned girl is visibly the odd one out in the squad and appears to be a city-dweller.

But who among these Maoists had avidly captured the solitary chirping cuckoo on camera, moments before pressing the trigger of the landmine?

---

prostrate, face down, hands on their heads, most of them in underpants and vests. The hands of some of the policemen are tied with a long rope.

A trailer is parked nearby. The Maoists and the freed inmates get into the vehicle. The Maoists raise slogans – 'Maovadi zindabad!' – as one of the two abducted policemen follows them. His hands tied, his shirt torn, he is paraded before the crowd and abducted in full public view.

The Maoists hoist their red flag over the jail, the camera stays on it for a while. During the entire recording, no reinforcements arrive, none of the surrendered policemen tries to retaliate. The rebels complete the raid without any resistance.

The last frame is of the jail bursting into flames.

death / iv

In Raipur yesterday, a CRPF officer described to me the last journey of a soldier who dies on the Maoist front.

The body is embalmed after the inner organs are removed. The head, stomach and buttocks are injected with a mixture of formaldehyde, glutaraldehyde and methanol. The coffin is draped in the tricolour. A policeman, perhaps a friend of the deceased, carries the coffin to his home. If the policeman takes a train, he doesn't keep the wooden box with him in the passenger bogey. It is loaded in the goods compartment, with sacks of letters, bikes and furniture.

After travelling by train, the coffin begins a road journey to the home of the deceased. The policeman gets signatures on an official document from the family, confirming the receipt of the corpse.

What happens to the tricolour? Is it used for another deceased soldier, draped over another coffin? Does the national flag carry the smell of many corpses through its life? Do the police and the army have a stock of such flags that are used only for the last journeys of corpses? There is no standard practice. I spoke to the police from various states, the paramilitary forces and the Indian army and navy. In some places it is handed over to the family as a souvenir, some bury it along with the corpse. Some quietly destroy it as well – perhaps the only instance in which the national flag meets such an end.

Three years later, on 17 January 2017, as I was tracking polling booths located at high altitudes in the Himalayas, one such flag crossed my path. It was snowing. In the mountainous Parsari village of Chamoli district lived an old woman named Bhagirathi Devi with a tricolour some men had given her a few years ago.

Her son, Murli Singh Bisht, a soldier with the 24th Assam Rifles battalion, had died on duty a few years ago. Some days afterwards, the coffin had arrived draped in the flag. 'They asked me to…' She forgot exactly what they had told her. 'What did they say?' she turned to ask her teenaged grandson, Anurodh. 'Hoist it on 26 January and 15 August,' he said, and stepped inside to fetch the flag from a box. It still carried the smell of his father.

An old tale of a coffin and war came to mind.

A poor blind man lives in a village with his children. His younger son has been drafted into the army and sent to a battlefield. One day, the family learns that the son has been killed in battle. But the old father refuses to accept it. Days later, army men arrive with the coffin, draped in the national flag. The coffin is buried in the village with a guard of honour. The blind man still doesn't believe that his son has died. The family ignores it and lets the old man be.

However, they soon face a bitter situation as the government wants to provide monetary compensation to the family for the young man's death. But the father, the person whose signatures or thumb impression are required to receive the amount, refuses it on the grounds that his son is still alive. The poor family, realizing that the money could pull them all out of poverty, pressures the old man, but he doesn't relent.

One night, unable to face their taunts, he leaves for the burial ground with a spade. Soon, the family and the entire village join him. The blind man reaches the spot and begins digging frantically. The crowd wants to stop him, but they cannot. They don't want to face the decomposed body. But they also secretly hope that it will finally confirm the death, and that they can then easily persuade the man to sign the document.

The father continues digging the earth, and soon the soiled coffin gleams in the dark. He breaks open the wooden box, and as he blindly gropes inside with his fumbling fingers, relief shines upon his face, leaving the family stunned.

The coffin is full of stones, placed neatly, one next to the other.

dream / iii

The other face of death gleamed in the words of Padma Kumari. I met her at her Hyderabad home in August 2014. Padma had been in jail when her comrade husband Suresh was killed in a police encounter. 'They asked me to go and take a last look at him, but I didn't. I knew that his corpse had been badly mutilated. I wanted to retain his smiling face in my memory,' said the woman whose eyes had not lost their twinkle despite spending years in the jungle and in jails. 'My bond with him was not just personal. He was my leader, a leader of my Party.'

Padma was released from jail a few years after his death. In 2007, she married a journalist, a member of the Revolutionary Writers Association, but Suresh's face remained with her. She joined the Amarula Bandhu Mitrula Sangham – an organization active in Andhra Pradesh and Telangana which the relatives of Maoists killed in police encounters had formed, relatives who had also led a long guerrilla life. Nearly 90 per cent of its members are women. They bring the corpses of killed Maoists from other states, hand them over to their relatives, and ensure a dignified cremation. The pallbearers of the Death Vehicle.

On 18 July, the founding day of the Mitrula Sangham, the dead are remembered in many cities of Andhra Pradesh and Telangana. Over 6,000 guerrilla revolutionaries in these two states have been killed in the past forty years. Though, over the last two decades, guerrillas from Bastar top the death chart, there is no such organization for them. The corpses of the adivasis for whom there are no claimants remain unidentified and are summarily cremated by the police.

* * *

The pallbearers of the Mitrula Sangham also brought back the body of Kishenji in November 2011, and handed it over to his family in Peddapalli, Karimnagar district. He was killed by the CRPF in an encounter which was believed to have been engineered by a woman who had been 'planted' in his camp. The Maoists allege, and the photographs of his post-mortem also suggest, that the paramilitary force had brutalized his corpse.

The night of 25 August 2014 is extremely humid, but there is not a drop of sweat on Madhuramma's face as she speaks without pause at her Peddapalli home. She is eighty-eight and speaks only Telugu. The journalist who is visiting her doesn't understand the language, so her grandson Dileep becomes the interpreter. Dileep, Kishenji's nephew, teaches psychology at a local college. The family seems prosperous. A big house with several trees lining the courtyard, air conditioners installed in the rooms. Several awards take up a shelf in the living room. Who was the recipient?

Madhuramma still remembers that November afternoon when the police had blockaded the roads to Peddapalli, yet a crowd of over 70,000 people had gathered for her son.

'You didn't stop him when he was leaving home?'

'How could I? Indira amma had imposed Emergency. He had to go underground. I do feel sad, but I am proud of him. People here respect him a lot.'

The old woman refers to the former prime minister as 'Indira amma' in a casual tone. Her aplomb is obvious. Her husband Mallojula Venkataiah and his father were freedom fighters. This award, Dileep points at a plaque, was given to Venkataiah by Indira Gandhi on 15 August 1972, three years before his son was to go underground, to be followed by the younger son Mallojula Venugopal Rao, alias Bhupathi, now a CPI (Maoist) politburo member.

The grandsons and sons of freedom fighters become the most wanted guerrillas of the country, and stake their lives for the revolution.

death / v

Autumn. Spare me, Autumn.

'When did you arrive?'

'Before daybreak. Didn't you ask me to meet you under the mahua tree ... Where have you been? See, so many people are already here ... All the mahua will be finished soon.'

'Don't worry, so much has been shed today. Come, let's start.'

Those were the days of autumn. The forest gleamed with dry leaves. Mahua drizzled down from early morning to noon. Tiny white flowers. The earth found itself carpeted by them. The mahua trees turned bare, poured out an entire year's worth of intoxicant in the month of March.

Mada and his wife would pick the white beads scattered amidst the dry red leaves. They would collect the desires of an entire year in their backyard. The night would dance on petals of mahua. The forest and the river were their adornments.

But that was earlier...

In January 2012, Podiyami Mada was found dead in a police station in Sukma. A Naxal, the police said, hanged himself in the lock-up. The entire village crossed the forest and blocked the road. The body was arriving from Jagdalpur in a government ambulance, via Dantewada. The ambulance had deliberately taken a longer route to avoid the villagers and ensure a quiet cremation. But the news had carried, people had dumped logs on the road, the ambulance was forced to stop at Gadiras.

Thundering screams. Men and women, in frayed lungis and saris, thump the ambulance to get its door open. Village women climb in – a coffin of transparent glass is lying in the vehicle. Underneath the glass, a body wrapped in white. The women beat the glass with their fists. Glass hits glass. Bangles snap into shards. The glass of the coffin is durable. Government property, shock resistant.

Away from the screams, Podiyami Kosi, who has the first and the last right over the body, is on her haunches. An unshapely bundle. Motionless. With Mada's five-month baby in her. She doesn't know that the medical report of her husband says that he was badly thrashed before death. His private parts were swollen. There was no police case in all of Bastar against him to prove his Naxal links. He did not have any rope in the lock-up. Just a shawl with which, the police say, he 'hanged himself' from a three-foot-high peg.

A policeman reveals that Mada had been apprehended by the CRPF a few days ago. They poured petrol over his private parts, set them on fire. Unaware of this, Kosi is hunched quietly. Carrying the remains of her 'Naxal' husband in her. Her head on her knees. You take photographs of her and of the women banging the glass coffin, immersed in the shame of being destined to view the world through the eye of the camera and the news. Why can't you quietly listen to this death and to the screams? The question lingers, but you step down from the ambulance only after being certain of having taken many photographs from different angles.

Two months later, the forest sheds itself again. Mahua drizzles down again. This March morning, she goes alone with a basket, picks the white flowers. Kosi still looks as she did on that tattered January afternoon. Muted. A little swelling of the belly. Perhaps. Perhaps not. A baby of 220 days barely registers its presence on her figure.

The constitution of deprivation is decided before birth.

Kosi goes alone to pick mahua. She will perhaps also take a rickety bus to the collector's office, stand in a queue to receive the death certificate of her 'Naxal' husband.

Her husband's younger brother was working in a southern state. Hearing about the death, he has come to live in Sukma. 'I won't let my brother's death die, I will ensure punishment for the killers,' he says. He is perhaps unaware of the crumbling earth beneath his feet. In the last two months, he has not been able to get even the post-mortem report. His struggle has remained an internal one, and will remain so. The mere consolation of holding one's ground. Scratch at it, and what emerges is merely a dry, cold wind that blows away the white buds of mahua.

Many years will pass. Living in Sukma's Pairmapara village, all he will manage to do is submit a few applications to the collector, the police superintendent, the local councillor or the legislator. He will carefully keep a Xerox copy of the application – which will carry a seal of acknowledgement from the government – in his file, show it to visiting journalists, narrate the entire tale right from the beginning.

(March 2012. Sukma.)

death script / vi

A corpse. An imaginary corpse. One lying under a mahua tree in the sun. Another echoing in your consciousness. You are reading an email you received the night before. Someone has asked you some questions which you have read twenty-two times in the last forty hours. This is November 2013.

Staring at the screen, you recall that last week, at dinner with a friend, you suddenly found yourself imagining his death. The many ways he could die or be killed. A quiet death when he is asleep, or a bloody police encounter that leaves thirty-two bullet holes on his body. Or a crushing accident, his body mangled by a vehicle. Sipping mushroom soup, you conceived the obituary of your friend sitting across from you at the table. The taste of garlic lingered for a while upon your tongue.

Last night, you received a phone call from someone close. Handset held against your left ear, you imagined him collapsing to the ground, his stuttering voice piercing your eardrums, as you gathered only the last vestiges of his shrieks. A thousand miles away. You enacted your most frequently recurring nightmare – you were not with him in his last moments. You have been living for a long time with an imagined fear. In vivid detail, you have visualized his death – in your absence, someone else washes him, covers him with a white sheet. His naked body, his genitals which you had once glimpsed dangling from his underpants years ago. Last night, you added another paragraph to *The Death Script*. He dies on the phone line, you the sole listener to his last cries emanating from the handset. As he collapses, you think of the twenty-four hours it will take you to reach him, hours in which rigor mortis will gradually set in.

Rigor mortis. These words have entered your vocabulary after your encounter with the forest. The old man lives alone in a decaying house. The domestic help comes in the morning. You will call the neighbours to take care of the body. The door is bolted from the inside. They will break it open to find him on the floor, frothing at the mouth.

'Will you visit me this winter?' he asked. You moved the handset from your ear and brought it close to your eye. It was his voice, his soul had not sprung out of the receiver after his death. He repeated the question. *The Death Script* that was being written within you paused, then instantly resumed after he hung up.

A mosquito trapped in a cobweb hanging from the ceiling flapped furiously, not to release itself but from mere habit – it had, by now, consented to captivity. Seeping through the walls, the November night percolated into your veins. In your eyes, suddenly, flashed the image of the girl who had played with her five friends near a river, whose village you had visited on a rainy September evening twenty-six months ago.

That evening, you didn't realize that you had entered the script of death, becoming simultaneously its writer and a character in it. You could grasp it only after four months, while writing about a man who had died in police custody, and witnessing his pregnant wife who was waiting by the road under a January sky, her head on her knees.

* * *

This November night, you read the questionnaire on the computer screen mailed to you by a researcher from the US. She wants to interview you about your experiences of the war zone in Dandakaranya. She has also added that you can, should you wish to, respond to the questions anonymously. You wish to add other questions: Can one be a reporter without betraying one's subjects? Can one be a Death Reporter without deceiving the deceased one writes about?

Betrayal perhaps impregnates the idea, the moment one conceives the written word. Novelists or journalists often yearn for sorrow. A novelist may admit to it, but can a journalist ever address the reader and say, 'I was always in search of sorrow. My words sought a home in the grief of others'?

The questionnaire from an unknown researcher has given you an anonymous space to confess. Death, you have often told yourself, invaded you in the jungle as you began stalking the corpses. With the questionnaire flashing on the computer screen, you feel that this is the occasion to admit that death has been an eternal resident of your universe, always moored in your imagination. The jungle merely pulled it out of the crevices of your being and placed it on your palette.

Long before your arrival in the jungle, you had published a short story about a young writer who, unable to compose any work of worth, sets out to write the greatest obituary ever, the obituary of his veteran mentor – who is still alive. The young man lives with the guilt of not having offered anything worthy to the old man as guru dakshina. To overcome that guilt, he conceives of this obituary, hoping to get it published the morning after his mentor's death, leaving the world stunned by his ability to write such a masterly tribute overnight. Over the years, he writes several drafts of the obituary, imagining the death of his mentor in multiple ways, killing his guru over and over in his imagination. Heart attack. Run over by a truck during his morning walk. Found dead at his desk – the despair of an unfinished novel. A Hemingway-like suicide. A Woolf-like end. The imagination of the young writer touches the skies, but the old man doesn't die. Death echoes within the writer, day and night. He visualizes the old man dying everywhere, his body going up in flames on the logs, but he doesn't die.

The story ends with this sentence: 'Were you writing the obituary of the old man, or addressing and recording your own self? Were you not the old man who, in the guise of a young man, was writing his own obituary?'

The Death Script had, perhaps, made you its captive long before your arrival in Dandakaranya. You were, perhaps, locked in an eternal wait for the jungle. The jungle never needed you. You needed it for your survival, to write your own tale.

FOUR

dream / iv

Abujhmad. District Narayanpur. Any month, day, hour or moment of any year.

'Mad' denotes a hill of bushes and dense jungles. 'Abujh' is uncharted, unexplored. The police, state, politicians – no one knows what smells and smoulders inside this grove. An ocean of green. Several thousand square kilometres. Forget a census of people, trees or animals, this is perhaps the only zone in India that is yet to see a routine administrative survey or a count of voters. The state began mapping Abujhmad in 2017 – it's going to be a long journey. Very few recognize the kinds of animals, birds, rivers and rocks that lie inside. Electricity, telephone, internet – there's nothing. It is now the headquarters of the Naxals in the country.

The last battle with the insurgents, the police say, will be fought in this forest of mahua. The police began venturing inside only recently. When the CRPF made its first entry in Abujhmad in 2012, they expected mythical ten-headed creatures, but they found that what seemed like Naxal bunkers on Google Maps were barns and scaffolding to trap animals. 'This operation was a blind gamble,' a CRPF commander later conceded.

When the first general elections in India were held in January–February 1952, Lahaul and Spiti were cut off from the country due to snow. But the Election Commission had conducted the polling there in 1951, before the advent of winter. Ramachandra Guha termed this election 'the biggest gamble in history'. But perhaps its checkerboard did not reach Abujhmad. There is still no polling booth for several hundred square kilometres. People walk for hours to reach some makeshift booth in a ruined school.

Abujhmad is a mysterious and maddening invitation. Of mirages and death. The wafting fumes of the woods, the flashing shade of the leaves. A step inside, and you are lost in the vortex. When you are lost elsewhere, you retain the feeling of being lost – an awareness that prompts you to gather yourself, latch on to a familiar sound or smell and begin to return. But nothing remains in Abujhmad. Return becomes impossible. The verb 'to return' turns into ashes. The jungle stands before you like an invincible question that cannot be satiated by any answer.

One can come here to romance with death, or with the novel. Death and the novel are joined at the hip. One has to sever all ties and summon the ghosts within to begin writing a novel. Death arrives in a similar manner, in the garb of an old accountant, carrying a logbook and an umbrella tucked under the arm, seeking an account of one's life. It is uncertain whether dying in Maghar takes one to hell, or dying in Kashi to heaven, but to take one's last breath in Abujhmad does create the possibility of becoming a novelist in one's next life, if there is such a thing.

Trudging through Abujhmad, you are followed by a fear. The fear that, given your utterly unfamiliar attire, a bullet shot from behind some tree – a bullet that is more afraid than you are – will blow up your head.*

---

* Years later, I heard about three kinds of bullets from an Indian army officer. Bullets that have your name on them, bullets that don't have your name on them, and bullets that carry the tag 'To Whom It May Concern'. The first two are very few in number, but they exist with absolute certainty. The one marked for you will seek you out in the remotest hiding place, in the depths of the seas, in the heights of the skies. The one that is not for you will leave you unscathed even if it hits you in the chest or the head. It will always find some intervening factor, a metal badge in your pocket, a helmet. (A policeman once told me about a bullet that entered the right cheek of a man, who happened to be yawning at that very moment with his mouth wide open, and exited through the left, causing just a minor wound in his cheeks.)

The third kind are numerous. They are not marked for you, but they are not unmarked either. They are on the prowl for random targets, they may

But living with a blank white paper is infinitely more dreadful than the fear of death.

If no one else, Abujhmad will be witness to the flames that consume you.

---

come from any direction, hit anybody anywhere. This is the unknown and unsuspected enemy that will eventually consume you and that you need to guard against.

dawn / i

February–March 2014. Abujhmad.

It was a long wire, over 200 metres. The three of them clutched torches between their teeth, uncoiled the wire, and laid it through the bushes, before fixing a Claymore mine and a trigger on opposite ends. This February night, with dew dripping from the sooty sky, they looked like ghosts on the prowl, or perhaps they were on the prowl for ghosts. Their comrades washed dinner plates in a tiny stream nearby, spread out tarpaulin sheets over rocks, and warmed themselves around a fire. This forested patch, deep in Abujhmad, was the night's halt for this Maoist squad. Rajnu Mandavi, the squad leader for tonight, kept the trigger with himself and asked the others to do a final check on the Claymore. Perfect, they signalled.

It was my third night with them. My heart was pumping fast. 'You said landmines are for the police?'

Mandavi nodded.

'Why did you place it here?'

'They can come at night.'

'But you said this place is safe? You also have informers in the villages?'

'They also have informers.'

'You expect an attack tonight?'

Mandavi deciphered my changing expressions. 'Our sentry will blow the whistle. I will set off this mine, some of them will be killed. We will open fire, give you cover. Run behind the hill.' Mandavi lay down on a tarpaulin sheet and pulled a blanket over his face.

'My bag? My belongings?'

'Leave everything here and run.'

Before stepping into the conflict zone of Bastar, one is required to hang one's life on the branch of a mahua tree. The looming possibility of having to scamper in the middle of the night, away from the spraying bullets and grenades of chasing policemen, defines Dandakaranya. If any moment could be the last one, every moment will be felt with unparalleled force, and every move will be determined by just one desire – to survive.

Since then, I slept with my shoes on, my laptop held tight in my arms. It was the beginning of my three-week stay with the Maoists.

* * *

Always on the move to evade the enemy, a guerrilla rarely spends consecutive nights in the same place, hardly sleeps for more than a couple of hours at a stretch. We travel around ten to fifteen kilometres a day, through hills, rivers and forests. 'Can you walk fast?' a cadre asks. We must cross that hill today. I increase my pace to match their steps.

At least one cadre is posted on hourly sentry duty at nights, while the others remain on alert. These are frosty nights in Abujhmad, but the Maoists sleep on rocks or in open fields with just a thin blanket and an endless sky over them. One night, a sloth bear almost attacks the camp.

At 6 a.m., the morning drill begins when, after a roll call, the squad leader assigns the day's work to the cadres, including who will bring the wood for cooking, who will go to the villages for meetings, etc. Sometimes, the whistle goes off at 5 a.m. It's still dark, but the leader has suddenly decided to change location. Maybe he has received some information on his walkie-talkie. Maybe it's just a survival technique.

Eight minutes is what the Maoists get to pack up and move. Their belongings, containing one plate in the name of a utensil, clothes and basic toiletries, all fit into one 'pithoo' bag slung over the shoulder. Their hands remain free to carry weapons. A loaded rifle always on the shoulder, even when they go to bathe. There are no buckets, just steel mugs, used both for cooking and for drawing water from streams for bathing.

Water and wood form the bedrock of guerrilla life. At many places, a little digging, a little scraping sets free a tiny stream of water. Wood is a valuable comrade. Hold a log like a torch, use it for cooking, or to make a fire on cold nights.

* * *

21 February, 8.40 p.m. Incessant rains for the last few days. We had erected a small tent. But today's rains flooded it. Our belongings got drenched. We quickly dug trenches around the tent to keep the water from entering. We are now huddled under it. The falling raindrops twinkle in the beams of our torches. The police, someone says, will not venture out in the downpour – we are safe tonight. We laugh merrily in this gruelling hour of night.

We can curl up and accommodate ourselves under a small tent, but where do we cook? If a fire is lit under the tent, its rising flames will damage the plastic. Having gone hungry for one night, we chopped off thick branches the next morning, pitched them in the earth, and placed several layers of bushes over them. It became a small hut. Its architectural design came from Naresh. He and two guerrilla women had joined us a day earlier. They are from another division of the Maoists. Initially, I took Naresh to be Telugu, but later I learnt that he is from Kanker. One of the women with him has thick, flowing hair and a dark, taut face. I have not yet heard her speak. I imagine the unheard voice. An indecipherable secret code lingers on her face.

* * *

A major factor that has enabled the Maoists to retain territory in Dandakaranya is their intelligence network which is denser than the jungle foliage. While the government has not been able to conduct even a proper decadal census in the interior areas, does not know the coordinates of many villages in Bastar, has wrong names on voter lists, frequently mentions schools and forest rest houses that ceased to exist long ago as polling booths, the rebels periodically update their database on the 100,000 square kilometre area of Dandakaranya – spread across the states of Chhattisgarh, Telangana, Maharashtra and Odisha – with regular reports to their bosses.

Their notebooks list hens and goats, as well as the quantity of food grains with each family in every village in their territory. Even if a single rooster goes missing, or a villager does not return from the city after a routine visit or gets late, the Maoists come to know.

One evening, cadres are passing through a village when they discover two villagers are not home. Could they be police informers? Could they have been arrested? Tension mounts as the Maoists decide to stay in the village for the night. The duo returns the next morning. The delay was nothing out of the ordinary, but the Maoists know their survival depends on not taking chances. The villagers are let off only after thorough questioning.

* * *

With his sweet smile and a twinkle in his eyes, Jaylal looks younger than his twenty-two years. An INSAS rifle slung over his left shoulder covers nearly half of his five-foot-three frame. The other shoulder is weighed down under a pithoo bag. Every so often, he adjusts a black pouch that is always slipping down his thin waist, a pouch that carries a pen-gun and a dagger. The pen-gun is a deceptive weapon. It looks like a fountain pen, but instead of ink it contains a small cartridge.

Jaylal heads a local organization squad overseeing Party work in nearly ten villages spread over 1,000 square kilometres in Abujhmad. In the Party for seven years, he has never participated in an encounter, nor is he ever likely to. 'My task,' he says, 'is to prepare the masses for a new democratic revolution.'

He joined the Balak Sangathan, or the child unit, of the Party when he was in school. His family land had been acquired for a proposed steel plant of the Tatas in Bastar around 2005. A lot of adivasis joined the Maoists in protest against the acquisition. A decade later, the company had to abandon the plant as it couldn't secure iron ore, but the boys who had taken up weapons continue to fight the guerrilla battle.* Jaylal's wife is also a guerrilla, deployed in another area committee.

---

* In 2004, the central government informed the Lok Sabha that 1,343,346 hectares of forest land was under illegal encroachment across the country. The figure rose to 1.9 million hectares in 2016. In 2004, the two states that had the maximum presence of Maoist guerrillas were Andhra Pradesh and Chhattisgarh. Of the 1,343,346 hectares of encroached forest land, 150,495 were in Chhattisgarh and 295,383 in Andhra Pradesh. In other words, 450,000 hectares or one-third of the encroached forest land in India was in the two states that had registered the highest spread of insurgency.

The government data on encroachment is likely to be highly conservative as it doesn't include the acquisitions that remain legal on paper, but are actually forced or fraudulent. Consider this: the Panchayats (Extension to Scheduled Areas) Act, 1996 or PESA was enacted to safeguard the areas mentioned in Schedule V of the Indian Constitution. The act makes it mandatory to consult gram sabhas before approving 'plans, programmes and projects for social and economic development'. In June 2005, the Indian Farmers Fertiliser Cooperative (IFFCO) Limited and the Chhattisgarh government signed an agreement to set up a 1,320 MW power plant in the Premnagar gram panchayat area of Surguja district. The project required 728.41 hectares of land spread over five revenue villages – Premnagar, Chandanagar, Namna, Raghunathpur and Abhaypur. Since the Premnagar gram panchayat was under the Schedule V area, the gram sabha's approval was mandatory. Between 2005 and 2009, the district administration organized as many as fourteen gram sabha meetings, and on each occasion people passed a resolution against the proposed plant. Given such a clear mandate against the project, any democratic government should have dropped its plans. But the Chhattisgarh government played a great trick. In 2010, it converted the Premnagar gram panchayat into a nagar panchayat and took it out of the purview of PESA.

The government and industry, Jaylal tells villagers, want to snatch their land away. The nearly illiterate villagers, many of whom have rarely stepped out of the forest, listen with a dazed look as he talks about the 'false Independence of 1947' and the threat of 'revisionist Left parties', trying to convince them that with proper groundwork they can eventually 'encircle cities after capturing villages'. His work is purely political. Almost none of the cadres of his wing has ever figured in any police case or has a police record – a completely camouflaged army.

The political wing also builds two ground-level forces in villages – the Jan Militia and the Gram Rakshak Dals. The JMs are villagers who are not Party members, but mostly operate as informers for the Maoists and offer them occasional help. The GRDs carry minor weapons and act as armed sentries, the Maoists' first line of defence. From these two outfits are eventually drawn cadres for the CPI (Maoist). In between are placed the Jantana Sarkars, or revolutionary people's councils, which comprise elected villagers, that work under Maoist supervision and decide how government schemes such as MGNREGA will be implemented. In February 2015, over 10,000 Maoist-supported panches or village heads were elected unopposed in Bastar, a repeat of the 2010 polls. Together, these panches oversee government schemes worth nearly 100 crore rupees a year. A small fraction siphoned off is enough for the guerrillas' sustenance.

* * *

It seemed surprising, improbable even, to someone diligently studying and recording India's largest insurgency for several years. In the heap of textbooks for guerrilla cadres I read in their camps was one titled *The Political Programme of the CPI (Maoist)*. Its tone and tenor could easily pass for that of a right-wing document. 'Our beloved motherland India is among the most ancient, biggest and populous countries in the world. The native place of several nationalities, tribals and followers of different religions and beliefs, our India is a multinational country ...

Its civilization is among the oldest civilizations in the world. Our people are the inheritors of a rich revolutionary tradition and proud cultural heritage,' the beginning of one chapter reads – sentences that could be anything but the manifesto of a revolutionary party.

The textbooks term the Independence 'false', call Gandhi a lackey of the British Raj, but a chapter on foreign policy towards India's neighbours reproduces Jawaharlal Nehru's Panchsheel principles verbatim: 'Mutual respect for each other's territorial integrity and sovereignty, mutual non-aggression, mutual non-interference in each other's internal affairs, equality and cooperation for mutual benefit, and peaceful coexistence.'

Who wrote these books? It cannot be the work of a single mind. A committee of several top ideologues have drafted and approved the texts that are taught both to the cadres and the villagers.

The textbooks underline what the CPI (Maoist) constantly states about itself – it is not separatist or anti-national, but anti-system. The state cannot win this battle without grasping the distinction. Know your enemy. They oppose the electoral system, which they believe has not delivered justice to the marginalized. Hence, the anger against 'revisionist forces' – the Left parties that contest elections.* Even Ganpathy, who first headed the CPI (Marxist–Leninist) People's War (PW) and then the CPI (Maoist) until Nambala Keshava Rao, alias Ganganna, took charge in 2018, once considered a limited participation in politics.

On 23 February, a Maoist leader is teaching history to five villagers. The 'treacherous battle of Plassey' in 1757 that brought British rule to

---

* Among the ironies of the Indian Left movement are its fratricidal battles. Beginning with a series of splits and splinter groups in its ranks, the Indian Left has shed a lot of blood fighting against its own brethren – on the electoral streets and in the jungle paths, with ballots as well as guns. Even in Bastar, the rise of the Maoists coincided with the decline of the Communist Party of India.

India. The textbook is in Devanagari script, but the language is Gondi. While the government barely recognizes the need to communicate with the adivasis in their language, the Maoists print books for them in Gondi. The leader is comparing the cruel Ryotwari landlords propped up by the British with Salwa Judum, and ryots with today's labourers. Among the five, four are illiterate. It's perhaps their first introduction to the words 'Plassey' and 'Ryotwari'. Like goats locked in a barn, they look around restlessly. It is not clear if the teacher, who lived with them and began his mornings with mahua until a few years ago, is able to grasp what he is preaching.

A theatre of the absurd.

* * *

He has been with us for four days. At first, I was surprised to see a boy coming with the Maoists, carrying grains and utensils. A boy in his early teens, in a shirt and trousers. He seemed to be an adivasi, spoke Gondi, swiftly chopped wood, but his demeanour somehow did not seem like that of a resident of the forest. I was even more surprised when I had a word with him a day later. He spoke fluent Hindi, without slipping into Gondi even once. Where had he come from? Why was he here?

I wait for some private space to initiate a conversation with him. The guerrillas have begun trusting me, but I notice that they never leave me alone with any cadre. A guerrilla always accompanies me even when I go to pee, but this is an understandable precaution. I talk to them through the day, over meals, record interviews, take notes, but a few guerrillas are always with me to ensure that if any cadre speaks out of turn or, without grasping the sensitivity of my question, reveals any secret, then the others will immediately snap at him or ask me to change the topic.

I know that the Maoists induct young boys, but he does not seem to be a new recruit. He wears civilian clothes, not the guerrilla uniform. He performs minor tasks, fetches water from the river, makes fires, lazily participates in their morning drills, and often spends his afternoons resting under a tree, dozing off whenever he can.

I finally get some time with him on the fourth day. His village is in Abujhmad, but he studies in class eight in a residential school in Narayanpur. He was visiting his home for the vacations when the Maoists asked him to stay with them for a few days. He is desperate to return home and join school, but they teach him the significance of protracted revolution, the art of combat. And since he is more educated than many of them, he is also asked to read them their textbooks. When I enquire with the Maoists, I am told that he joined them voluntarily.

He is worried that if word gets out about his stay here, it will jeopardize his return to the school. The police will harass him. He might be forced to become an informer, reveal secrets of the Naxal life, and eventually embark upon a path of treachery. The police barracks and the village lanes of Bastar abound with such Adivasis who have lost their identity and are known by a common noun – 'mukhbir'.

I resolve that I will not let this happen. An IAS officer posted in Narayanpur is my friend. A sensitive man. I will ask him to ensure the boy's seamless return to school. Nobody – not the schoolteachers, nor the police – should bother him. However, all of this is still in the future. Will the marks of the guerrilla life ever be erased from his impressionable mind, and the allure of the rifles and explosives he is living with now be overcome? How will he bear the sacred duty of history, of protracted battle, that he is burdened with now? And what if he, in fact, ends up becoming an informer?

* * *

24 February, 6 a.m. Ma's birthday. We are about to change camp. We should have left last night – we had been given the signal – but it got late. The moon is waning these days. Only three more days to Amavasya, the new moon. Last night, I suddenly found this name enchanting – Amavasya. I said the word aloud repeatedly to hear its sound. I will call my daughter or the protagonist of my novel by this name.

* * *

27 February, 5.50 a.m. My urine smells of medicines. I had begun taking anti-malaria tablets before heading for the jungle. Crumbling for the past two days, I am now on more medication. The nights are spent in unease, tossing inside a sleeping bag. A little while ago, I went to relieve myself in the bushes. A guerrilla was with me, as usual. As my urine fell on the soil, a strange bitter smell wafted up to my nostrils along with a thin strand of warm steam. If I am not cured soon, the Maoists say, they will call the doctor. I know that a doctor has come to live with the guerrillas, leaving his medical career behind. But who is he? And is it just one doctor or several?

Stones and gigantic roots are strewn around the camp. We arrived here late last night. We couldn't clear up the ground before spreading out our tarpaulin sheets, or perhaps such a rocky surface could not be smoothed. Stones and roots hurt my back through the night.

Like mountain sickness, perhaps there is also a malady known as forest sickness. I have spent the last three days and nights at places that do not offer even a tiny sliver of sky. The camp is set up amid a grove of formidable trees. Thick branches and dense leaves have seized the entire sky. The eye cannot see beyond ten or fifteen metres in any direction. My gaze feels strangled.

Amid the hopelessness, I am opening up to the guerrillas. I occasionally teach them martial arts and a few exercises. We even tease each other.

On many occasions, as we are on the way from one halt to another, Jaylal suddenly blows the whistle, signals for us to stop and, gathering the rifle slung over his shoulder, disappears into the bushes. Seeing him rush off, the other guerrillas, who are older than him but his juniors by rank, break into laughter. I did not understand until they told me, with a chuckle, that Jaylal often has an upset stomach.

Rajnu Mandavi, who stays awake through almost the whole night on sentry duty, often takes a long compensatory nap during the day. He snores majestically. The women comrades giggle and call him 'motorcycle'.

I now frequently use and twist their vocabulary of 'revolution' and 'protracted battle'. They laugh at my inventiveness, and also borrow some of my usages. On the night of 18 February, we chatted around the fire. As I rose up, I stepped over a log. Embers fell on my mosquito net and on Rajnu's tarpaulin which served as his bedsheet and mattress. The embers left big holes in them. I apologized. 'No worries. One tarpaulin will not bring about a revolution. Thousands of tarpaulins are needed,' Rajnu said and all of us started laughing.

He was imprisoned in Narayanpur jail for more than two years. He was bemused by city life, or what was revealed of it to him through a prison. 'Even goons do PT in the city.' He made gestures of lifting weights. He could not believe that jails had such 'facilities' for prisoners. Once, he was taken to meet a senior police officer. Rajnu was flabbergasted by the flush in the officer's washroom. He enacts what he narrates, and the jungle roars merrily.

He knows little Hindi. When he speaks with me, the syntax of his carefully framed sentences becomes extremely creative. His most unique usage is 'mutton': The bullet yanked the mutton out of his body. The bear snatched away all the mutton. Mutton will come out if you fall from a tree. His Hindi doesn't have a word for meat or flesh. Any kind of meat is mutton – chicken, goat, even man.

On 22 February, a few guerrillas and I had gone to the river for a bath. We also shaved. Suddenly, Rajnu took out a stainless steel nail-cutter from a blue plastic case and, pointing at my nails, held it out to me. Surprised, when I returned it after clipping my nails, he pulled out the file attached to the nail-cutter and again held it out to me. I couldn't understand him at first. He filed his nails expertly, showing me how to do it. 'Do this as well,' he said.

* * *

War is an impossible thirst, an incurable addiction. Having inhaled the breeze from a battlefield, a human being no longer remains fit for homes that don't host corpses flickering with unfulfilled yearnings, where the smell of fresh blood doesn't waft through the courtyard, homes that do not see an assaulting squad knocking at the threshold. Have the residents of this Kurukshetra become captives of the pledge to revolution?

There are many eyes recording the war. Guerrilla fighters, Indian soldiers, residents of the forests, journalists, companies that have their gaze fixed upon the mineral wealth beneath the soil. Could it also be viewed through the eyes of a dog without testicles?

After walking for several hours, we had reached Horadi village an hour ago on the morning of 27 February, set up our camp at a little distance from the settlements. Guerrilla sentries had secured positions on the periphery. The others were preparing the meals. A few villagers were also with us. One of them was named Malo – he brought rations from the village along with three other boys. Malo had shown me some videos on his mobile phone earlier, saying that the police were thrashing the villagers of Bastar, to which I had immediately countered that, let alone being from Bastar, these 'villagers' didn't even look like Indians.

Suddenly a screeching echoed through the forest. Many goats, screaming and scampering, were racing through the trees. A man wearing a red T-shirt and blue shorts was chasing them with three dogs.

'One of them doesn't have balls,' Malo suddenly said.

'What?'

'Yes, god forgot,' another boy said and all of them broke into peals of laughter.

Since I didn't believe them, they called out to someone – a sound in which I tried but failed to locate a name or name-like syllables. Leaving the goats behind, the man came running towards us. Malo spoke to him in Gondi, upon which he called the dog – Mocha. The name was clear now. Mocha came running towards him. He had a smooth, dark brown coat. A taut body, long face, alert ears and eyes. Malo asked me to inspect him. Mocha had no testicles. I had seen a variety of dogs, had several pets at home too, yet I couldn't recall such a specimen. 'He has been like that since childhood,' someone said, and they all let loose a crazy guffaw. The name of Mocha's owner was Kande Ram – he was 'kana', or one-eyed. A narrow slit in place of his left eye. 'He has also been like that since childhood,' another boy said. By now, the Maoists had also joined us, having kept their rifles aside.

'Your dog doesn't have testicles. You don't have an eye. What a great pair!' I said.

The goats were safe. Mocha was resting beside us. We were all roaring with laughter.

The morning ended with me clicking a few photographs of Mocha. But later, as I would recall that morning, it often occurred to me that Mocha was also a witness to the war. Mocha reminded me of the great warrior Barbarika in the Mahabharata, who was beheaded by Krishna because he was apprehensive that the entire Pandava army would be annihilated if Barbarika joined the Kauravas. Krishna then placed his head on a hill so that he could watch the great war. With the right to intervene snatched away from him, Barbarika was now an impotent spectator. Later, when the Pandavas had an argument about who had displayed the greatest valour, they approached Barbarika's head for the answer because he had been witness to the entire war.

* * *

Last night, the silvery shadow of the moon, filtering through the dark trees, mingled with the yellow flames of the fire near us and carved figures on the white fabric of my mosquito net. I suddenly found that the net had dissolved into the sky. A mahua tree spread out over me like a divine assurance.

Last night, we had anticipated a police assault. Everyone was on alert. I was told to run to safety as soon as the whistle was blown, but soon, lying in my sleeping bag, I found myself counting the leaves of mahua suspended in the air above me. Shivering in the cold, I couldn't recall when I pulled the sleeping bag over my face and zipped myself in. In the morning, I found that I had slipped very close to the fire. Embers had visited me in the night, leaving holes in the sleeping bag.

Two days earlier, a villager had brought some material wrapped in newspapers. Four pages each of the newspapers *Haribhoomi* and *Patrika* dated 10 February. The hunger for the world – mine and the guerrillas' – accumulated over so many days, swooped down upon those pages. We competed with each other on who would read first.

The papers are from when I was still in the city, and so I already know of all the 'news' contained in them. Still, I've been devouring them for the past two days. Every news item, headline, brief and advertisement. Arvind Kejriwal is adamant about the Lokpal bill. India lost the first cricket Test to New Zealand by forty runs. Two CRPF personnel killed in Sukma, three Naxals in Bijapur. The news of India's defeat is verbatim in both newspapers. Both copied from the agencies. Even their box items are similar. Amazing news desks.

This camp doesn't seem to be very far from a path. We are on a hilltop, yet I have heard the sound of a motorcycle twice in one day. It should not be difficult for the police to reach here. I wonder why they have set up camp here. I will ask them to shift soon.

I've had numerous arguments with the police about why they assume every villager is a Maoist informer and harass them. I am now in the grip of a similar apprehension. I take every villager who visits our camp to be a police informer. Some carry deadly axes, some carry bharmaars. They look at me with suspicion. I gather the few Gondi words I know from their chat with the Maoists and try to weave the entire conversation. Perhaps they talk about routine matters like the goods to be purchased from the next weekly market, or the newborn calf in the village, but to me they look like police informers. Have they come here to reconnoitre? Is a police attack likely tonight?

'Are you certain?' I ask the Maoists after they leave.

'Don't worry. They are very reliable.'

'Okay. But don't reveal my identity.'

To suspect every little thing is necessary for survival in the forest.

Despite the constant fear, I eagerly look forward to lying under the white net at night. The sky, the trees and the stars trickle down the white threads and gather at the tips of my fingers, like a dream that can be unveiled only in the future. A dream that is not mine but someone else's, in whose veins I resonate. I am the dream of an obscure apparition.

And yet, I am often unable to sleep due to the chilling terror and the terrifying chill. The nights are spent counting the hours, waiting for the sun, the moment the silver branches floating above me turn golden.

* * *

One evening, some villagers arrive at the camp and take two senior cadres of our squad aside. Soon we are told that it is not safe to change our halt now, but we will have to leave very early in the morning – a command that I take to be an indication of a possible police attack at night. Though I might have mistaken the signals, I follow their instructions, clutch my laptop and slip into the sleeping bag believing that this could be my last night.

It remains quiet for a long time, but suddenly, at around 10.15 p.m., the jungle is drowned in the frenetic beams of torches and the sound of feet scampering over dry leaves and twigs.

The flashlights and harsh rustling remain unabated. Zipped up inside the sleeping bag, I try locating human voices. Has our camp come under attack? But why are the guerrillas not opening fire in retaliation? Have they all been killed or made captive? I peep out of the sleeping bag – the fire is still smouldering. All the tarpaulin sheets are empty. I cannot see anyone. Am I the only one left in the camp? But no one blew the whistle, nor was there any explosion of the Claymore mine. Was the enemy attack so ferocious that all the guerrillas were killed without a whimper? Such fierce fighters wiped out instantaneously? What should I do now? Should I run away? Or perhaps that's too dangerous, and it's better to remain lying down? The torches are now very close. A restless beam flickers upon my mosquito net for a while. Are they policemen searching for anybody who may still be alive? Before a spray of bullets emerges out of an AK-47 or an X95 rifle and creates countless holes in my body, should I get up and show my identity card? There might be CRPF or District Force personnel of my acquaintance in the police team.

Amid this, a white pond spreads out over me. Looking at the sky and the stars that have descended on the transparent white net, and the fireflies that are twinkling on the sihari and dumar trees that night, I find myself escaping gravity and reaching a distant galaxy that has been created only for me. If I am killed tonight, I will be reborn a firefly and twinkle in this forest. 'Mudko', a guerrilla had told me yesterday, was what they called fireflies in Gondi.

I recall the protagonist of a Russian novel who has been made captive by Napoleon's army. Lying on the ground, he stares at the stars. 'High up in the light sky hung the full moon. Forests and fields beyond the camp, unseen before, were now visible in the distance. And farther still, beyond those forests and fields, the bright, oscillating, limitless distance lured one to itself.' At that moment, the infinity of his existence is revealed to him, and he tells himself: 'And all that is me, all that is within me, and it is all I!'

dream / v

Which Russian emblem left its greatest mark upon the last century? Communism? Revolution? What was the most uttered Russian name on the planet in the last seventy years? Lenin, Stalin, Trotsky, Brodsky? Tarkovsky, Tolstoy, Dostoevsky? Gorbachev, Glasnost? Or Kalashnikov? Avtomat Kalashnikova 47.

The Kalashnikov rifle is a tantalizing thing. Its black metal gleams in the forests of Bastar.

The bang of the primitive .303 during my National Cadet Corps days in school still resonates in my memory. Firing practice at the army's shooting centre. Lying on the ground, the rifle's butt firmly placed against the shoulder, we aimed at a cardboard target. A terrific thud on the shoulder with the release of each bullet. A sensation running through the nerves. That rifle, which should have been shelved long ago, still adorns the armoury of the railway security guards and the police of states like Uttar Pradesh.

Bastar, on the other hand, pulsates with the sound of the most seductive and devastating rifle in human history. Over 100 million AK-47s have been produced so far, which took birth in a Russian factory the year India got its independence. Its closest competitor, the US-made M16, rests at a mere eight million. If every rifle was used by say ten or twelve people during its lifetime of nearly fifty years, then over 1.2 billion hands – a number equal to the population of India – have already held it.

Its poise, power and poison run through the body of the enemy like a hot knife through butter. Khrushchev's forces crushed the Hungarian rebellion of 1956 with this rifle. It caused the defeat of the USA and its standard-issue rifles, the M14 and its superior successor the M16, in the Vietnam War. The US soldiers would throw their weapons away in desperation and grab the AK-47s of dead Vietnamese men. The weapon which began its journey in the USSR found its way to the entire Soviet bloc and the non-aligned nations through import and smuggling.

Despite their technological might, the NATO forces couldn't find an antidote to this rifle. The tales of various armed rebellions across the globe during the last seventy years were written by the tip of its bullet. Whether in South America, Iraq or Syria, it is the weapon of choice for every guerrilla fighting against Western hegemony. In a delicious irony, the Soviet army was eventually trounced by its own weapon. This very rifle led the first and most decisive assault upon the Soviet fort. The US gathered AK-47s from across the globe and distributed them to Afghan fighters during the Soviet–Afghan War that began in December 1979. The Red Army could not face its own baby. By the time Soviet tanks withdrew from the hills of Afghanistan a decade later, Afghan guerrillas had snatched the mighty weapon from dejected Russian soldiers. Years later, it was the turn of the US to swallow poison. The Taliban boys pulled the Kalashnikov trigger and, using its grenade launcher, shot down US choppers in the mountains. Kashmir militants also owe their continued rebellion to this magical rifle. 'Made in Russia, a gift from Pakistan, it was known to have powers greater than Aladdin's lamp,' wrote a Kashmiri journalist. Never before was such an impossible weapon seen. Be it the deserts of Arabia, the snows of Siberia or the marshlands of Africa – hide it anywhere, fish it out a year later, and it will fire with the first pull of the trigger. Armies of many countries manufacture versions of it with or without a licence. The Chinese Type 56, the IMI Galil of Israel or the Indian INSAS – they are all its Midnight's Children.

A rare rifle that has books written on it by journalists and army generals. *The Weapon that Changed the Face of War*. *The Gun that Changed the World*. No single weapon has taken so many lives in human history. The atom bomb is controlled by top generals, its use decided by political and strategic concerns. But the rifle that pulsates at the touch of an index finger knows no moral commands. A truly communist weapon this – egalitarian, accessible, precise.

The most smuggled weapon on earth. In many places, say in Somalia, one can get it for a few dollars. Sling it over the shoulder and set out on a hunt. Cheaper and lighter than your weekly vegetable shopping. The only weapon imprinted on a national flag. Mozambique placed it at the centre of its flag as a symbol of freedom earned after an armed struggle against colonial rule.

A copper fire springs from the barrel, creates a dense spray of metal in the air. Sixty seconds, a torrent of 600 bullets. In a split second, the bullets will rush 2,500 feet downrange. The gas from the release of one cartridge swiftly sends the next one into the chamber. A push of the palm and a new magazine is loaded. Easier than learning to ride a bicycle or kneading flour. The bicycle may skid, bring the rider down, bruise the knees. The equation of water and flour might be difficult to get right, the flour may not gain the requisite elasticity. But this rifle will always roar. A nubile and nimble beauty slung over the shoulder. A flame perched upon the index finger, below which lies the bewitching magazine of cartridges. No rifle on the planet has such a distinctively curved magazine.

An invincible lust before which all addictions available to humanity look childish and obscene. You might be a follower of non-violence, but listen to the whisper of this weapon. It will seduce you into its embrace, mutate you beyond recognition. The first dream of a novice soldier. The last love of a veteran fighter. The eyes of Maoist guerrillas gleam as they narrate their addiction to the rifle.

Could such an intoxicating weapon be the carrier of revolution? The weapon of revolution requires prudence and an adherence to ethics and principles which, guerrillas admit, is impossible with this rifle. Can an insane yellow cartridge ever dream of a future? Can the tip of a bullet write the destiny of a society?

Two things come to mind:

First, after watching militants the world over playing with the rifle, the Russian soldier–inventor said that, had he known the destiny of his weapon, he would rather have invented a lawnmower to help farmers.

Second, Mikhail Timofeyevich Kalashnikov wrote poems in his childhood and continued writing poems even after joining the Red Army.

The most devastating weapon in human history had to be created by a failed Russian poet.

dawn / ii

February–March 2014. Abujhmad.

There's only about a month left before my sister's marriage. Wedding preparations must be on at home. It's my fifteenth day here. I don't know how many more days it will take. The external world is limited to radio broadcasts. I must have missed many phone calls, my inbox must have received hundreds of emails.

Nobody knows where I am – or *whether* I am. Even I don't know my coordinates. They never tell me our location, just walk through the hilly forest. I sometimes wonder whether we are travelling in circles. Are they fooling me? Do they make me walk for five hours, drain me out, and then set up a new camp at just a little distance from the previous one? I often find the trees and the hills similar and begin wondering whether last week I had come across a similar clearing, that perhaps we had stayed on its other side. As they name the villages – Horadi, Kutul, Garpa – I try to map the coordinates. Before beginning this journey, I had memorized the geography of Abujhmad and satellite images of the area which I had obtained from the CRPF. I try to place the villages on that map in my mind, but I also recall that when the CRPF had first entered Abujhmad in 2012, they had found that many villages marked on the maps of the Archaeological Survey of India were located far beyond their coordinates. Many other villages had no existence on the ground.

In such an Abujhmad, I am waiting for their boss, the general secretary of the Central Committee, Muppala Lakshmana Rao, alias Ganapathy. I have been sending him messages via his comrades, but the only reply I've got so far is: 'Wait. Stay where you are.'

* * *

'Not at all,' Fulo Devi laughs when I gather the courage to ask whether she feels unsafe or uncomfortable among so many men in the camp. For the last three days, twenty-four-year-old Fulo has been the only woman in a squad of six – seven, including me. The men share all responsibilities with her – weapons training, kitchen work, fetching water from the stream. In any office, institution or college in the city, or at a picnic or tour, the presence of a woman amid six men cannot be easily imagined without a little sexual tension. If the atmosphere is austere or disciplined, little may seem to occur on the surface, but someone is likely to try their luck. I recall the image of a lone and vulnerable woman in a squad of dacoits or policemen in Hindi movies. But not here. Fulo and other women are simply comrades for the guerrillas.

Rice, lentils and occasional vegetables provided by villagers form the diet of the guerrillas. However, the Maoist rulebook makes special provisions for women cadres: two kilograms of groundnuts and half a kilo of jaggery a month. If groundnuts are not available, an egg a day. Guerrillas give money to the villagers and get them purchased from weekly markets in distant villages. In areas lacking the most basic facilities, special food rights are among the several privileges women guerrillas enjoy. In turn, women, mostly adivasis, constitute around 40 per cent of the cadre base in Dandakaranya, forming the spine of this insurgency. I have also seen several young women, seemingly from cities, in ambush videos prepared by the Maoists. They are seen holding weapons and celebrating the killings of policemen. The CPI (Maoist) marks International Women's Day on 8 March by making village women in Dandakaranya aware of their rights. In the calendar of days they celebrate, such as May Day and Lenin's birthday, this is the only one not linked to the Left movement.

As the secretary of the Kutul Area Committee of the CPI (Maoist) in Abujhmad, thirty-year-old Ranita – a class-five dropout adivasi from

Kanker – commands the zone where some of the topmost insurgents live. Strong arms, cracked heels visible in chappals. 'Pitrisatta' or patriarchy is what drew her to the movement.

'Patriarchy wants a woman caged in the family like a bird,' she says. Ranita joined the Maoists at the age of fourteen, when her parents were trying to marry her off. 'I knew some cadres working in my area. I didn't want to marry so I approached them. They said, "You're young, you can't join," but I insisted ... The Party has done a lot for women here. It has ended patriarchy in Bastar, something your governments have not been able to do. Remember the Delhi gangrape? You'll never hear about such incidents here,' she says, drawing figures on a rock.

She oversees around twenty-five Jantana Sarkars, or village councils – the ground unit of the CPI (Maoist) 'government' in Dandakaranya. 'Three decades ago,' she says, 'women in Bastar faced all kinds of exploitation. Now they are treated at par with men.'

She laughs off the police claim that women cadres are sexually exploited by senior leaders. 'If that were the case, you wouldn't find me or many other women around.'

The Maoists impose severe restrictions on man-woman relations. Their codebook prohibits male cadres from even bantering with their women comrades. Premarital sex is banned and the punishment is stringent – three months' suspension from the Party for a member, six months' suspension for an area committee member, and one year suspension for a divisional or zonal committee member.

A guerrilla army, cadres say, cannot sustain itself without such restrictions. There are certainly incidents of misbehaviour – some are ignored, some invite punishment. But no underground organization can survive if half of its force is sexually exploited. It will soon explode with internal rebellion. Also, a battle will not only be prolonged if a guerrilla army sees the participation of women, it will also be increasingly difficult to defeat them. When Jaylal says that the Party wants as many women in its ranks as men, I am reminded of the Indian freedom struggle which suddenly acquired a new momentum in the 1920s after women got involved in large numbers.

Before Fulo joined us, Paike and Lakhme were the other women guerrillas in our squad. All three very different from each other. Fulo's face resembled a peahen's on some evenings, and on other evenings a doe's. Lakhme's face was tough, her hands and fingers rugged. Paike had a sturdy physique and spoke very little. I always doubted her, perhaps because I couldn't decipher her. She also seemed to view me with suspicion – I wondered whether she took me to be a police informer. Whenever she conversed with others – such conversations were not frequent and I was unable to grasp them because they were in Gondi – I felt that she was complaining or cautioning others about me. Before I could get comfortable with her, she was sent to another squad.

But what strikes me now, as I write the final draft of this work, is that although men and women cadres cooked and washed utensils together, meals were usually served by the latter. Food was cooked twice a day – morning and evening. Women rarely served the leftover food to the men at the following meal. They either ate it themselves or gave it to visiting villagers or, on rare occasions, threw it away – this, when the Maoists use their resources with extreme frugality. I carried two plastic bottles from Raipur. One I kept for water, another for the loo. The next day, a guerrilla gave me a one kilo pouch of Nestle dairy whitener, its left corner snipped off. 'Use this instead. A bottle has better uses.'

* * *

The female guerrillas dress well. They oil their hair and tie it tightly into a braid. The Maoist rulebook provides for a hair clip and a bundle of rubber bands for every woman, but with the rider that these are necessities and 'not to be used for beautification'.

There are essentials for both men and women, including soaps, oil for rifles and cooking, torches, pens and notebooks. Cadres do not make the purchases, villagers do it for them at weekly fairs or from cities.

Male cadres are entitled to some curious provisions. The nights and mornings of villagers are rarely consummated without the local drinks of mahua and salfi. They laze around under its spell. Chhattisgarh also has a charming addiction for gudakhu – a tobacco-based tooth powder. The Maoists have banned intoxicants for their cadres, but they are aware that such habits die hard, so each squad gets a fixed monthly quota – 200 grams of tobacco and twenty bundles of bidis, but with the strict instruction that they will try to quit. Tobacco and bidis also bring some amusing moments to the disciplined guerrilla squad. They are usually kept with the squad leader. One has to ask him for it, but who will make the first move? The leader is also craving for a smoke or a pinch of tobacco – but he is the leader, how can he initiate it? Everyone is feeling the itch, but no one wants to stake the first claim. After prolonged hesitation, signals are conveyed through sidelong glances and the pouch opens. Dry tobacco leaves are rubbed on palms, and after the initial sheepish smiles the entire squad breaks into carefree laughter.

* * *

Fulo is weaving a dream this afternoon. She can always be seen writing letters. After lunch, before the evening tea, or before retiring at night with a torch clasped between her teeth – yellow light illuminates the paper, words flow from her pen. The torch is often not visible in the dark. Wrapped in light, words seem to emerge from her mouth. To whom does she write these letters? Sometimes, when she is reclining against a tree with a Maoist textbook on the revolution, she writes on a paper tucked between its pages.

The squad changes its location almost daily. But irrespective of their location, near a river or surrounded by boulders, amid the looming fear of a police attack, the letters continue unabated. Letter-writing is fast disappearing all over the world. The guerrillas are the loyal artists of a dying art.

I wrote four letters to various Maoists during my stay. One was to their supreme commander, Ganapathy, for an interview. On

28 February, Jaylal returns after two days. My message, he says, has reached them. They might arrange an interview with Ganapathy. He also gives me a book – *War and Peace in Junglemahal: People, State and Maoists*. Senior leaders have asked me to read it before I meet them. Its first page has 'Chandra' written on it. Whose name could it be?

While I wait to meet Ganapathy, I interview top leaders. One day, I am introduced to the chief of one of the two Maoist battalions in Dandakaranya. A battalion has two companies and eight or nine platoons. It's hard to gauge from Ramdher's smiling face that he heads a battalion. An adivasi from the Kutru region of Bijapur district, he was brought into the Party by Lanka Papi Reddy. 'He's my recruit,' Reddy smilingly told me later.

Ramdher moves with a squad of five armed guerrillas, his bodyguards. Shantila, a woman in his squad, has gorgeous tattoos on her wrists and chin. (Perhaps on her forehead too. It has completely slipped my memory what the tattoos were.)

The Maoists attacked the CRPF last November in Bastar and looted a Carl Gustaf under-barrel grenade launcher (UBGL) along with many grenades. They had earlier looted one each from Jharkhand and Gadchiroli. Ramdher is a military expert, and though the Maoists have not used this deadly weapon so far, he explains its operation to me in detail: how one grenade, effectively launched, can destroy a police post, and how to escape in the face of a UBGL attack by the enemy.

It suddenly strikes me that I have seen this face earlier. Perhaps in a video of a Maoist ambush of the police. His comrade friends later confirm that the 2009 Rajnandgaon attack in which twenty-nine policemen were killed, including the district police superintendent V.K. Chaubey – the only IPS officer ever killed in Chhattisgarh – was planned by Ramdher.

Ramdher assures me that I will soon meet Ganapathy.

* * *

Besides letters, the radio is their only other connection with the outside world. Every squad has a radio, tuned all day long to the BBC and to All India Radio in Hindi. A radio with a black belt. When the squad is on the move, it is slung across a cadre's shoulder; at a camp they hang it on a tree.

On 18 February, silence descends upon the squad, stationed atop a hill for the day, as the radio blares out news of the surrender of twenty-two cadres in Andhra Pradesh. The following day, a couple surrenders in Rajnandgaon. A woman cadre knew the man, Bhagat. She had taken part in an ambush with him and cannot believe such a fighter has surrendered. Almost every cadre has a memory of this battery-run instrument, dangling from a tree, announcing the death of a fellow comrade or spouse in an encounter. 'It was as if my friend was dying inside this radio. I wanted to break it into pieces and pull him out.'

28 February brings a change of mood as the same radio gives news of Maoists killing five policemen in Dantewada. Someone says: 'So many of these policemen get killed, but they still don't give up.'

Rajnu often turns philosophical at such moments. 'It's a long battle. We shouldn't be disheartened by the killing of our cadres or celebrate the killing of policemen. Neither happiness nor sorrow, we have to take the middle path,' he counsels.

On the same day, 28 February, they hear about the arrest of Sahara chief Subrata Roy and rejoice. 'If all capitalists like him were arrested and punished for their wrongful acts, then there would be no need for revolution,' says Ramdher.

We listen to the news and discuss politics, the Constitution and the revolution. They are particularly curious about Arvind Kejriwal, who has just resigned as the Delhi chief minister. His party is emerging as a major force before the Lok Sabha polls that are just a month away. 'What kind of politics does he promise?' Ramdher asks. The CPI (Maoist) spokesperson Abhay rejects the party. 'The Aam Aadmi Party (AAP) was nurtured in an NGO background and on imperialist and NRI funds.

It will not go into the roots of this system. It does not have any solution for the basic problems of the oppressed classes,' he says.

The AAP, they claim, is a dummy outfit formed by powerful people with ulterior motives. 'It is serving as a safety valve to divert the people's erupting anger into peaceful and parliamentary solutions, and is trying to cash in on it,' Abhay believes.* In the 1880s, a similar safety valve argument was made to denounce the fledgling Indian National Congress.

Almost a year later, in January 2015, when Narendra Modi equated Kejriwal with Naxals during the Delhi assembly poll campaign, the country's prime minister confirmed his inability or unwillingness to grasp an insurgent movement that has been raging in the country for the last five decades.

* * *

All of us here have a torch, as a basic necessity. I didn't have one when I arrived. A guerrilla would show me the way on the nights we travelled. Later, they asked a villager to get one for me from the weekly market in Sonpur village. The squad leader refused to take money from me. When I insisted, other squad members also said, 'Don't take money from him.' I eventually managed to give him fifty rupees. Fulo also has a similar torch, the same colour and model. When she notices mine, a faint shadow of surprise appears across her face. She looks at me for a long time. I can sense something brewing within her, but she prefers silence. Two days later, when the other squad members are away for daily work, she lets me into her thoughts.

---

* Few would have bought the Maoists' stand on the AAP in 2014, a party that was then promising new politics. But the AAP government's silence during the February 2020 killings in Delhi a fortnight after their second successive victory in the capital, amid the accusations of becoming another version of Hindutva, does, at this moment, seem to lend some credence to the Maoists' words.

The torch belonged to her comrade friend Bandu, who was killed in a June 2010 ambush in Kongera. His wife Rame was arrested in 2009 when, severely ill, she was visiting a doctor in the city. She is now in Jagdalpur jail. Fulo and Rajnu participated in the Kongera incident that saw the killing of twenty-seven CRPF personnel. Around 150 Maoists laid ambush and attacked the police team of around sixty, who had left for a routine patrol from Dhaudai police station in Narayanpur district.

Three of her friends were also killed – Bandu, Ramesh and Shankar. Bandu was the commander of the platoon that had launched the attack. Ramesh was a section commander. Both carried AK-47s. The CRPF commandant, Fulo recalls, fought valiantly. 'The old man was very brave.' Two of his juniors wanted to surrender amid the gunfire but he did not let them. 'I will shoot you, he warned them, if you surrender. But they took off their uniforms and ran away.'

Less than a month later, on 31 March 2014, another torch crossed my path. In an election rally of the Congress vice president Rahul Gandhi in Kondagaon, Bastar, before the Lok Sabha polls, an old man named Dasaram was looking for his 'three-cell torch'. He and his neighbours had been herded in from Lawagaon village, some forty-five kilometres away, for the rally. The policemen at the entrance made him deposit his torch, but now that the rally was over, he couldn't find the policemen. 'Where can we file a complaint for the torch?' his friend asked. 'The three-cell torch,' Dasaram corrected him. His village didn't have power. A torch was not only indispensable but also hard to get, available only in weekly fairs or town markets. The rally ground got deserted, but Dasaram was still searching for his three-cell torch.

After telling me about the Kongera deaths haltingly and at length, Fulo became quiet. Her torch was in my hand now. I tried to gather its shape. It had been somebody else's four years ago. If I switched our torches and gave mine to Fulo, she wouldn't know the difference. Comrade Bandu's torch could become mine. But I didn't do so. It also occurred to me that my torch could be someone else's, might have been used in an ambush too. Perhaps weapons had been snatched away from corpses in its light, many letters to lovers and friends were written under its white beam on dark nights…

I never needed the torch after that Abujhmad trip. Its batteries ran down. I changed several cities, lost or left behind several of my belongings during every relocation, and though I never replaced its batteries, the orange-coloured torch has always remained with me. As I write these lines under a table lamp, it lies quietly in my desk drawer.

dream / vi

> Comrade, lal salam.
> How are you? How is your committee working? You must be aware of the police ambush four days ago. We fought very well. Comrade Hunga and Comrade Minta were martyred. We killed eight policemen. Stole seven rifles. Police operations have increased. You please take care. Your area has more frequent ambushes.
> When will you come here comrade?
> Lal salam.

I have only one desire. By nourishing this desire, I am perhaps betraying the person who writes me, because whoever writes a letter doesn't want anyone, besides the person it's addressed to, to read it. Still, I, a letter, am living with the desire to be read by someone who I am not written for. A desire that the handwritten words on my yellowed pages might inspire a stranger, give birth to an urge within the reader to unearth the yearnings and fears, the friendships and passions wandering across Dandakaranya.

I have the desire that someone might read me and prepare an encyclopaedia of letters that guerrillas write to each other amid rifles, explosives, blood and death. Letters that are never sealed in envelopes, never posted in letterboxes. Letters that are written on the sheets of notebooks, the papers folded and stapled, and handed over to villagers or comrade friends. The unstamped letters that cross many hands, hills, rivers and days before they reach the person they are written for. Nearly 750 letters are exchanged every day among the Maoists in Dandakaranya, moved hand to hand, considered the safest mode of communication. However, not all of them reach their destination, some are intercepted by the police and celebrated as 'sensational discoveries'.*

A letter by a cadre to his guerrilla lover recalls the moments they spent together, reposes faith in the revolutionary struggle. A squad leader writes to his friend that the ground situation has changed a lot since they met a year ago. Letters that are never opened in between and immediately destroyed by the receiver after reading, letters that carry rare tales of guerrillas which will remain buried forever in the mahua forest.

The words of these letters weave an imperishable space, they chronicle the secret desires of a fiercely disciplined party. In the *Brihadaranyaka Upanishad*, Gargi's final question is: 'What pervades the ether, what is the final reality?' And Yajnavalkya replies: 'Akshara.'

Akshara – 'the letter', and also 'the imperishable'. Akshara – that contains the entire cosmos, and that can never be destroyed. The dreams

---

* Vladimir Nabokov was just about twenty, in love with a girl, when, facing the wrath of the Soviet regime, he was forced to leave his country forever. He left a vast estate behind, and yet, he recalled decades later in his autobiography *Speak, Memory*, as he set out with his family on a small ship carrying a cargo of dried fruits, all that reverberated within him was the letters that would never reach their addressee. '[T]he sense of leaving Russia was totally eclipsed by the agonizing thought that Reds or no Reds, letters from Tamara would be still coming, miraculously and needlessly, to southern Crimea, and would search there for a fugitive addressee, and weakly flap about like bewildered butterflies set loose in an alien zone, at the wrong altitude, among an unfamiliar flora,' he wrote.

Valentina Evgenievna Shulgin became Mary in his first novel and Tamara in his autobiography but, Nabokov's biographer Brian Boyd would tell us later, 'on his lips she was always Lyussya'.

of the Maoists recorded in my pages are the last letters of this revolution. The dream will survive the warriors.*

---

* Among the souvenirs the Indian army brought from Bangladesh after the 1971 war was a Pakistani letterbox. A rare instance in military history of an innocuous red tin box becoming a war souvenir.

I try to imagine the disposition of an army that brings a letterbox as a memento of victory. The soldiers, bruised and wounded, their clothes sullied with the blood of the enemy and their own, yet their gaze retains space for the bright redness. It also, perhaps, contains some letters.

An armed brigade, hundreds of miles away from home, sifts through the letters written by the citizens of an enemy country. Barely any soldier reads the languages these letters are inked in (presumably Bangla and Urdu). A few curious soldiers bring some letters home. Others manage to find a local resident who knows the languages to read it out for them.

The letterbox now quietly hangs in a corner of a hill, in the Army Museum at Shimla. The tale of the wounded brigade and the letter reader remains engraved on its red tin, like verses on an ancient shrine.

dawn / iii

February–March 2014. Abujhmad

These days, we listen to the Asia Cup commentary on the radio until late at night. Rajnu has a deep interest in Mahendra Singh Dhoni. He calls him Mahendra, and not by his popular name Dhoni. What does Mahendra look like? How much does Mahendra earn? 'Mahendra is a sportsman, he must be very strong,' Rajnu says.

Mahendra is injured, he's not playing today. I suggest that, since a slot has become vacant in the Indian team, Miriya must go and grab it.

It is Sunday, 2 March, the India–Pakistan match. It will begin in the evening. Rajnu stakes his revolution on it. 'If the revolution is to be successful, India has to win,' he says. Excitement rising within the squad, the guerrillas decide to hold a match. They begin stretching their muscles. The leader sends his cadres to neighbouring villages to get a ball. With plenty of logs around, a bat can be easily fashioned. Teams are being decided. I will captain one team, the squad leader will captain the other, and a match between the cadres seems set to begin near a stream.

But a ball can't be found. The Maoists' best chance is twenty-four kilometres away, at the Tuesday market in Sonpur village.

Meanwhile, Pakistan is chasing well and Rajnu looks uncomfortable. Night has fallen, dinner is over, the cadres are lying on their sheets, but some ears are still fixed on the radio.

There is a sudden turnaround. Bhuvneshwar Kumar takes two wickets in the forty-ninth over, and R. Ashwin claims the ninth Pakistani wicket on the first ball of the fiftieth. Pakistan still needs ten runs. 'I told you, India will have to win for the revolution,' Rajnu smiles.

Then Shahid Afridi hits consecutive sixes. Pakistan wins by one wicket. Rajnu looks around, and quietly lies down on his tarpaulin sheet.

* * *

Miriya has been living with us for the last few days. He is a village boy, around seventeen years old but very short. He has an endearing smile and vulnerable eyes of the sort I have never seen on any face. His parents died of tuberculosis when he was a child. He lives with his elder brother and his wife. A few years ago, the brother was visiting Narayanpur for routine work when the police arrested him on the pretext of being an informer and put him in jail. He was released eventually.

I often tease Miriya, saying that I will stow him in my bag and take him to Raipur with me. When the policemen will check my bag at the Kurusnar police post, the exit point of Abujhmad, I will tell them that there is a monkey inside. If they ask me to open the bag, I will warn the policemen that it will bite them. Miriya will make the screeching sound of a monkey and the scared policemen will run away.

Everyone laughs, Miriya even more heartily than the others.

I often do want to take him with me. He could study in Raipur. But I also feel that I am being selfish. He is a resident of the forest, innocent and vulnerable as a rabbit. At first, I thought that his name was Miriya because everyone called him that. Later I learnt that 'Miriya' in Gondi is what 'Chhotu' is in Hindi – a kid.

* * *

'Several bharmaars were recovered from the Maoists.' This is a recurring sentence in police files after a violent incident. When seventeen villagers were killed in Sarkeguda and Kottaguda villages during CRPF firing in June 2012, the forces had shown the recovery of three bharmaars from the spot as proof of Maoist presence.

One can only laugh at this. The muzzle-loading bharmaar gun which has a long iron barrel fixed to a wooden butt, no longer exists in the Maoist armoury. The guerrillas used it some fifteen years ago when they did not possess quality weapons and had not learnt the technique of causing underground explosions – when Dandakaranya was relatively quieter, and CRPF battalions had not entered Chhattisgarh.

The bharmaar uses gunpowder mixed with iron pebbles. It is to be refilled after each shot, takes several minutes to load, has a short range and can, at most, injure someone. It is not an assault weapon. Several homes in the interior villages of Bastar use the gun for occasional hunting or to protect themselves from wild animals. 'It's been with us for several generations,' says a resident of Beril Tola village. Since the gunpowder is not easily available in villages, it is hardly put to use and mostly serves as a trophy. With a gun slung over the shoulder, boys swagger around, much like the boys in any other place. Manku Ram of Orchha Paar village spent several months in jail after he was arrested in 2004. 'They thought I was a Naxal because I had a bharmaar,' he laughs.

The police betray little understanding of a Maoist attack. 'Hundreds of armed Naxals attacked us. The firing continued for hours,' is the police's refrain after a Maoist assault. 'Absolutely wrong!' the Maoists say. Around ten guerrillas are sufficient for an attack. Nor do they need their central leaders' permission before an assault as the police believe. 'What would I do if I get information that a police team is in my area? If I want to consult my seniors, a letter is the only safe mode, and it may take twelve to seventy-two hours. I cannot trust walkie-talkies these days ... So I will quickly assemble my cadres, take position and launch an attack,' Rajnu says. 'We only have to plant an improvised explosive device or lay a Claymore mine – explode it and fire. If there is no time for an IED, then just fire. Some policemen will be killed in the first volley, others will scamper for cover. Some will run away, leaving their weapons behind. The entire ambush will last not more than ten minutes.'

Major assaults are obviously prepared well in advance, strategies chalked out on maps. Rajnu had participated in one such attack years ago. It had lasted several hours, but he vividly remembers having fired only twelve rounds. 'We cannot waste our bullets like the police do.' The Maoists are always short of ammunition, use every bullet judiciously. Target practice is done with airguns and balloons.

A squad doesn't keep the stolen weapons. A report accounting for every single bullet is sent to senior leaders, who then decide the number of weapons a unit will get. The Maoists have the best rifles – all looted from the security forces – but less than half of the cadres in a squad get automatic rifles. The remaining carry a .303, or a single shot or twelve-bore gun – the last two are assembled by the Maoists in their small manufacturing units in Bastar.

Anything can be converted into a bomb. A pen, a glass, a camera, a utensil. Add gelatine sticks to explosive powder, seal it tightly in a container, and connect it with a wire. That's all.

The whole world is turning into a damned bomb.

* * *

Despite their commitment, the revolution seems impossible. They will be killed, they are aware, before the revolution. 'It's a protracted battle. I will die, but the revolution will take place,' almost all of them say. But a little conversation with them betrays that the dream of 'the Red Flag on the Red Fort' is amorphous. Few know where the Red Fort is. For many of them, it's just a battle for 'jal, jungle aur jameen'.

Naresh is a member of the Raoghat Area Committee. The soil of Raoghat contains high-quality iron ore. If the government wants to acquire land elsewhere in the country, Naresh says, it negotiates with people. But in Kanker, several battalions of the Border Security Force are deployed. 'You want my land. I resist. You post a thousand gunmen outside my home. What will I do?'

He was a carefree youth. One day, the police arrested him on the pretext of being a Maoist informer. He was thrashed badly in jail. 'After my release it occurred to me that, if I want to remain alive, it's better to become a Naxal.'

With the revolution nowhere in sight, how do they live with the looming fear of death? If one motive is to save their land, the second is the idea of being 'recorded in history'. 'When a villager dies, he is remembered only by people from his village. If I die, all of you will remember me. The Party will write books and print pamphlets about me,' a cadre says.

This is astonishing. Within three decades, the Maoist leaders have firmly planted their ideas within the Bastar adivasis. If the rebels freed them from the harassment of forest guards and patwaris, and taught them about their rights, they also sowed their ideology in the forest. The 'historical responsibility of revolution' suddenly descended on a people who had been living beyond the pale of history. The community that swayed on mahua in ghotuls and worshipped their local deity Budha Deo found Lenin and Mao seizing their consciousness. Family, gods and romance were now impediments to the revolution. History arrived and gripped the jungle in its claws.* The struggle to 'find a place in the annals of history' became the paramount goal of the adivasi.

For not all lives are remembered. Comrade Mangal was killed in an encounter a few years ago. The Maoists erected a memorial to him

---

* History also weaves its own myths. The final drafts of this tale of Dandkaranaya's rebels were written in an imperial study, a circular glasshouse, of the Viceregal Lodge in Shimla that had served as the personal office of the British governor for many decades. The summer capital of British India was witness to the chalking out of strategies to control freedom fighters and revolutionaries. One-fifth of the planet's population, from Aden to Myanmar, was governed from the study that allows both the sunrise and the sunset to seep in through its tall windows.

The Death Script of the jungle was completed on a mountain, at the former desk of the colonial ruler.

outside his village Balibeda, but the villagers erased his name from it. 'They feared that the police would come to know he lived here,' says his younger sister Simri. Draped in a black sari, with a baby in her arms, she points at the memorial.

In vulnerable moments, they admit that their fate will not be very different from that of Mangal. The might of the Indian state is enormous. Party pamphlets will never be enough. Cities will gradually slip into the forest and villagers will eventually move to the cities, but there seems to be no return from this path. The master strategist Ramdher admits that the revolution will not be possible in his lifetime, but he sees no alternative to the struggle.

The outside world often seems far beyond the reach of their elusive dreams and ideology. Cadres who have been with the Party for a decade and can hold forth for hours on 'the significance of protracted battle, and the dangers of neo-imperialism and globalization' sit wondering one night where the 'neo-imperialist America' is.

'Where is America?' a woman cadre asks, resting next to a fire after a dinner of rice and papaya curry. She is astonished, as are the others, when told that, the earth being round, America is almost on the exact opposite side of the planet from where they sit. Or that it is day there at this time. A majority of the Gond adivasi cadres have not stepped out of their forested zones since joining the Party. Others have never seen roads, or known electricity and telephones.

'I have heard there is something in the cities for summer. How does it work?' a cadre asks about fans. Another can't believe that people in cities use gas for cooking and don't need wood.

'How big is Raipur? How many houses does it have? How many vehicles?' asks a third.

They believe they will die without learning the answers to these questions. 'I'll be killed the moment I step out. Now we will only be able to get out after the revolution,' says Jaylal.

I remember an old incident. When the collector of Sukma, Alex Paul Menon, was in the custody of the Maoists in April 2012, a young guerrilla approached him with a humble request: 'Sahab, I had applied for a handpump mechanic's job. Could you please look into it after you are released?' The Maoist, a Gond adivasi tasked with guarding Menon, in a vulnerable moment, revealed the fragility of his existence and the insurgency to his hostage.

'When one loses the way, one asks a passer-by or looks for signposts, but what about birds? What happens if a bird from a flock returning to its roost in the evening strays and gets lost in the sky? The clouds it had seen on its way in the morning have changed their forms. The whole sky must appear the same to it ...' I asked Naresh and Jaylal, staring at the sky one evening.

It was 3 March. 'What an observation! Yes, how will it find its way?' Jaylal wondered.

A bewildered parrot was flying in rapid circles above us, piercing the sky with its screams. It seemed to us that it had lost its way. But we couldn't do anything about it.

* * *

Meanwhile, after several assurances about the interview with Ganapathy, I received the final reply from his close confidant, Chambala Ravinder, alias Arjun. He expressed regret that the meeting was not possible this time, but 'hoped' that it would be 'as soon as possible'. *Your task couldn't be accomplished despite staying for so long, we're sorry for this* – were the last words of his letter.

Among the most powerful and respected Maoists, Arjun soon replaced Ramdher as the Abujhmad battalion chief before he surrendered to the Telangana police with his wife, Wetti Adime, just a few months later. Considering the nature of a Maoist surrender, which involves long negotiations with the police through their informers, and the time it takes to secretly leave the forest, it was likely that giving up arms was already on his mind at the time, and he may have been discussing it with the police when he gave me the assurance of an interview with his boss.

Such are the ironies of their lives...

* * *

I had regular debates with the Maoists over several issues – state, democracy, revolution. Jaylal presided over a controversial Jan Adalat or people's court in 2013. Kawasi Chandra, a resident of Konger village, was clubbed to death before his wife, parents and children by around 200 villagers. Jaylal ordered the public killing because the Maoists suspected him of being a police informer. 'We wanted to convey a message through Chandra,' Jaylal says. 'The villagers had decided the punishment ... Such lessons are necessary sometimes.'

Ask him what's the difference between them and the police whom they accuse of torturing adivasis, and Jaylal looks towards the evening sky. A flock of parrots is returning home. After a long pause, he tries to defend himself, but then says: 'Yes, you are right. It is bad.' But he also adds, 'Maybe it's for the senior leaders to decide.'

Ramdher too admits that the killing of the state Congress president Nand Kumar Patel and his young son Dinesh was a major mistake during the Darbha attack. 'A day before, Patel had given a statement against fake encounters. As we listened to this news on the radio, we said, oh, what have we done?'

Always argumentative, they are not unwilling to accept shortcomings in their ideology and procedures. When they bring up Mao and say, 'All property is bad, monetary incentive for work makes one dishonest,' I ask, 'I earn a salary. If I work hard, I get incentives. Do you think I am corrupt? Why do you believe everything that Mao said?'

'We will discuss it with senior leaders.'

Several theoretical foundations of their movement can be challenged, but since the state remains unwilling to engage with them and unable to comprehend them, the adivasi guerrillas continue to believe that weapons are the only option.

The lives of many guerrillas are consumed in fighting for the jungle. Besides the top leaders, very few have stepped out of the forest. As villagers of Bastar, their life centres around mahua, salfi, rice and tamarind chutney. Upon joining the Party, mahua gets replaced by a constant anticipation of death.

The city has moved closer in the last ten years to sell its products. Electricity has still not arrived, but some homes on the city's periphery have got batteries, TV and DTH. It has made villagers a bit more familiar with the city, but they continue to suspect it. DTH can drastically mutate the jungle in no time. Abujhmad needed other amenities before TV channels.

Some senior Maoists have solar batteries, which they use for screening videos of police ambushes on their laptops to junior guerrillas. They also screen propaganda documentaries of their movement made by their supporters, and occasional movies, like *King Kong*.

A senior leader gave me three pen drives containing many videos. Since then, my laptop is placed on a high boulder every night, and the squad avidly watches the ambush videos. A guerrilla recalls that he had participated in the ambush being played onscreen, another remembers that he had lost his comrade friend in the assault. One story unfolds on the laptop, many others reverberate within the cadres. They locate themselves in the narrative – I will be visible in the next scene ... I was hidden behind that bush on the right ... I made an escape from here.

One night, I play Theo Angelopoulos's *Ulysses' Gaze*. They don't understand the language or the subtitles, but are fascinated by the images, particularly of Lenin's mammoth white statue being dismantled somewhere in eastern Europe.

The laptop soon becomes the most precious object in the camp, as all cadres eagerly wait for night to descend and the laptop to be turned on. Sometimes I want to tease them. I deliberately delay switching it on – the battery is not fixed properly, a wire is loose, the socket is not working, I need two twigs, not thick ones but thin to plug the wire into the socket, not thin ones but thick to suspend the battery from the tree, peel off the wire a bit, show me the torch, not on my face but on my hands. The guerrillas run around to bring me the material I need. Women cadres snap at the men for their delay in providing me the material. I also remain cautious lest they learn about my mischief, though we have become so close by now that even if they get to know they will not get angry but will only play a bigger prank in retaliation.

* * *

Besides the laptop, the other eagerly awaited celebration is that of the monthly feast. The Maoists make a provision for a 'mutton' feast once a month for every squad, a separate fund is earmarked for it. It is a night of grand celebration. The date of my departure has arrived, but the day of the 'mutton' feast is still far. They want to give me a farewell. I have been with them for three weeks. What have we not learnt about each other, shared with each other? Much of it can never be recorded here, or elsewhere. We ate together, chopped logs, bathed in the river. They joyfully used my shaving equipment. We slept under the sky, mocking the bears and the mosquitoes. We were amazed by the mudkos. I learnt Gondi from them, they learnt Hindi from me. We lived through countless moments of impending death – the marks of death on our memories will last forever.

I am leaving tomorrow. How can 'mutton' be cooked today? How can they withdraw money from the Party fund in advance? The Maoists hold a quick meeting and decide that they will talk to their bosses about it later, but today they have to give a farewell to their guest. When they gleefully inform me about the farewell feast, however, I disappoint them. I am vegetarian.

They don't believe it. How can anyone live without 'mutton'? How do people live in the city? But a farewell feast is a must, so a cadre suggests jalebis for me. The market is several hours away, but a villager is asked to leave immediately on a bicycle. By the time the jalebis that are already several days old arrive, they have turned dry and yellow. But we all sit on the ground and savour the sweet together. My faith in the world gets reaffirmed.

* * *

The next day, I began a long and melancholic return journey to Raipur. My rucksack was much lighter because I had given most of what I had carried to the Maoists – my medicines, mosquito net, soap, shampoo, shaving kit, etc. My soul had been scorched. I was too overwhelmed to look beyond my memories of the jungle, but life outside had also been waiting for me. Soon I was on a flight to Delhi, where I wrote what was the last diary entry of those Abujhmad days.

> *14 March, 12.30 p.m.* The Indian Express office, Delhi. Waiting for the editors. They immediately called me to Delhi after my return from Abujhmad. Three framed black-and-white photographs hang on the office wall – Sanjiv Sinha, Priya Chandrashekhar and Vijay Pratap Singh. Two dates and two sentences underneath each photograph: how they died on duty. If mine becomes the fourth, what will be written underneath? Who among my colleagues will write these sentences, and who will edit them?

FIVE

delusion / v

'Will you become our intellectual?'

I was surprised.

'Our biggest weakness is precisely this – that we do not have any intellectuals.'

A forest, somewhere along the Jharkhand–Bihar border. 16 April 2013. The Lawalong block of Chatra district. Some twenty-five young men, ranging from sixteen to thirty years of age, were on guard with AK-47 and INSAS rifles. Three of us were sitting amid the columns of trees – I along with Akraman, alias Ravinder Ganju, and Guddu, alias Sagar, whose real name no one was willing to tell me.

A little while ago, these two commanders of the Tritiya Sammelan Prastuti Committee (TSPC) had made their young fighters perform an armed drill for me to establish that they were no less than the Maoists.

Until a few years ago, many of them had been cadres of the Maoist Communist Centre (MCC) and the CPI (Maoist), but they separated from their parent organizations following ideological differences and formed the TSPC. Now they enjoy some power in Chatra and Latehar districts. The police instigate them and help them fight against the Maoists.

There are many splinter outfits of the CPI (Maoist) in Jharkhand that lure uneducated and unemployed youth to guns. They are limited to a primary, sustainable violence – extortion, mostly under the aegis of the police.

Akraman's gang suddenly shot into the limelight when these boys killed ten Maoists and captured around two dozen others on 28 March in Chatra. No one had ever seen such images of the Maoists – vulnerable, their hands tied. In no state other than Andhra Pradesh had they ever been able to neutralize so many Maoists in one go. Who were they? Where did they find the strength and weapons?

Having described their enmity with the Maoists, Akraman and Guddu suddenly said, 'Our biggest weakness is that, unlike the Maoists, we don't have any intellectuals. Will you become our intellectual?'

'I'm a mere journalist ... nothing more.'

'This is precisely the role of the media and intellectuals. Without your help, the Maoists would not have reached this level,' they said, their voices brimming with certainty.

They knew that the Maoists were spread across the country, while they were limited to a few districts of Jharkhand. They would vanish in no time if the police stopped nourishing them, and hence they wanted to strengthen themselves. If the residents of the forests lead the battle of a guerrilla movement on the ground, urban educated people create an ideological base for such banned outfits and argue for the inevitability of the battle. The Maoists could not have made such a long journey without this base. The TSPC youth had similar aspirations without being aware that, sitting on the other side of the jungle, their chief thought otherwise.

'Who is an intellectual? Can't you intellectuals intervene and bring this to an end?' It was their chief, Brajesh Ganju. Dark, rugged, with rough, curly hair protruding from under his cap. Exhausted by the guerrilla war spanning over two decades, the man now wanted to spend the rest of his life with his wife and son. 'We don't want violence, but if we lay down our arms, the Maoists will kill us. If I have to die, then I'd rather die on the battlefield. I will fight, I'll also teach my son to fire the rifle,' he told me haplessly, seeking an urgent intervention to end the battle.

The police also didn't want them to withdraw at this stage. 'Don't lay down arms,' an officer of the Intelligence Department had sent a message to Brajesh. The Maoists called the TSPC the 'pet dogs of police'. Sitting deep in the forest, Guddu laughed it away. 'We also hear that the police are using us. But its opposite can also be true – maybe we are using them. We have just begun our struggle. We don't want a tussle with the police at this moment.'

Brajesh was in his early twenties when he left the MCC after spending several years with that outfit which was dominant in Jharkhand and Bihar. Many others also left the organization, and when the MCC and the Communist Party of India (Marxist–Leninist) and People's War (PW) merged to form the CPI (Maoist) in 2004, rebels like Brajesh formed the TSPC around 2005.

Though TSPC fighters deny a caste dimension to their fratricidal wars, many of them – including Brajesh – belong to scheduled castes and had revolted against the MCC's Yadav leaders. The caste system has invaded even the ultra-Left rebels.

* * *

The Naxal insurgency in Jharkhand is fundamentally different from that in Dandakaranya. The latter has a single outfit, the CPI (Maoist), whereas Jharkhand has many ultra-Left groups that carry a vicious enmity for each other. The police cheerfully watch their battles, hoping that the mighty Maoists will spend themselves in confrontations with the splinter outfits. The Jharkhand administration and citizens make little distinction among the CPI (Maoist) and the other groups. In Jharkhand's annual reports sent to the Union home ministry, outfits like People's Liberation Front of India – a bunch of goons operational in just a few districts, whose sole business is extortion and related offences – stand at par with the Maoists.

The two prominent guerrilla zones, Dandakaranya and Bihar–Jharkhand, offer crucial signposts to the Maoist movement. The contrast between them counters the popular perception that political instability combined with poverty leads to revolutionary activities. Poverty may cause some violence, but not necessarily lead to revolution.

In 2000, the year the PW leaders formed the People's Liberation Guerrilla Army, the states of Jharkhand and Chhattisgarh were constituted. Many areas of both states were extremely deprived then, and continue to be so. Jharkhand's polity has been very unstable. Apart from the majority government of 2014, Jharkhand had seen eight chief ministers and three terms of president's rule in the preceding thirteen years. On the other hand, Chhattisgarh has had strong chief ministers, just three so far, always with a decisive majority in the assembly. Yet, while the guerrillas have diminished in Jharkhand, they continue to retain their territory in Bastar.

'We began as a class struggle, but it fizzled out. In Bihar and Jharkhand, our movement reflected the anger of the landless against the landlords, not a desire for total revolution. Once they got land, the Party could not lead them to the desired goal,' says Palamu-based Satish Kumar, now a leader with the All Jharkhand Student Union, a political party with a presence in the state assembly. Kumar joined the PW in 1982, was part of the armed struggle for around twenty-five years before he left the Party and contested the 2009 assembly polls on a Jharkhand Mukti Morcha (JMM) ticket.

Many guerrillas of Jharkhand have joined politics. Among the most prominent is former Palamu MP Kameshwar Baitha who, as a CPI (Maoist) leader, was named in several killings and encounters. He was arrested, but fought and won the 2009 Lok Sabha elections on a JMM ticket while he was in jail. He joined the BJP before the 2014 general elections following the Modi wave, but switched over to the Trinamool Congress when he did not get an election ticket.

The boundary between insurgency and politics is barely distinguishable in Jharkhand. Many relatives of TSPC cadres are in politics. Mamta Devi, the wife of Brajesh's deputy Kohram, alias Laksham Ganju, has been the chairperson of a Zila Parishad or district council.

Brajesh's younger brother Ganesh Ganju, who contested the 2009 assembly elections on a JMM ticket, later joined the BJP, and then won the 2014 elections from Simaria again as a JMM candidate. His voice is tender, and doesn't betray the fact that his elder brother heads a banned outfit. He is missing his left hand – a bomb exploded in it many years ago. His muscular arm ends abruptly in a mound of flesh. He drives a bike, somehow managing to press the clutch by stretching out his arm. If the motorcycle had gears on the left hand, like a scooter has, he would have found a way to change gears too. He was often on the phone when he was driving me around Lawalong, with the cellphone pressed between his neck and shoulder.

He reminded me of the eponymous character from Sarveshwar Dayal Saxena's poem 'Mantu Babu' whose index finger had been chopped off by the police so that he couldn't pull the trigger of a revolver. But Mantu Babu only laughed – he could still press it with his middle finger.

* * *

The highly politicized society of Jharkhand also caused the Maoist movement to fizzle out. While Chhattisgarh has only two major parties, the BJP and the Congress, the tiny state assembly of eighty-one seats in Jharkhand sees contesting claims from at least six major parties and an equal number of minor ones.

The political and administrative vacuum across several thousands of square kilometres in Bastar offered an easy laboratory for the Maoists. In north-west Jharkhand, the government remained absent for years, remote areas had no electricity, but politicians were aplenty. People had an easy window for grievance redressal – a politician next-door who would do anything to retain his voters and would never want them to approach a banned outfit. When social angst finds a vent in the political space and politicians tour their constituencies to secure voters, space for revolution fades away.

This is also true for other zones. After the 2004 MCC–PW merger, Satish Kumar was made a member of the Uttar Bihar, Uttar Pradesh and Uttarakhand Special Area Committee of the CPI (Maoist). The Maoists believed that the impoverished area provided perfect conditions for their growth, but it was not to be because of the entrenched polity in the region. 'There was not much to do there,' Satish Kumar said.

He was among the select comrades who attended the Ninth Congress of the CPI (Maoist) held in 2007. 'A fresh call was given to make Jharkhand another rear base. We thought it was possible, but it did not happen, and probably never will,' he recalled those days. 'Maoists do not have families in Dandakaranya, certainly no children. In Bihar and Jharkhand, feudalism and family bonds are very strong. There is always a yearning to return.'

The Bihar–Jharkhand comrades tend to follow a distinct pattern. They go underground, then make a return, spend a few years with their family before going back to the guerrilla life. The circle continues, repeated contacts with family push the revolution away until they eventually return home.

Another distinction lies in the leadership. The Andhra Pradesh comrades who led the Party in Dandakaranya had been moulded by student movements. They could easily influence and guide the residents of Bastar. The comrades of Bihar and Jharkhand could hardly match the ideological commitment of the Andhra Pradesh leaders.*

---

* Once the cradle of the rebels, Andhra Pradesh has managed to check the violence but overground support continues. On 24 August 2014, some 100 Telugu writers, journalists and academics gathered at a community centre in Hyderabad to celebrate the tenth anniversary of the CPI (Maoist) and urged the audience to support the violent movement. Among those present was the award-winning poet K. Siva Reddy. The day-long gathering kicked off a series of events in Andhra Pradesh and Telangana to mark the anniversary. Outside the hall were sold books on Maoists, glorifying their lives and achievements.

Fratricidal battles have also weakened the Maoists in Jharkhand. On 24 June 2012, the CPI (Maoist) issued an appeal to the various banned armed groups in Jharkhand, urging them to stop fighting with each other and join hands against the police. The ceasefire didn't last even one month, but the appeal by the mighty Maoists hit a delicious irony. They often term these outfits 'counter-revolutionary' and 'reactionary'. They have rarely announced a unilateral ceasefire with the police, but calling these small outfits to the negotiating table confirmed their realization that they were faltering in the state they once wanted to convert into another 'rear base', a state they believed had 'material conditions' more conducive to the revolution.

Jharkhand could never be another Bastar. With or without the support of the intellectuals.

Such public events could invite police action at most places in India, but not in Hyderabad, one of the biggest IT hubs of the country, a city that has many former Naxals occupying eminent public positions, including Allam Narayana, the chairperson of the Telangana State Press Academy. Speaking to me, he expressed regret that 'his middle-class background' led him to leave the Party, but added: 'They have made great sacrifices for people. I have the highest regard for them. I consider their violence a reaction to government tyranny.'

death script / vii

'Naxal literature', on the basis of which many people are arrested, is often a ridiculous proposition that the police construct around some proper nouns. When the police are unable to provide any evidence of an arrested person's involvement in prohibited activities, they point to the recovery of 'Naxal literature' from the accused.

In February 2012, the police arrested a woman named Rekha from Bhilai, following the arrest of her husband Deepak Parganiha in Kolkata. Both were termed the 'urban face of Naxals'. Deepak was an award-winning technician with the Steel Authority of India Limited's flagship Bhilai Steel Plant before he went underground in 2009. He was allegedly a member of the Central Technical Committee of the CPI (Maoist), but the 'Naxal literature' recovered from Rekha's home had some odd components – images of Bhagat Singh, the works of Marx and Engels, Brecht's poems. *In the dark times / Will there also be singing? / Yes, there will also be singing / About the dark times.*

Curious, a policeman asked his boss what was so 'Naxal' about these books? His boss scolded him. Not that his boss had some enmity with the accused. He just firmly believed that this constituted 'prohibited literature' and its recovery from someone confirmed their Maoist status.

The allegation and the offence are in search of a person. Kafka's protagonists often found themselves in the clutches of similar laws. In the Penal Colony. Bastar.

Argue with policemen, and they will tell you that they got themselves transferred to this difficult terrain only to ensure the safety of citizens. If the argument continues, they will throw at you the provisions of the Indian Penal Code and the Indian Constitution, many copies of which adorn the shelves of their offices. They won't tell you why they keep so many copies of these books. You can pity them for their ignorance, or write against them. They consider themselves to be your only saviours. Whatever the nature of protest, unless it is approved by the Constitution or is in the form of a notice by the Human Rights Commission, it leaves no mark on their skin.*

* * *

I realized the extent of the state's failure to grasp the tale of Bastar in the summer of 2012. Many children in the interior areas of Bastar

---

* There is another face of the police. Reporting from a conflict zone can often be difficult without the police's help. Since there aren't many internet or scanning facilities in such terrains, news reports are sent from the offices of the police superintendent or the collector. The batteries of cameras and laptops are charged by generators at police stations.

The police remain aware that the report the journalist is typing on their office computers goes against the administration, the papers he is secretly scanning are actually lifted from a file of the police station, the pictures he is sending on email are of a man who died in the lock-up, and their publication in the newspaper will create an uproar, but the station officer deliberately ignores it. Even if his constable signals about it, he waves it off: 'Let them do it. They are media-wallahs. Doing their work. It will help everybody.'

These are the moments when the police place their constitutional oath before immediate administrative requirements. One such policeman is Rajinder Kumar Vij, a senior IPS officer in Chhattisgarh. This chapter fondly remembers him.

There is a tendency among writers and intellectuals to disparage the police. However, if the khaki uniform, believed to be merciless, has retained a space for exceptions and emergencies, then the artists and activists who proclaim themselves to be considerate and compassionate must also review their compulsive distrust towards the police and find space to hold a dialogue with them. After all, there aren't many writers and intellectuals who will offer you a seat in their homes, give you a table and chair, pen and paper, computer and scanner, all so that you may write against them and expose their misdeeds.

drop out of school at an early age. The government blames the Maoists for forcing them to quit studies. Exploring this further, Dantewada Collector O.P. Chaudhary, who has now joined the BJP, found that the Hindi alphabet and words taught to Gond children were often alien to them, unconnected with their cultural symbols. He asked his staff to create a new alphabet and books for them. The Hindi alphabet teaches a for aam (mango), the new alphabet has a for aak (leaf in Gondi). The Hindi alphabet has i for ikh (sugarcane), the new one has iru (mahua); d for davaat (ink pot) is replaced with dadam (shadow); y for yagya (sacrificial fire) is replaced with yayo (mother); instead of r for rishi (sage) there now is rimma (lemon). Perhaps the most significant intervention that reflects the creativity of those who wrote the new alphabet is that they did not include two of the last three letters of the Hindi alphabet, ksh and jn – sounds that don't exist in Gondi.*

Some letters in the English alphabet taught in India have no connection with the soil. X for xylophone. How many Indians have ever seen a xylophone? William Wordsworth's 'Daffodils' prompted a similar discourse in Caribbean countries. In their postcolonial readings, Caribbean writers questioned the utility of having in their school curriculum a poem about a flower that didn't grow on their land. The writers coined the phrase 'Daffodil complex' to express and counter the colonial hangover.

One must obviously read literature from various cultures, but if the curriculum ignores the cultural uniqueness of its geography, the

---

* The language question is not without its inherent complexities. If there is a need to keep Gondi alive, the adivasis have other aspirations too. An adivasi of Sukma became a close friend of mine. He was in his early twenties. We often drove together into the jungle on a bike. He also travelled with me to Andhra Pradesh and Odisha. He had studied up to class ten, and was always keen to learn English phrases from me. Once he asked me, 'How do you say "do you love me" in English?' I said, 'Why do you need to know that?' 'If I ask her in English, she will get a VIP feeling.'

students may feel a rift between themselves and their textbooks, as has happened in Bastar.

In the primary classes of many schools in the Hindi-speaking zones of India, students are often asked to write short essays on several topics – 'Diwali', 'My Favourite Player', 'My Home', etc. One such essay is on the cow. For many children, the first sentence in their Hindi notebook usually is 'gai hamari mata hai' (the cow is our mother). But when they write it in English, the first sentence becomes 'The cow is a domestic animal.'

My childhood school and the small towns of Uttar Pradesh are now well behind me. I've lived in several metropolitan cities, have had some exposure to world cinema and literature, fiercely oppose cow politics. But I still cannot write in Hindi that 'gai ek paltu pashu hai' (the cow is a domestic animal) in the same way I cannot write in English that 'the cow is my mother'. The cultural codes of a land are reflected in its language, a dense network of bonds woven around words and sounds. A language nourishes its practitioners, anchors them in the reservoir of myths and memories that emerges from the culture. A community is tied to its language by an umbilical cord. Sever it, and people are pushed towards amnesia.

A lot of Hindi-speaking people eat beef and do not hold any sentiment for the cow – and they are entitled to it. But the discourse may change for many others as they switch from English to Hindi. They will still be opposed to cow politics, will support the right of people to eat beef, but the cow appears in a new perspective as the language changes.

The cow is usually not a mere domestic animal in Hindi. She can be seen ruminating at leisure in the middle of roads and lanes, froth dripping down her jaw. Many of us share a childhood bond with her. We have fondled the soft flesh dangling underneath her neck. Our mother would keep the first roti of the day for her. We would then look around for a cow, dangle the roti before her, entice her, before she swished forward and seized it with her teeth. During our childhood, we were often confused between a he-calf and a she-calf, and our mother would scold us for giving the roti to the former. Many years later, when I saw the bulky and stout cows on a farm in the US, they looked like completely different beings. Massive animals, dreadful too. In absolute contrast to the Hindi cow and her naive and vulnerable gaze. I wondered how one could fondle the necks of American cows ...

displacement / iv

The only act for which the Raipur journalist Prafulla Jha was convicted of sedition was translating what the police believed to be 'Naxal literature' – translations that he had done many years before the case against him was framed. Among the incriminating seizures recorded in the charge sheet was a Hindi book, *Premchand ki Sarvashreshth Kahaniyan* (Premchand's Best Short Stories).

The July 2013 conviction of Jha epitomizes the absence of civil society in Chhattisgarh, an absence that enabled the Maoists to grow in Bastar and convert the adivasi zone into their laboratory. It also led the state to foist the label of 'urban Naxal' on citizens.

A vibrant civil society, as evidenced in the experience of Andhra Pradesh, creates a buffer zone between the insurgents and the state, raising questions, forcing both sides to introspect, cede hardened positions and come to the negotiating table. Few lawyers, teachers, journalists or writers in Chhattisgarh have challenged the state's or the insurgents' narrative. Student movements, which can be so crucial to making ground for peace, have been absent in Chhattisgarh.

Almost all the major voices on the Maoist issue in Chhattisgarh are from outside the state, making it easier for the government to dismiss them.

Several media groups in Chhattisgarh have business interests in the state – coal fields, iron ore and thermal power production. Journalism becomes a carrier of their commercial agenda.

Well above sixty years old, Jha was arrested along with seven others in January 2008. The Chhattisgarh police termed the arrests its 'biggest success in cracking the urban network of Maoists'. But the court didn't rule him a Maoist, nor did it find that he was a member of any banned outfit. His interrogation report called him 'a Gandhian who would never resort to or support violence'. Still, in July 2013, Jha became the first Chhattisgarh journalist to be convicted on charges of sedition and for attempting to wage a war against the nation. There was not so much as a murmur in the Chhattisgarh media against this conviction of a journalist on a charge that many considered to be absolutely baseless.

In the Raipur office of *Dainik Bhaskar* in the mid-1990s, Jha was sometimes seen translating articles that his colleagues thought was 'Maoist literature', which later built the case against him. Speaking to me at the Raipur jail in 2013, Jha laughed at his colleagues' perception: 'It was not Maoist literature. I translated several articles from a special edition of the *Economic and Political Weekly* on the Nepal Maoists and got it published, too, as a booklet in Hindi – *Loktantra ki Dagar par Nepal* (Nepal on the Road to Democracy).'

Raipur was then a mofussil town. Among his friends with whom he discussed political economy was a young lawyer Vijay Reddy, alias K.R. Reddy. Few knew his identity, but Jha was not unaware of it. A resident of Karimnagar in Andhra Pradesh, Reddy lived with his wife Shanti Priya, alias Malathi, a son and a daughter in Bhilai. Reddy went underground in December 2007 before it emerged that he was Gudsa Usendi, the spokesperson of the Dandakaranya Special Zonal Committee of the CPI (Maoist), a post that was later held by Sukhdev (whose life is narrated elsewhere in this book). Among those arrested along with Jha in January 2008 were his transporter son Prateik, Shanti Priya, her friend Meena Chaudhary, and four others in a case of supplying arms and other material to Maoists. Four years later, in April 2012, Malathi, Meena and Prafulla were among the persons whose release the Maoists sought in return for the freedom of Alex Paul Menon, the abducted Sukma collector. Perhaps Vijay Reddy wanted to repay the debt of friendship.

The police admitted that Jha had only done some translations, but they still deemed his arrest and conviction necessary 'to teach others a lesson'. The interrogation report (IR) of an accused is usually at complete variance with his stand in court, as police enquiries build a strong case by attributing many statements to the accused that he later rejects before the judge. Jha's IR, his defence in the court and his long interview with me were identical. His IR had not a shred of evidence against him.

Jha was actively involved with the People's Union of Civil Liberties. Except for a few years as an editorial writer in newspapers like *Dainik Bhaskar* and *The Hitavada*, he worked mostly as a freelance journalist, he even brought out occasional publications. He got his post-graduate degree in anthropology and researched on 'migration and cultural change'.

His friend Vijay Reddy was among the topmost PW men entrusted with the task of spearheading the urban movement in Chhattisgarh. While Reddy's fellow comrades were establishing a base in Bastar, he came to Raipur in the late 1980s, studied for a degree in law from Pt Ravishankar Shukla University, befriended several journalists and set up a home in Bhilai. Reddy's interviews and articles featured in Chhattisgarh papers and news channels. The term 'urban network of Maoists' was yet to gain currency as the rebels allowed easy access to journalists in their Bastar camps.

Raipur and Bhilai hosted several senior Maoists for years, who went underground only around 2010. Rebel operations in the cities of Chhattisgarh aided the guerrilla war that was being waged from Dandakaranya. Reddy lived in urban Chhattisgarh for twenty years and became friends with many influential people before disappearing. The police don't even have a photograph of him except for one passport-sized picture that has him dressed in lawyer's robes. After his disappearance and Malathi's arrest, their children moved to Hyderabad.

Despite being a convict who was contemplating filing an appeal against the verdict, Jha readily discussed his friendship with Reddy, even as other Raipur journalists avoided talking about the Maoist spokesperson. 'I first met Reddy in October 1988. He was a brilliant law student and circulated Maoist literature,' Jha told me. 'Reddy arranged for the visits of several journalists to the Bastar camps of the Maoists. One even took a laptop for them. But I never went. I never felt the need.' Jha's investigation report corroborates this. It notes that although Reddy often insisted, Jha never visited the Maoist zone.

Several journalists in Raipur were friends with Reddy, but only Jha was arrested. 'I was a freelancer, had no banner. They could easily lay their hands on me.' Prateik's work as a transporter for Reddy, the police also admitted, eventually prompted his father Prafulla Jha's arrest. 'If you arrest a son who is involved in such activities with his father's friend, then the father also comes into the ambit,' said an officer. Even the son, the court noted, was not a Maoist. It attests to Jha's honesty that, speaking with me, he admitted Prateik should have known whom he was working for.

His friends in the media fraternity, Jha recalled, swiftly deserted him after his arrest. His daughter Priya said to me: 'Several journalists visited us. After his arrest, we requested them to take up our case. But none of them wrote about him.'

After spending nearly seven years in Raipur jail, Jha returned home on 27 September 2014 to find that his city's landscape and sky had changed almost beyond recognition. 'Are these the same roads? I asked my wife. She assured me that we were in Raipur,' he said, his wife Kavita blushing nearby, reminding him that his release came a day after he had turned sixty-nine.

Despite such a long imprisonment, the 'Gandhian' Jha did not hold a grudge. 'Yes, I was wrongly convicted and I will fight against it, but I utilized my time inside for reading. I read a lot,' he said, relaxing with family at his Raipur home.

The first book he asked for from the jail's library was Tulsidas's *Ramcharitmanas*, followed by Bal Gangadhar Tilak's *Gita Rahasya* and Gandhi's *My Experiments with Truth*. 'I'd read these books several times earlier. But behind bars, I found rare wisdom in their pages. Gandhi was the only Indian who blended the Ramayana and the Gita in his life.'

He soon aroused curiosity among the jail staff who wondered how an atheist Naxal could read religious literature. So he told them: 'Neither am I a Naxal, nor are these books religious.' He had suggested these books to them as 'compulsory reading to learn about Indian society and culture'.

Because of his daily schedule as a 'devout brahmin' involving early morning prayers, the jail staff soon began calling him 'Maharaj'.

'I was treated very well in jail,' he said, and praised the Raipur jail superintendent Dr K.K. Gupta. His release was due in January 2015, but his sentence was commuted by a few months.

How did the family survive all those lonely years, especially his old wife Kavita without her husband and son? She recited a somewhat erroneous version of Tulsidas's famous couplet from the *Ramcharitmanas*, only to be corrected by her husband: 'Hoi hai soi jo Ram rachi rakha / Ko kari tark badhaave shakha' (Everything will take place according to what Lord Rama has ordained / Why argue and prolong the matter).

Quite a statement from a family believed to be 'hardcore Maoists'.*

* The case also saw the conviction of Bilaspur's cloth merchants, Naresh Khubnani and Ramesh Khubnani, and a Raipur tailor, Dayaram Sahu. They were not convicted of sedition or criminal conspiracy, but under Section 8(3) of the Chhattisgarh Public Security Act for 'assisting in the management of an unlawful organization'. The Khubnani brothers were convicted for supplying cloth to Vijay Reddy for Maoist uniforms, Sahu was punished because he had stitched the uniforms. The trio claimed that they were absolutely clueless about their customer's identity. They, the Khubnani brothers contended, merely sold cloth to one Sunil Chaudhary who claimed to be from Industries Detective and Security Services, Raipur.

The court deduced that, since Sahu 'failed to attach his tailor mark on the stitched uniforms, he knew these were Maoists'. The brothers, the court noted, did not apply their intelligence. 'Why would a Raipur company place cloth order in Bilaspur and incur unnecessary transportation cost? Even if one accepts that the accused did not have information that it was going for Naxals, when they got the order next time they should have verified whether the detective services existed or not. Since they did not do it, the only conclusion is that, despite knowing these uniforms were for Naxals, they accepted the orders.'

Bilaspur, incidentally, is just 120 kilometres from Raipur, and has traditionally been a bigger city and market than the state capital. The Chhattisgarh High Court is also in Bilaspur. The frivolous conviction of a journalist, a tailor and cloth merchants in a Maoist case went uncontested in Chhattisgarh. 'Hardcore Naxals Convicted', the front pages of local media screamed.

dream / vii

A Marquezean tale, this. Some seven years ago, a young man named Annu Lal Bhandari had lived in this village. A mythical geography. Mahua, teak and pine. No electricity or telephone. A postman would arrive once a month with occasional messages from the outside world.

Annu played the shehnai, dholak and other local musical instruments with his adivasi friends during festivals. Tunes and songs of the forest. A talented man, he mimicked the voices of birds, women, kids, and performed occasional street plays too. Once, he visited the district headquarters of Narayanpur, came across a wedding procession that had bands and other instruments.

And so it began.

The Arcadio Buendia of Abujhmad, he brought 'modern music' with him and a second-hand Casio synthesizer. He managed to arrange for a truck battery from somewhere. The evening assemblies of the village turned musical. The entire wilderness became curious. He soon taught his friends how to play these instruments and set up Abujhmad's first orchestra – Ma Danteshwari Club. Perhaps the first 'entrepreneur' in a vast forest that lives off mahua and subsistence farming.

Soon, Annu and his orchestra became famous across the region. He got invitations from the other end of the forest to perform at weddings and festivals. As his troupe flourished, some village youths whom he had tutored and who had been part of his orchestra, formed two more bands – Kudum Tula and Ma Sheetla. Kudum Tula is the younger brother of a Bastar deity, Ma Sheetla is Ma Danteshwari's distant cousin.

Today, they charge anywhere between 1,000 and 3,000 rupees, depending on the occasion. Boys from other villages visit Annu for music tutorials.

Some fifteen kilometres away, a village chief told me: 'Ask anyone in Abujhmad – the music of Sonpur.'

(27 March 2012. Sonpur, Abujhmad.)

death script / viii

Tales are often the sites of resistance and protest. By asserting their identity through their tales, communities oppose the imposition of moral codes and laws upon them by external authorities. While it can be a self-conscious act expressed through printed literature (Milan Kundera's tales, for instance, opposed the intervention of the USSR in Czechoslovakia), the resistance may also reach from one generation to the next through oral traditions.

Several local communities living across the forests of central India often treat Hindu deities with irreverence. They roast them over a fire of mahua wood, make delicious pickles out of them, and gatecrash the great Sanskrit tales. Let's begin with the proposition that such a creative subversion of Sanskrit texts reflects the community's desire to respond to the cultural power of the language and the ethos it represents. Admittedly, despite the attempts to standardize Hindu deities they do not have a monochromatic personality, as various communities often mould them to meet their cultural requirements. Yet, the tendency to subvert divine tales is perhaps most prevalent among people who live in forests or marginal areas, beyond a codified and dominant language patronized by the state, who are considered to be on a lesser plane by the city dwellers, and for whom a creative rejoinder is often the most effective form of resistance.

A marvellous instance of such resistance is witnessed among the Ramnamis, a poor community of Dalits in Chhattisgarh. They live on both sides of the river Mahanadi, spread across the three districts of Raigarh, Baloda Bazar and Janjgir-Champa. A brilliant rupture in the story of Rama led to the formation of the community around 125 years ago. Prohibited by brahmin priests from chanting hymns to

Rama on the pretext that by taking the name of the god they would defile him, the Dalits, in retaliation, began tattooing his name on their body parts. Hundreds of tattoos all over their body, even on their sex organs. By engraving Rama on their private parts, they took the great lord to such hidden places and moments which the city priests would find blasphemous.

They also subverted the interpretation of famous couplets from Tulsidas's *Ramcharitmanas* that are insulting to shudras. One such couplet is: 'Pujiya bipra sil gun hina / Sudra na gun gyan pravina.' Its widely accepted meaning is: Even a worthless brahmin deserves to be worshipped, a shudra never holds any virtue or knowledge. The Ramnamis overturn the interpretation and say that a brahmin who lacks any virtue should be killed, whereas shudras are always virtuous and knowledgeable. Their interpretation is not without its linguistic merit. The word 'pujiya' or 'pujna' which they emphasize has another meaning too – if on the one hand it means to worship, the phrase 'puj diya' also signifies thrashing someone badly or killing them.

Another example is that of Dhankul Jagar in Bastar. Dhankul Jagar or Teeja Jagar ranks among the four folk epics of the region. The adivasi women, called Gurumai or Gurumata, recite it over several days during festivals. Men play the chorus in the recital of this epic whose story, briefly, goes like this:

Lord Shiva happens to get enamoured of a young girl named Bali Gavra, who incidentally is his grandniece and also a distant cousin of Parvati. Completely under her spell, Shiva makes several advances but she takes no interest in him and rejects him. Not one to lose heart, Shiva continues to pursue her relentlessly. He tries to woo her even when she is busy in tapasya.* It is a rare creative turn. In prevailing myths and

* Tapasya denotes austerity and meditation towards an end. It is often translated as penance in English, but penance indicates an atonement for wrongdoing, a feeling of being apologetic. Tapasya need not be an expiation for one's sins.

tales, it is usually Shiva who is distracted from his tapasya by others, mostly demons. But in the Bastar epic, he is seen to be disrupting the tapasya of a girl.

After demonstrating many a great trick, Shiva eventually persuades her to marry him. As the newly-wed couple reaches home, Shiva, apprehensive of Parvati, conceals Bali Gavra in his long hair. When Parvati finds his body smeared with turmeric, which is applied during weddings, he lies, saying that he had gone to the wedding of a friend. Parvati soon finds out about Bali Gavra and is incensed by the presence of another woman in her home. She curses the young bride and subjects her to immense torture which pushes her to suicide. In profound grief, Shiva wears her ashes around his neck like a garland and begins doing tapasya. Many years pass. Bali Gavra is reborn and is now called Dili Gavra. Unable to face Shiva's grief, Parvati visits Dili Gavra's parents with her husband's marriage proposal. Dili Gavra's parents rebuke her, reminding her of the atrocities that had forced Bali to commit suicide. They eventually agree after Parvati promises that she will never abuse Dili Gavra. Shiva marries Dili. Wishing the couple marital bliss at Kailash mountain, Parvati withdraws from their life.

This is an extraordinary tale. In the popular Hindu imagination, Shiva is a devoted and monogamous husband. In the entire pantheon of Hindu deities, Rama and Shiva are among the few gods who are not seen chasing after women. Perhaps only once does Shiva get enamoured with Mohini, the female form of Vishnu. However, such instances are exceptions. Shiva is not a deviant and flippant god like Indra. In this regard, he is considered even superior to Rama, whose behaviour towards Sita on crucial occasions remains questionable. Young girls observe fasts to find a husband like Shiva.

One may challenge the proposition that such a depiction of Shiva marks the creative response of the Bastar adivasi to the cultural code of the city by contending that, since the adivasis usually treat their local deities with irreverence, it did not require any special effort on their part to portray Shiva in this subversive manner. The noteworthy aspect, nevertheless, is that the dominant narrative in the city portrays Shiva as Parvati's devoted husband and the great lord of death. Instead of accepting such a form of Shiva, Bastar gave him a diametrically opposite trait. Even if it is to be taken as a regular practice among such communities, it stands in opposition to the narrative promoted by the city.

Another example is that of the Mahishasura festival that has been celebrated by an adivasi community in Bengal and Jharkhand over the past few years. The Asurs, designated as a particularly vulnerable tribal group by the government of India, believe themselves to be the descendants of the demon Mahishasura and abuse his slayer, the goddess Durga. The festival of Durga Puja celebrates the killing of the demon, but the Asur community observes it as a period of grief, and thus subverts Durga's tale as recorded in the Durga Saptashati – one of the foundational scriptures of the Shakta Sampradaya. This narrative about Mahishasura might have been prevalent for centuries, but it has gained prominence recently as an obvious political assertion, so much so that even other adivasi communities and scheduled castes have begun observing Mahishasura Shahadat Divas (the day of Mahishasura's martyrdom) as a mark of their opposition to a section of the Hindu culture that worships Durga.

The clues to such subversion perhaps lie in the bond between the city and the forest. The forest has been the natural habitat of many communities for several centuries. Their bond with the forest has informed their lives, their worldview and their arts.

Old Sanskrit texts betray an ambivalence towards the forest. It was the seat of sages, a sacred space for retiring to and for gaining wisdom. The third ashrama of life, vanaprastha or gradual detachment, was realized in the forest. Young princes regularly visited the ashrams of sages to receive their teachings and blessings. It was also a wilderness that offered asylum to kings when they were sent into exile. Marvellous beings like yakshas and gandharvas lived in the forest who supported princes in their endeavours. The epics of the Mahabharata and the Ramayana are built around the exile of their protagonists to the forest. However, it was also the abode of demonic creatures like rakshasas whom the kingdom always considered its enemy and sought to tame and annihilate. If it was the habitat of sages who had taken a vow to protect Vedic dharma, it was also inhabited by communities who did not necessarily follow the dharmic code.

This fluctuating characteristic gave the forest a distinct personality in the literary and cultural imagination of the city. For the city, the forest was simultaneously a geographical unit whose autonomous status was to be maintained, yet one that on occasion needed to be dominated and even destroyed. The forest was subjugated through both physical and cultural force. Epics and myths of the city carried its moral and religious code to the forest. The confrontation between the city and the forest took place in the battlefield as well as on the fertile land of stories. The city could physically overpower the forest, but the forest knew another mode of resistance – subversion of the city's epics.

There is perhaps no historical evidence to ascertain the psychological and cultural reasons behind the subversion, as storytellers of the forest have not left behind any record of their intention. However, a tale that is composed and modified by several generations over hundreds of years invariably echoes the voice of its society. If the contemporary retelling of tales like that of Mahishasura, and the recent confrontation between the Dalits and the Marathas over the interpretation of the Bhima Koregaon battle are useful signposts, then such narrations can be easily read as a political rejoinder to the perceived hegemony of the city. For such communities, the tale is not deadwood but a vibrant, living entity that carries the dreams and anxieties of a storyteller to subsequent generations.

* * *

Until about 150 years ago, the city had a multilayered bond with the forest. It was not a binary, not the inevitable opponent of the city. The first major assault on the forest was made by the British who cut jungles to lay railway lines, announced rewards to kill wild animals, and notified various indigenous communities as criminal tribes. Independent India launched the second attack when its cities learnt about the mineral wealth buried in the forest. The forest is now a mere geographical entity full of minerals that have to be hurriedly extracted at any cost. The forest is now considered to be inhabited by savages who need to be tamed and, if need be, annihilated.

In the Nehruvian era, when the union government had appointed the anthropologist Verrier Elwin as its advisor on tribal affairs for the Northeast, the country debated a policy on tribals, and whether it should preserve the forest or introduce industries in the area. In the foreword to Elwin's 1958 book, *A Philosophy for North-East Frontier Agency*, Prime Minister Jawaharlal Nehru wrote that 'we should not over-administer these areas or overwhelm them with a multiplicity of schemes. We should rather work through, and not in rivalry to, their own social and cultural institutions ... We should avoid introducing too many outsiders into tribal territories.'

Once, Elwin brought to Nehru's notice that tribal life moved in circles – they sat around a fire, sat in a circle to eat, and so on, but 'the newly built offices and schools [in Assam] followed straight lines'. Soon after, in a note from 1 August 1958, Nehru chastised the Assam chief minister B.P. Chaliha: 'If a school or dispensary is built in a tribal village in a manner which is completely different from the village style, this is a foreign element which sticks out from the rest of the village ... if we have to make the tribal people at home with our officers, then our officers should not live in a building which is completely out of keeping with the surroundings.'

This view faced opposition from people who believed that it would convert the forest into a museum and its inhabitants into artefacts. Yet, the dialogue between the two sides created the possibility of a richer forest. Such discourse has been diminishing over the last few decades. Except for some activists and writers, few speak for the forest. Those who do, receive the 'anti-development' or 'anti-national' tag.

The emergence of a hierarchy between the city and the forest is mutating the tales of the forest. Earlier, the storytellers were content to subvert the myths of Durga and Shiva, but now the battleground has shifted. The fight of the adivasi in the central Indian forests is straight and clear – to save their 'jal, jungle aur jameen'. The forest's tale has gradually turned into a mrityu katha – a death script. Old storytellers are disappearing. They are now the combatants in the ongoing civil war between the state and the Maoists – some have donned the khaki uniform, others have joined the guerrilla brigade. Two brothers born in a Bastar village suddenly find themselves in opposing armies. Whoever survives in the end, the destruction will match that of the Mahabharata war. Bastar will be devastated. Hundreds of Bhishmas will await their end lying on a bed of arrows, many Guru Dronacharyas will be treacherously beheaded by their beloved disciples, because storytellers would have already been forced to sacrifice their thumbs and tongues.

Tales offer a sacred space to human beings to record and live their yearnings, lusts, jealousies and loves. Tales liberate both their narrators and their audiences. A civilization that snatches away this space gradually moves towards ruin. The Naxal tale is a reflection of ruin.

In Sanskrit epics, sages and princes came to live in the forest and brought with them the breeze and fragrance of the city. Now the brokers of the city arrive to measure and acquire land. Dantewada houses India's richest iron ore deposits. Come what may, the state and the market want the mineral. Several local adivasi politicians, including Congress leader Kawasi Lakhma and CPI leader Manish Kunjam, have been demanding mining rights on their land. But the state doesn't concede that right.

Pointing to Essar's massive beneficiation plant,* a Dantewada resident once told me, 'People come from outside and erect buildings on your land. You continue to live in huts. You eat red chilli chutney, but they feast on chicken and paneer. How would you feel?'

A sage wrote in the ancient Sanskrit text, the Yog Vasishtha: 'The world is like the impression left by the telling of a story.' The ongoing violence in Bastar perhaps reflects the yearning of a tale which, having been stifled, has now chosen the mode of death to record itself. A tale that the state does not want to – or perhaps does not have the moral strength to – hear and comprehend. When the epics of the city reached the forest in the previous eras, it responded by weaving its own tales. The forest is now reciting its death script to the city, but the city continues to believe that it can drown the voice of the forest. The city remains oblivious to the fact that, facing death, the tale of the adivasi will retreat into a dark corner and, reinventing itself, will endure in an even more formidable form.

* In December 2019, ArcelorMittal and Nippon Steel acquired Essar Steel India Limited, which ran their Dantewada plant.

death script / ix

In what language does the Indian media write the script of Naxalism? How does the media weave the narrative of this battle? The May 2013 Darbha attack in which several Congress leaders, including Mahendra Karma and Nand Kumar Patel, were killed was the gravest Maoist assault on any political party in India.* What should one expect from journalists after the Darbha attack?

'Topless hokar force ko uksati hain Maovadi yuvtiyan' – Maoists women go topless to provoke security forces – an 'exclusive' report of the Hindi daily *Patrika* announced on its front page on 2 June 2013. 'During encounters in the forests of South Bastar, women Maoists go topless, hurl abuses ... make vulgar gestures to distract jawans.' The report quoted some unnamed policemen as having narrated such experiences to the reporter: 'Jawans made a sensational revelation.'

On 29 May, the same newspaper described another supposed operational method of the insurgents: 'Maoists drink fifty-rupee-a-litre mineral water ... lassi to beat dehydration.' In extreme heat, the report said, Maoists carried mineral water bottles and lassi in ice containers. The accompanying photographs were of a large ice container with a few packets of Amul lassi and a Qua mineral water bottle. 'Around 500 empty bottles of Qua mineral water were found at the spot [of the Darbha attack].'

---

* There were attacks on political convoys earlier too – the convoy of the Andhra Pradesh chief minister N. Chandrababu Naidu was attacked in October 2003, and that of the West Bengal chief minister Buddhadeb Bhattacharya in November 2008. But both survived.

It did not occur to the reporter and the editor that a guerrilla squad couldn't carry such costly items in the jungle. The bottles and the container could also belong to the Congress leaders in the convoy. A Congress leader later told me with a smile that the container was indeed his.

In March 2010, Chhattisgarh's prominent news channel Z24 broadcast a report titled 'Jenelia ki Lal Kahani' (Jenelia's Red Story) after the Bastar police had arrested a woman named Jenelia. The report was produced even before her interrogation could be completed and the police could establish her Maoist connections. The channel then submitted a CD containing the report and a copy of the script, along with the CD of another story, to the PR department of the Chhattisgarh government and demanded ten lakh rupees plus service tax in payment. Government officials paid them four lakh rupees, adding a note saying, 'The channel did not repeat the programme on prime time. Also, most of it was file footage.'

In February 2011, another major news channel, Sahara Samay, submitted a written proposal to the PR department for producing a 'special programme focusing on how various government departments facing Naxal challenge are running development activities'. The cost: twenty-five lakh rupees plus service tax for the programme 'to be aired on national channel, NCR channel, MP–Chhattisgarh, Bihar–Jharkhand and Uttarakhand channels on twelve occasions'. On 3 March, the government gave Sahara Samay permission to 'produce and telecast special programmes on Naxalism'.

Naxal incidents have become a product to be sold and purchased in the news market.

Chhattisgarh has been the Naxal capital of India for nearly four decades. Its news channels and newspapers are expected to have a reasoned dialogue with the insurgency. But such are the headlines of prominent Hindi papers: 'Naxal-affected children met the president', 'Naxals looted fourteen roosters in broad daylight, terror prevails in the area after the incident'.

The children were not 'Naxal-affected'. They belonged to districts that had recorded police–Naxal violence. The headline should have been 'Children of Naxal-affected areas met the president', but 'Naxal-affected children' directly links the children with the guerrillas, instantly catches the reader's attention. They will carry the Naxal tag, their sole identity, to their schools, perhaps for their whole life. The media's proposition might also then establish that, since Rajnandgaon is a 'Naxal-affected district', its resident Raman Singh was a 'Naxal-affected chief minister'.

The English newspapers of Delhi match the chord with the phrase 'Naxal-infested area', the word 'infested' denoting unwanted creatures, vermin. If a discourse considers any geography infested and its residents vermin, a nuanced reading of the issue is thrown out of the window. A large section of the country, aided by the media's narrative, seems to believe that every resident of Dandakaranya is a Naxal.

* * *

In the history of the Nobel Prize, only two journalists have received the award for literature. One of them also wrote great fiction, but both extensively reported and commented on wars. (We can also add a third journalist, but he was primarily a novelist who had an early stint in journalism.)

It's not without reason that reporting on war is placed on a high pedestal in the world of letters. War causes even giants to falter. Yudhishthira uttered only one (half) lie in his entire life, and it was during a war. A deliberately twisted sentence that brought about the killing of his revered guru and left an indelible blemish on the Dharmaraj.

War is a unique matrix of self-love and self-abnegation. One requires a high degree of love for one's land in order to kill another. Yet, it is impossible to enter a conflict zone without staking one's life. These two extremes are, perhaps, not opposites but reflections of one another. War dispatches also necessitate a tight-rope walk between these two poles, balancing love and destruction on opposite ends. A slight slip, and the artist falls. If journalism is about not expressing one's prejudices, but contesting and confronting one's preferences, then reporting on a conflict one's country is engaged in marks a very advanced stage of the confrontation. A country needs soldiers to safeguard its territory, it also requires journalists to judiciously interpret and translate the war that soldiers fight.* Not everyone can be a soldier, not everyone can write on war – a shapeless entity that changes its form and hue in the blink of an eye.

* * *

Bastar and Kashmir share a remarkably similar physiognomy and biography – gorgeous woods, ponds, hills, and an ongoing battle between the Indian security forces and armed fighters. The nature of insurgency in the two zones is obviously different, but both geographies and societies challenge the legitimacy of the Indian state.

---

* In 1961, a woman in her mid-fifties landed in Jerusalem to cover the trial of the Nazi general Adolf Eichmann for *The New Yorker*. A German-Jew, who had to flee during Hitler's regime before finding herself in a detention camp in France, she was then living in New York. The tone of reporting by a Jew, who personally suffered the Nazi horror, about the trial could be easily anticipated. Yet, her dispatches first confounded the newsroom of *The New Yorker*, then bitterly divided the Jewish community upon publication.

Hannah Arendt's *Banality of Evil* is a classic of journalistic writing. Instead of condemning the general, the man who brought horror to her community, she tried to 'understand' him and his deeds, and noted that 'he was simply unable to think'. In a situation when it was perfectly normal to be swayed by emotions, the writer remained committed to her vocation, rewriting and revising her dispatches many a time. 'Tolstoy wrote *War and Peace* in less time,' a member of *The New Yorker* staff commented when Arendt missed her deadlines.

Out of all the hate mail she received after the publication of her articles, one read: 'The soul of six million martyrs, whom you desecrated, will swarm about you day and night.' The Israeli authorities approached her to stop the publication of her book. But Arendt didn't budge because she knew that trying to understand was not the same as forgiveness.

There are some important distinctions as well. The contours of Kashmir are arranged in apple-pie order – neat rows of trees, trimmed layers of clouds, articulate and assertive people. Bastar is disarrayed – a puzzled mass of wilderness and streams, shrivelled and lost residents. Kashmir is zealously conscious of its identity, Bastar remains mostly oblivious to it. Both the struggles are to save their land and identity, but the Naxal insurgency in Bastar is essentially a secular struggle, whatever the word may mean. The Kashmiri militancy over the years has come to firmly root itself in Islamic religion. The religious foundation doesn't, of course, delegitimize the struggle but nevertheless restricts its catchment area and makes it vulnerable to the genuine claims of the non-adherents. Also, and more significantly, in its entire history the Kashmir militancy has not had perhaps a single woman cadre. Unlike in Dandakaranya, where armed women constitute some 40 per cent of the Maoist force. A people's movement is characterized as much by its capacity to inflict violence as by its composition and constitution.

Kashmir attracts writers, filmmakers, journalists. Let alone outsiders, few people from Chhattisgarh make a trip to the interiors of Bastar.

Bastar was once a part of Madhya Pradesh, the seat of high priests of art and literature, but the jungle hardly found an entry into their creative world. Many of these luminaries travelled around the world, but they rarely wrote about the southern tip of their province. The painter J. Swaminathan brought the adivasi art of Madhya Pradesh to Bhopal. He reached Patan, discovered Jangarh Singh Shyam, but remained oblivious to Abujhmad.*

---

* Nirmal Verma is a remarkable exception. The protagonist of his novel *Raat ka Reporter* (*Dark Dispatches*), a journalist named Rishi, has a brief stint in Bastar. Though the region is never described, its shadow looms over the novel. A conversation between him and his editor illustrates Bastar as well as the vocation of journalism:

> When he returned from Bastar after wandering there for two months, Rai Sahib was surprised by the large bundle of his notes, 'Is this a report or an

Ever since Naxal footfall began in Madhya Pradesh in the 1980s, police officers posted in Bastar began informing their political masters in Bhopal about guerrilla presence. At times the Naxals even launched attacks in the mainland: on a December night in 1999, they dragged the state's transport minister Likhiram Kaware out of his village home in Balaghat district and chopped him into pieces. Yet, the concerns of Madhya Pradesh's artists did not include Bastar. Their indifference might have been inadvertent, but it is difficult to give them the benefit of doubt. Bastar's grievance is genuine, as not only did the state and administration ignore it, but so did most writers and artists. If guerrillas from Andhra Pradesh had not entered the area, if police vehicles had not been blown up by landmines, few would have taken note of this land.

The situation has not changed much. Chhattisgarh has never had a permanent correspondent or a cameraman from any major English news channel. After a Naxal attack, their crew flies in to put together a few prime-time packages. The comrades become a story only when an attack on the police provides a readymade headline. No media, print or electronic, has had a Naxal beat. Kashmir, in contrast, attracts media from all over.

The popular perception of Maoists is largely distributed in a quadrangular formation – pastoral guerrillas, corrective forces of history, extortionist butchers, and disillusioned youth. Choose the Maoist that suits you. They thrive in the shadow of India's collective indifference and appear mythical. A myth becomes formidable, supernatural, if not

---

autobiography?' What Rai Sahib had said with a cynical laugh was perhaps the dream of every reporter. A journalist's secret hope is to discover that everything that may happen to him in his personal life is related to the events printed in a newspaper – that there is a relationship … [H]e rewrote, on fresh and clean paper, his report on Bastar. And while he wrote, he remembered that Rai Sahib used to say that a good reporter is one … who escapes the enchantments of karma.

explained. An underground insurgent needs this aura to survive. An insurgency is as much a reality as it is a product of myths that society weaves around the insurgents.

Violence or armed insurrection is just one aspect of the Maoist's curriculum – which due to its obvious newsworthiness and our collective voyeurism erroneously dominates the discourse. Remain hypnotized by their violence and miss the complex matrix they weave in order to operate: attack the enemy, awaken the masses, attract the intellectuals.

The ignorance of India's top journalists about the issue is appalling. Soon after the April 2017 attack in which twenty-five CRPF men were killed in Sukma, a senior news anchor, tweeting his demand for a 'mine-proof vehicle for every CRPF patrol', wondered: 'Is that an anti-national question to ask?' Of course not. Except that it could be a tactical blunder. First, such unwieldy vehicles have not proved trustworthy in the terrain of Bastar. Second, several of them have been destroyed in landmine blasts in Dandakaranya. Since such vehicles are easily identified by the guerrillas, the forces prefer 'neutral' civilian vehicles without any police insignia.

At times, the ignorance turns delicious. Soon after I interviewed a Maoist leader in 2012, a top English news channel called me for a possible 'live' with the rebel. When I explained the absurdity of this request, they switched to seeking some visuals of the comrade, or at least a 'phono'. This illiterate editorial response to the Red insurgency is accompanied by authoritative tweets from their editors.

The flag of journalism in Bastar is mostly carried by local journalists who work on meagre salaries for Hindi newspapers and channels in Chhattisgarh. They face daily risks, strike a difficult balance among the Maoists, the police and their editors, yet are derided as 'stringers'.

Let me recount an archetypal incident which reflects bravery, compassion and dedication – traits necessary for conflict-zone reporting: G.V. Prasad, a commando with the Greyhounds, Andhra

Pradesh's elite anti-Maoist force, went missing during an encounter with the rebels in the jungles of Sukma on 16 April 2013. Three days later, a Bijapur-based journalist, Ganesh Mishra, went on a motorbike with another journalist to gauge the situation. They found Prasad's decaying body near a pond in Kawargatta village, amid thick forest, about ninety kilometres from the district headquarters. Mishra could have safely returned to Bijapur, but he drove to Bhadrachalam in Andhra Pradesh and informed the police, who then requested him to bring the body back. The next morning, he set off again on his bike, this time alone. He reached Kawargatta, loaded the body in a tractor that the police had arranged, and brought it back. 'The Andhra police asked me to go and retrieve the body. They probably thought that the Maoists might attack them if they went inside. His relatives also requested me,' Mishra later said.

He is not alone. Bastar has many such journalists who occasionally help both the police and the villagers. They even become intermediaries when the Maoists hold someone hostage, and help secure their release. They often break the first stories, collect photographs and videos that are soon minted by journalists in the capital city. The photographs and information regularly tweeted and written about by the capital's journalists are procured from these 'stringers' who are not given any credit, adding yet another dimension of treachery to this war.

Bastar lives on thus – perched on the cliff of neglect, misinformation, ignorance. Can one still blame solely the Maoists for converting this forest into a war zone?

displacement / v

A Raipur night that does not end. Around 5,000 people have been camping near Budha Talab under a forty-five degree Celsius sky for a month. Gathering their meagre belongings, they are returning home tonight. Residents of tribal areas of Chhattisgarh, they cook food in government schools under the Midday Meal scheme. One cook for one hundred students. Salary, 1,000 rupees per month. 33 rupees daily. Less than one-third the minimum wages notified by the government, which always complains that nobody wants to work in distant schools. These men and women, most of them illiterate, have been cooking food in the schools of Bastar and Surguja for several years. They formed an informal association of cooks and came to the capital demanding an amount equivalent, at least, to what a labourer gets under the MGNREGA, a law of the Union government that provides mandatory work at minimum wage for at least a hundred days in a year to a household.

Since schools were closed for the summer vacations, they managed to get away from their homes for a month, lived under tarpaulin sheets and spent their entire savings hoping for an increment.

What did they finally receive?

A monthly increment of 200 rupees – 2,400 for a year.

That's all? A daily increment of less than 7 rupees? Much less than the minimum wage?

What could we have done, they say, and narrate a tale.

Soon after their arrival in Raipur, a leader of a local leftist trade union spotted a crowd of villagers sitting under the sun. It won't help you, he told them, but if you hold your protest under our banner, the government will feel the pressure and eventually accept your demands.

The village cooks took the educated city man to be their well-wisher. He fastened his union's red flags over their tarpaulins. They wanted to hold protests at prominent places like the chief minister's residence and the secretariat, but the union man assured them that he had been negotiating with officials on their behalf. The cooks remained at Budha Talab, away from the gaze of the media and public.

He paid them a sudden visit today afternoon. Your demands have been met. An agreement has been made with the government. A 200-rupee increment. You can leave now.

Didn't you tell him that it was hardly an increment?

We did, but he said that it was sufficient for this round. We'll see about next time.

Next time? Will you be able to undertake another twenty-four-hour journey from your villages? To bring yourselves together from the entire state on a common platform?

We don't know. He told us to leave today, that only this much is possible now.

His phone number?

No, only these pamphlets.

The pamphlets he distributed do not have any phone number.

It is a night of terrible humidity. Someone in the crowd says that the office-bearers of the association returned to their villages in Bastar two days ago.

How could they have left earlier if the agreement was signed today? What is this agreement? Where are the documents? Who signed on your behalf? The cooks' association? Who represented the government?

The cooks have no answers.

They have the numbers of the president and vice president of their association. It's past 2 a.m., yet I don't hesitate to call them immediately. Nobody would expect a phone call at this hour, certainly not the two cooks who must have reached their villages a little while ago.

At first, they are unable to grasp who has called them and why. Eventually, I gather from them that the 'agreement' had been arrived at a day before, between the union man and a government officer without any involvement of the association or their office-bearers. The union man had managed to convince the two office-bearers to leave earlier. The others were to be informed at the last moment to curtail their options.

It is 2.30 a.m. now. Some of them are leaning against street lamps, exhausted. Their helplessness and anxiety churning, making knots in their stomachs. Old women gather their crumpled bundles. They begin shuffling towards the bus station to start the long journey back to their villages. Their apparitions shimmer in the pond like bewildered and defeated ghosts.

A giant statue of Vivekananda stands in the middle of the pond. People come here for boat rides during the day, but at this hour the boats are quietly anchored to the shore like birds whose wings have been clipped. The bus station is quite far. Few of them have a direct bus to their village. They don't know when the next one is. This Friday night will not be buried in history before devouring countless hopes.

5,000 people lived in the state capital's heat for a month, out in the open. They cooked and ate the rice they had brought with them. Bathed under taps. Not a single eye saw them. No one from the media, no politician visited them. A conspiracy ensured that they remained beyond the public gaze. For many of them, it was their first visit to Raipur. What memory of the capital and the state are they returning with? How will they remember this month of May? The May of Labour Day. A burning pond, red pamphlets and red posters.

This much is sufficient for this round, we'll see about next time. The last words of the union man to the adivasis of Surguja and Bastar.

(25 May 2012. Raipur.)

death script / x

The attitude of the city towards the adivasi life brings to mind Leo Tolstoy's 'The Three Hermits'.

A bishop on a voyage finds a boatman talking about three solitary men who live on an island in order to achieve the 'salvation of their souls'. Curious, the bishop asks the crew to sail towards the island. When they're there, he asks the three men: 'How do you serve god?'

'We do not know how to serve god. We only serve and support ourselves,' one of them says.

'But how do you pray to god?'

'Three are ye, three are we, have mercy upon us,' a hermit replies.

The bishop, convinced that they don't understand the holy trinity, spends the day teaching them. The three barely grasp his words. He makes them repeat the prayer a hundred times over, and returns with a smug smile. Back on the vessel, the island lost in the night, he sees a bright streak of light chasing the ship. As it comes closer, he is stunned to find the three hermits running on the water, hand in hand, all gleaming white. 'We have forgotten your teaching,' they say with one voice. 'Teach us again.'

'Your own prayer will reach the lord,' the bishop crossed himself. 'It is not for me to teach you. Pray for us sinners.'*

---

* Ludwig Wittgenstein, who did not have much interest in fiction, was particularly fond of this tale for its obvious metaphysical meanings. Many decades later, Ramchandra Gandhi, another brilliant philosopher, invoked Tolstoy's three hermits during a lecture he delivered in the memory of his friend Nirmal Verma on 3 April 2007. He compared its last sequence with the end of Verma's story 'Kavve aur Kala Pani' (Crows of Deliverance). This was one of his last public lectures. He died two months later.

The city also wants to impose its language on the adivasis. Tolstoy's bishop eventually realized his mistake, but the city seems to have little compunction about its deeds.

* * *

The two terms, 'adivasi' and 'tribe', are used almost interchangeably to denote the communities that live largely beyond the margins of 'civilization'. The word 'adivasi' refers to the native residents of a land who, thus, also have the first right over all the forest and mineral resources lying therein. Whereas 'tribe' is an administrative-legal term to denote those communities that have been granted certain rights under the law. Also, while the word 'adivasi' always refers to the communities that live in or come from forests or relatively inaccessible terrains, tribes can also be found in urban or semi-urban areas.

However, none of these terms – adivasi, scheduled tribe or tribe – is a merely social-anthropological category. They have deep political and cultural connotations. Coined during the British rule, the nomenclature 'tribe' unjustifiably clubs together many diverse and heterogeneous communities of India into a monolithic block. Worse, since the contribution to the gross domestic product has become the overarching parameter of evaluating a community, the tribes or the adivasis, having a negligible footprint of production and consumption, are rewarded with obscene adjectives like 'backward' and 'anti-modern'.

Abujhmad has many cows and buffaloes wandering about, but the adivasis are not interested in selling milk in Narayanpur, they don't even milk the cows for themselves. The Maoists have tried to teach them to use bullocks for farming, but it hasn't become common. Iron is perhaps the only metal that has a word for it in Gondi. Since their bond with nature has been fundamentally different from the city's, economic production has never been their prime concern. The GDP parameter becomes redundant in Bastar.

If anything, modern thinking mandates that one evaluate a community by its intrinsic parameters. Imposing one's concepts on the other is terrible intolerance, backwardness. The contempt of the city towards the village has also entered the language and the Constitution. A resident of a country is called a citizen, not a villager. The constitutional rights are available to the citizen, whose root word is the same as that for city (the Old French *cite*).

Life suddenly assumes different hues once the lens of the GDP growth rate is taken off. One can then hear the poetry of silence and ambivalence that Bastar weaves. A family can pass an entire day with few verbal exchanges. There is little need to communicate even with immediate kin, much less with the outside world. Travelling through the jungle on a motorbike, I've often met people who, when asked for directions, readily come along to drop me to my destination. Their unplanned travel doesn't end there. They stay back in this village, without worrying that their family back home might be waiting or concerned about them, as there is no mode of communication to explain their sudden disappearance. Any home in the village will give them shelter in its courtyard, a little mahua and rice. The visitor will help the host in fetching salfi or hewing wood before making the return journey to their home in a day or two. Bastar is an epic of slowness that moves beyond the call of GDP growth, and that worries little about the twin ideals of scientific temper and rationality. I once thought that V.S. Naipaul was right when he termed the adivasis a 'stunted' species. My visits to Bastar erased this perception. Abujhmad refuses to surrender before modernity and responds to history with its own mythologies.*

---

* This is, perhaps, not unique to Bastar. I recall a conversation between a traveller and a 103-year-old villager in a Japanese movie:

> Traveller: What's the name of this village?
>
> Old man: It doesn't have one. We just call it 'the village'. But outsiders call it 'the village of the water mills'.
>
> Traveller: You don't have electricity?

A modern state governed by codified laws needs certitudes in its language and operations. It cannot afford to be ambiguous. A large population of India lives an existence that is almost an antithesis to the ideal. From giving directions about a place to making a statement under oath or even writing love letters, people often cherish prevarication. Not necessarily with an intention to mislead or deceive, but because they enjoy answers that don't bring any closure, but raise new and even confounding questions. It's the sign of a civilization that refuses finality, cherishes the unfinished, and swears by the contingent and contextual. A modern state and its interlocutors cannot easily appreciate this trait which appears even more entrenched in Bastar. A trait that has not diminished in spite of the introduction of history into the jungle by insurgents.

Writings on Bastar by outsiders, who perhaps cannot but use a modern vocabulary to decode the jungle, thus verge on becoming translated texts whose metaphors and similes may well be against the spirit and language of the wild. The narrative of Bastar, being written by various actors, several of them earnest, often faces this crisis. They transcribe and interpret Bastar in gestures that it is barely cognizant of. One such oft-used phrase is 'interior Bastar' or 'the interior villages of Bastar' – phrases used in this book as well. But very few of Bastar's residents are conscious of living in an 'interior' land. They don't divide their jungle into 'accessible' and 'remote' – words that denote the hierarchy created by the city for its own purpose and convenience.

Old man: We don't need stuff like that.

Traveller: What do you do for light?

Old man: We have candles and rapeseed oil.

Traveller: Isn't it dark at night?

Old man: The night is supposed to be dark. We'd be in trouble if night were as bright as day. I don't want a night so bright that I can't see the stars.

If one converses with a community in a language it doesn't speak, if one remains ignorant about their language and writes about them in an alien tongue, then one's narrative can never escape the possibility of being incomplete and, at times, distorted. I often felt a formidable linguistic disconnect with the adivasis. For almost every question of mine, they had an answer for a question I had never asked. I repeated the question, paraphrased it, elaborated and explained it, still our conversation often remained tangential. It also reflected the distinct epistemic character of Bastar. The adivasis live in a cosmos that does not require many questions, much less answers. A moment is often complete in itself. Their life is at complete variance with the city – which is founded on questions. During my travels in the adivasi zone, I met a number of people, raised a lot of questions, about personal topics like love and sex, and also about minor issues. But I cannot recall anyone ever asking me even one simple question about my life or work. Even the guerrillas, with whom I stayed on many occasions, hardly had anything to ask me other than discussing their revolution and ideology. The only questions that came were from the senior Maoist leaders, and were about Indian politics and society. Not a single adivasi was ever interested in my personal life, my hometown or my education, whereas I was always keen to know as much possible about them.

Bastar has seen many visitors from the city who have invested and surrendered a large part of their self in the adivasi land, often becoming genuine insiders. Yet, their narrative eventually speaks to their constituency in the city, from whom they seek to derive legitimacy. The coordinates and referents of their arguments often remain steeped in a lexicon alien to Bastar.

But don't my words also carry a similar possibility? One day, a Gond girl will read these pages, view me with suspicion, question my gaze, and reject every one of my words. *The Death Script,* she will record in her diary, was written to be erased.*

---

* One often takes to writing to register all that could not be recorded or accommodated elsewhere. There is also the naive hope that the word can atone for betrayals one has committed but managed to carefully conceal from the world. But if one narrates a tale to redeem one's past, the tale will always be suspended, eternally waiting to seek release. I recall an old diary entry:

> *19 August 2011, Raipur.* All that I have written so far, every word that has emerged from my pen so far, it occurred to me yesterday, is like a sinful relationship which one is unable to face after the tide ebbs, to call whose offspring one's own causes remorse. The words pierce you like a knife for having committed the wrong of writing them.

That was two days after I had arrived in this province and hours before I started the journey, with my luggage still lying locked in a hotel, for my first report on a Naxal attack.

SIX

displacement / vi

'If I say I'm happy now, I'd be betraying myself ... I have lost my identity as an individual.'

I was taken aback. 'Are you sure of what you're saying? I'm going to write this.' I wanted to be certain that he was aware that our conversation was 'on record', though there was no question of his not being aware of it.

We were in an office of the Intelligence Department of the Telangana police, in the supervisory presence of an officer of the special intelligence bureau. It was the humid August of 2014.

Until a few months ago, G.V.K. Prasad was known as Sukhdev, alias Gudsa Usendi. He was the spokesperson of the Dandakaranya Special Zonal Committee of the CPI (Maoist). The forty-five-year-old Sukhdev spoke several languages, was fairly erudite and, like many of his comrade friends, was a native of Warangal district.

He was a surrendered cadre now. The Telangana police had held a major press conference in January to showcase his surrender along with Lalita, a fellow comrade whom he called his wife. 'I surrendered,' he had told the media, 'due to my failing health and with the Party's permission.' The police provided him with a home and money for medical treatment. They also secretly spread the word that Lalita had led to his surrender.

A few days later, his boss, the DKSZC secretary Ramanna, issued a statement about his 'character flaws'. Lalita was not Sukhdev's wife, Ramanna said, but worked with the Press Department of the CPI (Maoist). 'Eloping with a woman and leaving his wife behind shows his character,' Ramanna said. Sukhdev had joined the Party in the 1980s, Ramanna continued, but left it in 1993 when 'the Party was facing several problems at both the military and organizational level'. He was re-inducted in 1997 'after the Party duly examined his conduct'. A few years later, once again, 'his weaknesses came to the knowledge of the Party'. Among his major flaws were 'ego, a bureaucratic approach and patriarchy'. In 1999, Ramanna said, the Party punished Sukhdev for having an affair with a woman. After his wife was killed in an encounter, he married another cadre Raji in 2003, whom he had now left behind to run away with Lalita.

When I met him in Hyderabad, I knew a little about his past. After his surrender, I met some junior guerrillas in Bastar whom he had once taught Maoist ideology and had urged to never lose hope as the revolution was inevitable. Now the lads called their former boss 'a bad fish'. 'Some people do it and the entire Party gets a bad name,' Rajnu Mandavi, half of Sukhdev's age, told me.

If the Party had been aware of his 'character flaws', why did Sukhdev remain in the fold for so long, and why was he assigned major responsibilities? Didn't such accusations after the exit of a comrade signify the Party's crass opportunism? Does one become evil merely because one doesn't want to be with you? The Party did not have an answer. It was nothing out of the ordinary, though. The Party often decorated surrendered comrades with such adjectives.

This thin man of medium height was aware that his former friends had declared him a fallen character. I was keen to know how he remembered his old friends, with whom he had spent decades after he had entered Bastar in 1987 carrying the dream of the revolution.

In utter disbelief, I listened to Sukhdev completely rejecting his life after the surrender in the presence of a police officer. 'There is no absolute happiness. A person like me … Even Ambani won't be fully happy. I was extremely happy in the forest. If I say that I'm happy now, I'd be betraying myself … I now have a shelter, three meals a day, but it's only for me. When I look at my surroundings, it [poverty and inequality] disturbs me. My worldly happiness troubles me …' His voice faltered, his eyes gleamed behind his spectacles. 'I have lost my identity as an individual. It won't be a smooth life for me in the city.'

When I had set up this interview, the Hyderabad SIB had suggested that I meet Sukhdev in the presence of an officer. I had agreed, but had my doubts about having a conversation in a police office. But it seemed that he had already decided what he wanted to tell me. At first, we spoke about his Party, and then he gradually opened up. He ignored the fact that a policeman was sitting in the room – perhaps one of those who had negotiated with him and enabled his surrender – and ended the interview with a statement: 'I'll be happy only when inequality ends.'

* * *

A week later, Lanka Papi Reddy repeated similar words to me. Reddy was among the first batch of guerrillas to have arrived in Dandakaranya from Andhra Pradesh in the 1980s. He had surrendered in 2008. One August afternoon in 2014, he was at his Warangal home, preparing for his daughter's first journey abroad. The districts of Khammam, Karimnagar and Warangal had been the birthplace and bastion of many prominent Naxal guerrillas. Many bright students left their careers and jumped into the vortex of the revolutionary battle. The Maoist movement after the 1980s mostly revolves around the young men and women of these three districts – in fact, such has been the dominance of the Andhra comrades that in 2014, as many as twenty of the twenty-four Dandakaranya Special Zonal Committee members and eleven of the twenty Central Committee members of the CPI (Maoist) were from this state. But the situation has changed dramatically. Many students from this region now go abroad for higher studies – one of whom was Tejaswi, the eighteen-year-old daughter of the guerrilla who was, and still remains, the topmost cadre ever to have surrendered. She was sitting on the sofa, listening to him intently.

Six years had passed since he came out and began a family life, but the revolutionary days still tormented Reddy, now a man of fifty-two. 'I was living a better life inside. I was fighting for a just society. It gave me satisfaction ... I'm now earning more, but I also witness evil all around me. Earlier, I beat up those who paid or took bribes, now I'm forced to offer bribes.'

When I told him that Sukhdev had also expressed similar sentiments to me, he wasn't surprised. 'I also never said anything against the Party.' Reddy even called Sukhdev after he had come out. Both of them were certain that neither would ever speak against the Party.

Reddy's revolutionary life was not beyond reproach. It had seen him fumble and falter. Many years ago, when he was a prominent name in the Naxal movement, the Party had punished him for 'misbehaving with a woman cadre'. He was then operational in Haryana and was a Central Committee member of the CPI (Maoist) – among its topmost leaders. Yet, it decided to punish him. A Maoist once told me in Bastar that, suspended on the rope of humiliation in Punjab, a place that had little revolutionary activity, Reddy finally lost himself and could see no way to come out of the hole other than a reluctant, perhaps forced, surrender.

I've met many surrendered guerrillas. A variety of reasons push them to surrender. Their resolve crumbles when they realize the improbability of revolution. Their desire for a family overpowers them. Few can lead a starved and parched life in the forest, with the ever-present possibility of a violent death. Staring at the sun every morning with the feeling that it might be your last ray of sunshine. The grand dream of revolution is often diminished by several diseases and infections that can afflict a guerrilla in the forest. A visit to the city for treatment involves the risk of getting caught.

The army of a country has medical care and a number of facilities that enable a soldier to remain deployed on the battlefront. The deployment also changes regularly – a soldier rarely remains on the front for long. In contrast, Maoist guerrillas spend their entire lives wading through the jungle, confronting hunger and mosquitoes, holding on to a dream, not without an awareness that they stand no chance before the might of the Indian state. They may ambush and kill some policemen every year, but 'the Red Flag on the Red Fort' in their lifetime is an impossibility. How long can one sacrifice oneself at the altar of protracted battle? They eventually get enervated, more in the soul than in the body, which pushes them to leave the forest despite being conscious of the torment that awaits them outside. They now find themselves doing what they had always considered evil and hateful.

But Lanka Reddy? He was not prepared for surrender. Following a transgression that he had committed at the peak of his revolutionary life, he was forced to come out, forsaking a path that had brought him self-fulfilment and personal honour.

dream / viii

Even her birth was a metaphor for rebellion. Her parents were members of a guerrilla outfit that considered procreation to be against the ideals of the revolution. Those were the initial years of the Naxal movement in Dandakaranya. The guerrillas of the CPI (Marxist–Leninist) People's War (PW) who had arrived from Andhra Pradesh wanted to make the wilderness their base and create an underground army. The local adivasis were to be its foot soldiers, with an equal participation from women. A baby in a woman's womb could divert the mother and the father from the revolutionary path. Her father was a top guerrilla leader, but he also wanted a baby.

Lanka Papi Reddy had prolonged arguments with his comrade friends over the issue. They tried to persuade him, but he wouldn't budge. In October 1996, several women, weapons slung over their shoulders, created a shed near a mahua grove, underneath which his wife gave birth to a baby girl. In the history of the Maoists in India, she was only the second child* to be born to guerrilla revolutionaries in the forest of Abujhmad that was, and still remains, the headquarters of the Maoist insurgency. Reddy named the baby Tejaswi – the radiant one. Did the father have even the slightest inkling that his baby, who received all but a cradle full of weapons at birth, would go to China two

---

* The first child was born to another Telugu guerrilla from Warangal district a few years earlier, who came out of the jungle with the baby, but she died soon after. Just a few children have been born to the Maoists in Abujhmad, but they have remained inside and have eventually joined the Party. Tejaswi is the only one to get an education outside.

decades later? This tale of father and daughter is a legend of the Maoist movement in India.

Eighteen years later, on the afternoon of 26 August 2014 in Hanamkonda town of Warangal district, I make an unexpected entry into their tale, adding another chapter to the legend. Tracing the lives of former revolutionaries, I arrive at Reddy's home. He tells me about his rich landlord family that had a strong political background. His father, an old Congressman, was a freedom fighter; his uncle, a communist leader. They had around 200 acres of land. During Vinoba Bhave's Bhoodan movement, his father had distributed a lot of land to the peasants. Reddy joined the Naxal movement with several friends in the 1970s. A few years later, his brother Murli Mohan Reddy was killed during the Emergency in a fake police encounter along with three other young men – one of whom was a student at the Warangal Regional Engineering College that, in subsequent years, went on to produce several prominent Maoist leaders.

Immediately after the death of his brother, Reddy went underground in May 1976 before he was arrested in November. He spent eight months in prison during the Emergency. The PW was formed in Andhra Pradesh a few years later, and Reddy left his family behind to enter Dandakaranya with a dream that emerged from the barrel of the gun.

* * *

We are in the living room of his home when a girl comes in. They both speak Telugu, a language I don't understand, but I can figure out that she is his daughter. I am intrigued. Before his surrender in 2008, Reddy was underground for three decades. When was she born? Who is her mother? Is it the platoon commander Saroja who laid her weapons down soon after he did, or some other woman? Did this girl spend her childhood and adolescence in the forest, amid weapons and blood? When and where did she receive her education? (For she seemed to be a fairly educated city girl.) Or had she been in Haryana with her father?

A lot is brewing within me, but I am unable to gather the courage to raise personal issues. I manage to sneak in a question about his surrender, but Reddy cites 'personal reasons' and asks me to avoid such topics.

But the tale doesn't stop there. The girl is still in the living room. I casually ask her about her studies, to which Reddy responds saying that she has completed her class twelve and is now going to China for a degree in medicine.

I am even more intrigued now. Does the Chinese government invite children of Indian Maoist guerrillas for higher studies? Is it some sort of clandestine cultural exchange?

'It's very difficult to get through to an MBBS here,' Reddy continues. 'Many students from Warangal go to China for their degree.'

By now I am beginning to get a sense that she had continued her studies outside, perhaps in a city of Andhra Pradesh, while Reddy was in the forest. But how? Where? And then, suddenly, a thread emerges that gradually unravels the tale.

'Will you practise medicine in China or return to India after your studies?'

The reply again comes from her father: 'I want her to return, serve the society, visit the place she was born in and work for the people in that area.' He looks at his daughter who gets up from the sofa and comes to sit beside him.

'What place is that?'

'Abujhmad.'

'Abujhmad? Was she born there? Where in Abujhmad?'

'You wouldn't know. Deep inside the forest flows a river called Nai Berad … Along its banks … I don't know if she'll ever be able to visit the river.'

The father and the daughter look at each other. Their gaze suggests that this is a tale the father has narrated countless times to the daughter, but it remains incomplete, and neither of them is certain that it will ever reach its culmination. She will never get to return to the forest where her father had once roamed with a rifle and where his former comrades are still battling against the state.

'Nai Berad! The river that flows along Balibeda village?'

'Yes, Balibeda! How do you know?'

'I've been to Balibeda. I stayed in the village for a few days, bathed in the river. It flows down almost straight, then takes a circular turn near the village. It's surrounded by old rocks and boulders. A little further, you have a wonderful grove of salfi trees. That's the village, right?'

'Yes, that's Nai Berad. It takes a circular turn!'

'I have photographs of the village and the river. Would you like to see them?'

'Photographs? Here? Right now?'

'Yes ... In my laptop, in the cab outside.'

The subsequent scene unfolds at a feverish pace, one moment falling on to the other, collapsing into the other. I run outside. A white Indica is parked nearby. I turn the handle of the back door. It's locked. All four doors are locked. The driver is nowhere to be seen. Whenever I go to meet somebody, the driver locks the vehicle and goes for a stroll. I call him and if his phone is switched off or he is far, I patiently wait for him. But today, I am annoyed that his phone remains unreachable. I bang the bonnet and roof of the car with my fist. The driver shows up after a little while. I take the laptop and run inside. They are still in the living room, waiting for me. I switch on the machine, hurriedly click on the folder of photographs that contains a subfolder named 'Abujhmad'. It has some 250 photographs, of which over a dozen are of Nai Berad. I am searching for one particular photograph. I don't want to run the slideshow, as many other photographs might be of his former comrades. I want to quickly find the river, and flipping through the thumbnails I stop at a photograph and enlarge it to fill the screen. This is the river, yes, this is the river. The father's eyes are glistening now. It has been eighteen years, but the river hasn't changed at all. Where is the place, which are the trees that recorded the first smile of his baby girl? The father is searching everywhere in the photographs. The daughter is also now tracing her first cries in the photographs. This was the river, perhaps this was the spot surrounded by trees, and this was the village. There are some photographs of the village too. The face of the village has changed somewhat, but Nai Berad has not. It still is what it was before history came to Abujhmad. Father and daughter feel the screen. The spot her mother had lain down to bring her baby into this world. The father is now aching to take a handful of the river and pour its water upon his daughter.

The daughter spent her first two years in Abujhmad. The darling of the women guerrillas, her infancy was spent in a cradle of rifles and ambushes before her father began worrying about her future. One night in 1998, he quietly held the baby, crossed the Godavari, reached his home in Andhra Pradesh and left her in the safe custody of his mother. She grew up in the care of her grandmother, absolutely unaware that her parents were fighting for the revolution.

Her father's homecoming was a big event. He was the first Central Committee member of the CPI (Maoist) to have ever surrendered. (Another Central Committee member, Jinugu Narasimha Reddy, alias Jampanna, surrendered in December 2017.) The surrender was staged before the Andhra Pradesh home minister K. Jana Reddy, and the government publicized it a lot. 'I remember seeing it on the news ... Grandmother told me that Papa was coming back,' the daughter would tell me later.

The second chapter of this tale was to begin now. The father had to 'reclaim' the daughter he had been forced to leave twelve years ago. He vividly remembers the 'struggle to reclaim his daughter'. He was a good photographer and was also good with computers. During his forest days, he had handled the technical wing of the Maoists. Now he would click photographs of his daughter, Photoshop them and post them on Facebook.

The father recited to her tales from his revolutionary days, the ideals he had lived for, but with immense humility. Later, in an email to me, he wrote: 'I am a surrendered revolutionary. I couldn't do anything major in life, achieved no success. I only lived for the ideals I had faith in.'

The father had other worries too. 'When she was preparing for her medical entrance exams, she lived in Hyderabad. It was several hours away, but every Sunday I cooked chicken for her and took a bus to meet her ... I won't be able to visit her in China.'

She was proud of her father who had 'lived for people'. Months later, she would send me a WhatsApp message: *I lve my dad sooo muchhh.*

Many years ago, many oceans and continents apart, Aleida Guevara wrote about her father: '[T]he more I read [about his life], the more in love I was with the boy my father had been ... as I continued reading, I began to see more clearly who this person was and I was very happy to be his daughter ... the man I love intensely for the strength and tenderness he demonstrated in the way he lived.'

Reddy would perhaps forever live with the haunting memory of his surrender to the police. His city life would always weigh heavy upon him. But returning from Hanamkonda that August evening, it occurred to me that not many fathers are destined to – or capable of – earning the faith and love of their daughters.

death script / xi

'I once visited a senior policeman at his office and found him in his socks. He had taken off his shoes,' he said and laughed freely. 'Some policemen even loosen their belts after entering their office. Such paunches they carry around! How will they hold a rifle?'

His laughter was innocent and warm. It showed self-confidence and even swagger, but it was free from the kind of arrogance that belittles others. At first, I listened to him quietly. I was only four months old in this province. He could laugh at senior police officers. I couldn't. But soon, I joined in his laughter.

It was the evening of 2 December 2011, at Raipur's Hotel Babylon. My first evening with the retired brigadier B.K. Ponwar. I did not need to drink to realize that a soldier who has spent his life on the battlefield carries a repertoire of tales that can unsettle the masters of magical realism. He was a young commando during the 1971 India–Pakistan War, and had served in several battlefields from Kashmir, to Assam and Tripura, to Bangladesh.

For the last few years, he had been teaching guerrilla warfare to India's security forces before they were dispatched to the Naxal front. As the battle between the state and the Maoist insurgents intensified, the government set up the Counter Terrorism and Jungle Warfare College in 2005 in Kanker. He was its first director, and continues to be so until today.

Sixty-two years old, wearing a tight T-shirt and a cowboy hat. He kept his hat on even in the bar, and took it off only after the first beer. He'd caught cobras in the jungle, roasted and ate them.

'You are taught since birth to be scared of snakes. But once the king cobra is in your stomach, what is there to be afraid of? It tastes like fish. That's it.'

'A snake can't bite me, a bullet can't hit me.' He laughed away the possibility of a Maoist assault. His white Ambassador could go up to 125 kilometres per hour. 'You require special training to hit a vehicle moving at that speed. The Naxal bullet will go past me.'

'The only companion of a solider is his weapon. A soldier goes to sleep with his finger on the trigger. His response time is just half a second.'

His life was reflected in everything he said. I had ideological differences with Ponwar, but I felt that this soldier had lived an intense life.

Listening to him, it occurred to me that not many writers could make you believe that theirs was the last word, that the blood on the umbilical cord that ties their words to an emotion is raw and unadulterated.

The diaries of Krishna Baldev Vaid record a recurring restlessness to write only that which is absolutely necessary for his survival: *Not a single word that doesn't offer me in totality.* Fernando Pessoa writes about the terror of recording certain experiences, the terror of being forced to record them.* A terror that was consummated in the works of Franz

---

* For some reason, this reminds me of a letter written by a Naxal. One of the founders of the CPI (Marxist–Leninist), Nagbhushan Patnaik was sentenced to death in December 1970. Awaiting his execution, he expressed his will in a letter to the jail superintendent:

> Dear Superintendent,
> Central Jail, Rajahmundry.
>
> I want to ensure the best utilization of my body. Your government merely wants to end my life. But you can remove all my organs before my death and use them for medical purposes. I dedicate my body for such purposes. Remove all my organs, blood, skin, skull and all the bones while I am alive.

Kafka – a man who was afraid of light, who wanted to hide himself in a dark attic, away from everybody.

Let me explain further. Squeeze out all the blood from my body, remove my eyes, cut out the other organs, and finally, remove my lungs, liver and heart before you declare me dead. All my organs should be preserved for people who require transplantation.

If the officers don't accept the above option, and want to follow the superficial meaning of execution by hanging, I have another suggestion for them. Squeeze my blood out and remove my organs to the point that I remain alive enough to stand on the scaffold, so that my execution order can be implemented and I am hanged from the noose until I die. After the orders have been followed, remove all the organs that can still be put to use.

I am providing a list of people who have a right over my organs, blood and skin – labourers, landless farmers, masons, students, schoolteachers, revolutionary intellectuals, small merchants, vendors, the exploited proletariat, beggars.

Nagbhushan Patnaik
Condemned Prisoner Number 2760
Central Jail, Rajahmundry
Eastern Godavari district

(Though several prominent leaders like J.P. Narayan demanded his release, Patnaik refused to write a mercy petition. The government later commuted his death sentence to life imprisonment, and he was released in 1981.)

dream / ix

A married Maoist couple is not, normally, deployed together. But I found Paike and Rajnu Mandavi in the same squad for a few days during my long Abujhmad stay. Both were from the Gangalur area of Bijapur. They communicated very little with each other. If someone had not told me, I couldn't have guessed that they were married. They had been in the same platoon before marriage. As their love blossomed, they told their leader Kiran, who got them married before a Maoist memorial in the presence of his comrade friends in 2010.

One day, I plucked the courage to ask Rajnu about how 'things happen' between couples under such discipline. I was apprehensive that he might get angry, but he replied very casually. Some gestures, and then we slip into the jungle. Other cadres understand, no one bothers us.

The adivasi community these guerrillas belong to live an almost opposite life. It's common for unmarried teenage girls to conceive. The village elders call an assembly, summon the boy and the girl, and soon she hops down to his home. No need for a formal marriage.

A community that had been living so naturally with love and desire, repressed or perhaps transformed itself, and brought about a fundamental change in its life overnight. There have been obvious aberrations. Many top Maoist leaders are seen in 'live-in' relationships. The Party sometimes ignores their transgressions – G.V.K. Prasad, alias Sukhdev, is one such instance – but some senior cadres, like Lanka Papi Reddy, are also punished for indiscipline.

I recall that, after describing family as fetters for the woman, Simone de Beauvoir concludes *The Second Sex* with a quote from Marx: 'The direct, natural, necessary relation of human creatures is the relation of man to woman.'

Many comrade couples live underground in cities to create an urban base. The spokesperson of the CPI (Maoist) Cherukuri Rajkumar, alias Azad, lived in the heart of central Delhi with his comrade wife Padma for several years. No one got wind of it until he was killed in an encounter in 2010. Since the mid-1980s, the couple, having decided not to have children, lived in hiding, moving from city to city across India, changing their names and identities.

'He was the brightest student in his engineering college, but we opted for a guerrilla life. Why? We dreamt of an egalitarian society,' says Padma, who now lives in Hyderabad. She was in Delhi when she learnt about Azad's death. The first thing she did was to destroy his hard drives and other confidential material. She came overground after his death, and spent some time in jail before she was released. The comrade son of her landlord was in a Jharkhand jail, the daughter-in-law out on bail.

Her questions remain unanswered. Is politics in India possible without money? Is power not confined to a select few? Why have the state and the market come together to grab the adivasis' land? The state may annihilate the guerrillas with its might, but without responding to these questions, its victory will never be an ethical one.

But can victory in a war ever be ethical?

* * *

Police forces receive extra allowances when they are posted in Maoist areas, yet most of them cannot wait for their tenure to end. Guerrillas have been living in the forest for decades without any salary. 'Mao banned all incentives before the revolution arrived,' a cadre says. But has the adivasi been able to grasp Maoism, or has Maoism grasped them?

Every July, the Maoists celebrate Martyr's Day in memory of their comrades killed in police encounters. At many places in Dandakaranya, they have erected memorials to martyrs, before which they gather villagers and remember their dead. On Martyr's Day in July 2012, I met the secretary of the Kerlapal Area Committee of the CPI (Maoist) in a village of south Bastar.

'The police and the CRPF are salaried forces. They can never fight an army that derives strength from ideology and conviction. These forces are like cotton bales, they occupy space but have no weight and will blow away in the wind. The army of ideology can move even the Himalayas,' Madkam Bhima, alias Akash, says. A rifle sits next to him, the magazine of cartridges tied to his waist. He was the leader of the squad that had abducted the Sukma collector in April that year.

I first met Akash a few days after the abduction. In another corner of the forest. Explaining the reason for abducting the young collector, Akash had asked: 'Do we have any other option?'

'But abduction is not an option either,' I had said.

This July evening, he repeats his argument. At a little distance, his squad is instructing a group of villagers to lift their right arms and raise slogans – *Long live Comrade Charu Mazumdar. Long live Comrade Kishenji.*

Men and women, young and old, wearing lungis and saris, have been summoned from nearby villages. They follow the instructions with blank faces. The sounds they are somehow able to make bear no link to the slogans. The sky is dark. The rain has just stopped, and can begin again at any time. Some have broken umbrellas held tight under their armpits, some have umbrellas tucked down the backs of their shirts. Their arms don't go up in unison – some are slower, some don't rise up fully, some don't budge at all, struggling with the umbrella. The guerrilla commander teaches them to raise their right arms, asks them to repeat the slogans again. Clearer and louder. The Gond adivasis still cannot grasp these words, their arms still don't go up in rhythm. An old man pulls the few remaining hairs on his head.

When the script doesn't get staged effectively even after several rehearsals, the deflated commander makes a compromise with the lazy arms and shapeless sounds but doesn't concede defeat. He now calls on the children. They go to school on the other side of the river, once a week. They cannot recall when they went last, but they are wearing the school uniform. The blue shirts provided by the government to schoolchildren have gathered several weeks' worth of dirt. Many children from the Bastar forests can be seen wearing blue shirts throughout the year, from morning to night, and again from night to morning.

The commander asks the children to write the names of martyred comrades in Gondi and read them out to the villagers. The children have never heard of these names. They cannot spell them correctly. While the children struggle with pen and paper, the villagers, tired of empty sloganeering, steal a break. Their role in the script will appear a little later. An old woman unties the knot of her sari and takes out a tobacco pouch. Two palms quietly spread out before her.

And love? Akash, who had lectured me on Maoism that evening, on the need to stay away from all enticements before the revolution, the fighter who was just twenty-six years old that evening, quietly quit with his beloved Hemla Hungi a year later in summer of 2013. Hemla was also a guerrilla and worked in the medical department of the Maoists.

Having learnt about their disappearance, I looked for them in the interior villages of Dandakaranya before reaching Bodaras village where they were last spotted. They had lived almost hidden in a hut on the village periphery for nearly forty-five days after leaving the Party, before they suddenly disappeared one night.

'I hope they were not killed by their former comrades?'

'No, no, there is no such information. Perhaps they crossed the Godavari and moved towards the south,' the villagers said.

It's been over five years since that evening in Bodaras. I hadn't been able to gather any more clues about them, and comforted myself with the thought that the couple had gone beyond the reach of the police and their comrades, that perhaps they even had a baby. But only recently I learnt that Akash was arrested on 26 August 2016, and Hemla in March 2018.

Both are in jail now.

delusion / vi

Suhag Nagri – city of weddings – that's what they call Firozabad. This small town in Uttar Pradesh supplies bangles for weddings all over India. The glass jewellery found an unlikely echo in an under-construction police camp in the forest of Dantewada one April afternoon in 2015, a day before five policemen in an anti-landmine vehicle were killed in a landmine explosion. I was a little distance away, in another police vehicle.

As he talked about his deceased colleagues, Shailendra Kumar, Constable 352, 17th Battalion, Chhattisgarh Armed Force, often took his mobile phone out of his pocket then kept it back. Perhaps to check the time, perhaps to steal a glance at the photograph on its screen. He was inside a makeshift cabin, guarding the camp's gate. His SLR rifle kept aim through a hole in the cabin's wall.

That twenty-three-year-old man was a resident of Firozabad. He had joined the Chhattisgarh police in June 2013 and, without any anti-Naxal training, was dispatched to the front two months ago. 'I have heard that, during training, they make us eat raw snakes ... I do not know anything about Naxals or why we are deployed here,' he said. A colleague prompted him, 'The security of the country.' Kumar repeated it, before he glanced at his mobile phone again and spoke about life in Firozabad.

How did he come to travel over 1,000 kilometres to join the Chhattisgarh police? The state needed more men for its battle against the Naxals. As it invited applications from other states for recruitment into its special battalions, many unemployed men rushed in. Finding him looking at his mobile phone yet again, I wondered whether he had left someone behind and, suddenly, the tale of a soldier I had read long ago came back to me.

Once, a villager was drafted into the army and sent to the battlefront. After a few months, his wife gave birth to a girl. The family taunted her, and eventually expelled her for giving birth to what they believed was an illicit child. She came to reside in a small hut outside the village. The girl grew up, turned four, but the soldier did not return. The girl, too, was taunted about her father. Whenever she asked her mother, the woman always assured her that her father had gone abroad for work, that he would return soon. It brought no relief to the girl, who continued to be ridiculed in the school and the neighbourhood.

One night, there was a massive storm in the village and the power was cut. It was dark all around. The girl cried out aloud, 'Where is my father? Why has he left me?' Her mother lit a candle. Her shadow appeared on the wall. Unable to console her daughter in any other way, she pointed at the shadow and said, 'He is your father.'

'Is he really my father?' the girl quietly asked.

Her mother nodded.

The girl slept peacefully that night. Her mother now knew how to quieten her. Whenever she came home crying, asking for her father, she switched the lights off, drew the curtains, lit a candle, and the shadow father came to the girl.

A few months later, the war ended and the soldier returned. Upon reaching the village, he found out about the expulsion of his wife. But he had absolute faith in her. The daughter, he knew, was his. He reached her home and found a girl playing outside. The woman was out, working. He asked her mother's name, and when she named his wife, he was overjoyed. He lifted the girl in his arms.

'Do you know who your father is?'

'My father? He visits me every night.'

The soldier was crestfallen. He wrote a letter, kept it on the table and returned to his parents.

The woman had also heard about his arrival. She rushed home, but found only a letter: *I did not expect this from you.*

She was devastated. She had been waiting for him for years, absolutely certain that he would embrace his daughter and they would begin a new life. She jumped into a nearby river.

The girl, the man thought, was the daughter of the woman he had once loved, after all. He couldn't see her being orphaned. He decided to raise her and brought her home.

Sometime later, there was another storm in the village. A power cut. Darkness all around. He lit a candle and his shadow appeared on the wall.

'Papa!' the kid screamed.

'Papa?'

'Yes. He's my father. He used to visit me regularly ... Where were you, Papa?'

The following day the soldier's body was found in the same river.

dream / x

'Could you do it?'

Perhaps he asked her, or perhaps he did not.

'Better worry about yourself.'

Perhaps she replied, or perhaps she did not.

What is certain is that they were both moving towards the west of the forest to visit a young doctor who would tell them: 'This operation could be fatal for her.'

To which he would respond: 'Then let her be the first martyr.'

That was the 1980s. The couple had arrived in Abujhmad from the south of the Godavari just a few years earlier. He was a member of the first batch of PW guerrillas, she came a little later. Before arriving here, they had carried out a few explosions in Andhra Pradesh, but that was insufficient for the revolution. They needed an army, and an uncharted wilderness to raise the army. But a sudden crisis had cropped up before them to which the forest had no solution.

They learnt that, on the western periphery of Abujhmad, in Hemalkasa village of Gadchiroli district, lived a city doctor. Both of them crossed the jungle and walked for a day to reach Hemalkasa late in the evening. It was difficult to trace an individual in the dark, but not impossible.

'I have no experience of this … I've never done this operation,' the doctor said.

'You can do your first experiment on her,' the guerrilla fighter said, implying that the doctor might have to do more such operations in the future.

She lay down on a broken wooden table in the doctor's hut. She looked at her man for one last time. He looked at his woman sliding towards possible death.

Thirty years later, none of them would remember the time of the day, the month or the season of the year when that first operation was performed. But the doctor vividly recalls that the couple did not betray the slightest worry or anxiety.

She didn't become the first martyr, instead she set the first milestone. Subsequently, the doctor operated on many such Maoist women. The operation was necessary for the revolution. Guerrilla women couldn't become mothers – it was against the spirit of the revolution. To avoid such risks, Naxal commanders had made stringent rules for male–female bonding. Yet, in the absence of contraceptives in the jungle, it wasn't possible to avoid pregnancies. It is not certain whether she was the first guerrilla woman to get pregnant, but it was perhaps the first instance of a doctor performing an abortion on a guerrilla in the battlefield of Dandakaranya.

It marked a beginning. Many more such operations would be performed.

The lover of the woman, who was then a young fighter, is now a politburo member of the CPI (Maoist), and among the fiercest revolutionaries of the country. Mallojula Venugopal Rao, alias Bhupathi. His brother Mallojula Koteshwara Rao, alias Kishenji, was killed in an encounter in West Bengal in 2011.

And the doctor? He soon became famous in Abujhmad. Besides the Maoists and the adivasis, even wild animals adored him. He tended to the injured animals, raised their calves. They became his friends – pythons, crocodiles, panthers, even a tigress which would go with him on morning walks wagging her tail like a Pomeranian. When a leopard, a deer or a tiger is born, their mother licks their bottoms, they open their eyes, defecate and grope for their mother's teats. The doctor would caress the bottoms of orphaned baby animals and give them a milk bottle.

Over twenty years later, he went with his wife to receive the Ramon Magsaysay Award in Manila. Prakash and Mandaniki Amte – the son and daughter-in-law of Ramon Magsaysay winner Baba Amte. The only family of which three members have received the prestigious award.

'Maoists came to me for abortion for their wives and vasectomy for their cadres. Abortion was risky for women, it endangered their lives ... There was also a possibility that if we did it once, they would come again for another abortion for the same woman. It involved great health risks, so I opted for the lesser evil – vasectomy. Also, I knew vasectomy was reversible,' Prakash Amte would tell me in the winter of 2012, sitting in his Hemalkasa home.

A few months earlier, in summer, I had come across another set of doctors who removed the uteruses of women in several villages of Chhattisgarh under the Rashtriya Swasthya Bima Yojna that provided cashless health insurance of 30,000 rupees yearly to below-poverty-line families. A doctor could charge 12,500 rupees for a hysterectomy. Agents of doctors lured village women in for 'free of cost' hysterectomies. They lapped up the offer. 'We faced monthly troubles and embarrassment because of this organ,' the women said, 'besides the perpetual fear of unwanted pregnancy, as our men were unwilling to use contraceptives. So we readily agreed, despite being aware of the side-effects.'

These were young women in their early thirties, in a way denouncing the epic metaphors poets had woven around this organ. For them, it was a 'bachhedani', a simple pouch that, stripped of all metaphors and mysteries, had no use other than holding babies for a while. 'Get rid of it once the family is complete' was the sentiment among them. In Raipur hospitals, a joke doing the rounds those days was that someone would soon file a Right to Information application to know the number of uteruses left in Chhattisgarh.*

---

* The metaphor returned to me when, in November 2014, I found myself writing about adivasi women who had died during unauthorized sterilization

The uterus tale takes a different turn in Dandakaranya. Living on the Abujhmad border, Prakash repeatedly figures in the tales of Maoists. Emptying the wombs of women, closing the tubes of male guerrillas through which their seed enters the woman's body, or simply treating their wounds and diseases.

Hemalkasa got electricity in 1993, a road in 1998. Before the road was built, the area used to get severed from Gadchiroli for five months during the rains and become an island. People stored up rice and lentils to survive those months. The Amtes had only two small huts when they came to live and work here in the 1980s – they used one as a residence, the other as a clinic.

Prakash does not have any inclination towards the Maoist ideology. 'By conducting vasectomy, at no point of time did I help the Maoists or their movement. I only performed my duty as a doctor on purely humanitarian grounds. I have provided medical aid to thousands of adivasis in the area.'

But without him, or another such doctor, the dream of the revolution could not have soared so high in Dandakaranya. The story of the Maoists could have remained incomplete. Still, there were also some rebels who did not approach him – for them, giving birth to a child was also a metaphor for rebellion.

---

operations in Bilaspur. Since the government doctors had to meet their targets of sterilizing women, lactating mothers, diabetic and anaemic women were herded in, mostly without their consent, for surgeries conducted in a crumbling building. All the thirteen deceased were young mothers, under thirty.

This metaphor, it now occurs to me, had been chasing me for a while. Several years before Bastar, I wrote a novella about a twenty-four-year-old woman who is forced to undergo a hysterectomy after contracting severe infection due to consecutive abortions. She is aware that at this moment she is incapable of even comprehending what she has lost. She takes the uterus back home, preserves it in a glass jar full of formaldehyde and places it in a showcase in front of her bed.

delusion / vii

How many years was I with the Party? Eleven? Twelve? Perhaps fifteen. Was there anything else besides the jungle in my life? I cannot recall. It has been twenty-six months since I got out and joined the Rajnandgaon police. It has been more than two years now, and still I often face the question: What is the difference between life in the forest and here? A journalist came to meet me a few days ago. He also asked the same question. When such questions are raised, I ask the woman who was with me in the Party, carried a weapon, and got out with me. She stares at me.

Superintendent Sahab had told me earlier that a journalist would come and ask some questions. Sahab had also told me what he was likely to ask.

I, my woman, my friend and his woman were in the room with the journalist. They had also been Naxal commanders like us earlier but, like me and my woman, they were now in the Rajnandgaon police.

The journalist's first question was what SP Sahab had said. I replied that I had undergone vasectomy The other commander had also got it done. Everyone who gets married or is seen with a woman undergoes vasectomy in Bastar.

The journalist asked repeatedly, 'Is it forced? How does it happen?'

'When we are asked to get it done,' I said, 'we get it done.'

'Who asks for it?'

'Big commanders ask us.'

'Do big commanders also go for it? When did you undergo vasectomy?'

I was twenty. My friend said he was around eighteen.

'At such a young age? Didn't you resent it? Everybody agrees to it, nobody resists?'

The journalist even asked my woman how she felt about it. What could she have said? What would I have said? What was there to feel about it? Everyone got it done, so did I. I don't know why he was asking this.

My vasectomy was after my marriage, the Gadchiroli commander had it before his.

The journalist then asked why we were now getting our tubes reconnected. I want to be a father, I told him. My friend also said that he wanted to be a father. The journalist then asked my woman, but she didn't reply. He said again and again that the reversal surgery is a huge thing. He also asked us whether any other Naxal had got the reversal done, or whether we were the first ones. Our photograph, he told us, would appear in Delhi.

Then, suddenly, he started asking us something else. I had told him that my operation was conducted by a doctor in Hemalkasa. The journalist latched on to that point. 'Are you certain it was that doctor who operated on you?'

'It happened to me,' I told him, 'wouldn't I know about it?'

'Did that doctor perform vasectomies for any other Naxals?'

I said yes, he does it for all the Naxals. All of them go to him. Some also visit Nagpur.

First he was asking about the vasectomy, and now he was asking about the doctor. I and my woman could not understand why. SP Sahab had told me to reply to whatever he asked, but he had not told me that he would ask such things.

He was also jotting down something in his notebook in English. I was unable to understand. Some big commanders in the forest, they write in English.

A week later, the journalist phoned me. He said that a photograph of me and my commander friend has appeared in his newspaper.

In Delhi. He had taken it with his mobile phone. I should, he said, ask SP Sahab to show me the photograph in the newspaper. He also said that the government would now give money to Naxals who undergo a reversal surgery.

'Why money for me?' I asked my woman at night. 'Is reconnecting the tubes that big a thing?' She was resting on a cot. We were in a room in the Rajnandgaon police lines. 'I don't know,' she said.

I pulled out the magazine of my weapon, counted the rounds – all intact. With a thump of the palm, I reinserted the magazine in the weapon. I always count the rounds before I retire at night, and keep the magazine in the weapon. I learnt this habit in the forest. My earlier weapon was stolen from the police. This one was given to me by the police. Before switching off the bulb, I stared at my weapon for a long time – the white stamp of the police on its butt reminded me that an area committee commander had a similar weapon. With exactly the same stamp. Where was he now?

I pointed the barrel of the weapon below my waist. Touched my skin with it. Which tube was closed? Which one was open?

(October 2012. Rajnandgaon.)

dream / xi

Jaabili.

The journey a word goes through, the many roads it takes to reach you.

An afternoon in August 2014. I am sitting in the Hyderabad home of Sneha Lata. She is a journalist, her husband Kasim teaches Telugu at Osmania University. The two of them also edit a journal on literature and politics called *Nadustunna Telangana*. Kasim is a Dalit. There's an interesting story behind his name. In certain communities of Andhra Pradesh, especially among Dalits, if a child dies early, the parents take their next baby to a Muslim shrine. The baby is given a Muslim name, though that doesn't mean a conversion to Islam.

Sneha's father Malla Raja Reddy, alias Satyanna, now a Central Committee member of the CPI (Maoist), was among the earliest guerrillas from Andhra Pradesh to slip into Bastar in the 1980s. In 1985, her mother Rathakka, alias Nirmalakka, left her five-year-old daughter with her relatives and joined her husband in Dandakaranya.

'I was an infant when my father left. I met him for the first time in a court after his arrest in 2007. I couldn't even meet my mother. I heard two months after her death that she was no more ... I always had this complaint against them – that they left me so early. My grandmother also complained that her son did not take care of her in her old age. But we knew that they were following a big dream. They got a lot of respect for that,' Sneha, wearing a red salwar and blue kameez, says. 'Many people respect me for being the daughter of such a man. Whenever I visit my home district of Karimnagar, people look up to me.'

Her elderly grandmother died in 2013. Her mother was killed in 1998 in a police encounter in Bastar. 13 August. Sneha recalls it vividly,

'There was a news article, all of three sentences in a newspaper: *Woman Naxal Killed in an Encounter.'* It did not occur to Sneha that the woman could be her mother. The news was soon lost. 'I heard only when Varavara Rao called me to his home on eighth October and told me.'

A few days earlier, someone had told Sneha's grandfather in their Shastrulapalli village that their daughter-in-law had been killed, but he hadn't believed it.

And Sneha's father?

'My memory of my father was composed of what others would tell me – he is very tall, strong, muscular, has a big moustache. That's how I made a mental picture of him. But when he was arrested in 2007 and I met him in the Karimnagar court, he had changed completely, had become old.'

That day, Sneha got only five minutes to meet father, but she often visited him when he was shifted to Hyderabad's Cherlapally Central Jail.

When her grandmother met her son there, she said: 'Enough now. Come home. I've grown old. Stay with me.'

But he didn't. During the meetings with his mother and daughter in jail, he told them tales of his guerrilla life, and that the revolution was the only way to social change.

With her parents away in the forest, Sneha's childhood was full of struggles. She undertook minor jobs to sustain her education. There was only one way to get some information on her parents. Whenever any Maoist from Andhra Pradesh was arrested, Sneha would visit them in jail and ask them about her parents. Often, the guerrillas would cheerfully tell her: 'I saw you a long time ago, when you were a kid.'

Sneha last saw her father after his release from jail in 2009. He immediately returned to the forest. A few years later, she gave birth to a son and named him Vasant. Elderly members of the family said that her son resembled her father in his childhood. She has now been living with the wish that her father meet his grandson at least once.

But this was in 2014. When will Purnima, or Jaabili, make her entry into the script? Four years later, on 30 October 2018, when I am writing the final draft, and it will occur to me that I should talk to Sneha. My memory or old notes might have missed something, or a new chapter might have got added to it. She will immediately recognize me. She will still be living in Hyderabad, and will express the desire to read extracts from my book.

'Your email?'

Her SMS will reach me. The email ID will contain a word, 'jaabili'.

Jaabili? I will Google it. It means 'full moon' in Telugu. Many popular songs in Telugu begin with the word. Jaabili. Full moon. Who is this person with such a beautiful name in her email address?

I will text her. It is Sneha's daughter, who was in her womb when Sneha visited her father. A mother goes to see her father in jail with a baby inside her, hoping that the war will end one day, that her father will come out and take his daughter's daughter into his arms.

SEVEN

death / vi

Our screams cut through the forest. We rip apart our frayed saris, beat our dry breasts – Dandakaranya breaks into a tumultuous cry. Our men try to pacify us, they pull us back by the arms. But on this Sunday evening, 19 May 2013, we are absolutely unwilling to return. We speak only Gondi, but we have also learnt a few Hindi words of abuse – from, who else, the policemen. We hurl those Hindi words back at them, pelt stones at the Gangalur police station and the adjoining CRPF camp.

Go back. Go back.

Residents of Ehadsameta village, we have walked for hours and crossed hills to reach Gangalur. On our return journey, we will be carrying corpses on cots, the corpses of our husbands and sons whom the police have handed over to us after their post-mortem. Some injured villagers are also lying on cots. We don't remember how many corpses shrouded in red and green saris we have ferried for cremation in our lives.

On Friday night, 17 May, the policemen fired at a gathering of the local festival of Beej Pundum in our village. Eight of our people were killed. Karam Joga and his thirteen-year-old son Badru, Karam Pandu and his fourteen-year-old son Guddu. Punem Lakkhu, a boy of fifteen.

We lay the corpses down at the police station's gate and rattle the lock. The policemen are hiding inside. Some are standing behind the wall. We want to break the lock and barge in. Two elderly women among us violently pull at the barbed wire around the CRPF camp. We are also carrying our cooking utensils, ladles and vessels. We hurl them at the CRPF personnel standing on the other side of the wire.

Stop killing the adivasis. Shoot us if you want.

Our men have done this earlier – hurled stones and abuses at police camps. It's our turn today.

First the police kill us, then they take away the corpses. You want to know how they treated the corpses of our husbands and sons? No, we can't describe that. Our language doesn't have the words for it.

* * *

These women, who look like dry twigs, have been standing in front of the police station for the last twenty-four hours. Do they even understand what was done to the corpses four hours earlier? Not every life ends with death. Death may beget new agonies.

The corpses had been lying under the merciless May sun in the middle of the jungle. Forty-five degrees Celsius. Bullets had hit them thirty-six hours ago. They had swollen obscenely, rotting, with an unbearable stink. Their male relatives stood nearby. And the CRPF soldiers, still on alert, guarding the corpses. Their faces covered with scarves, armed with X95 and AK-47 rifles fitted with under-barrel grenade launchers.

'Make an incision on the stomach,' a man ordered. He, too, had his face covered, and had a register in his hand. Dr B.R. Pujari, a government doctor. Suklu, a villager, came forward. A relative of one of the deceased lying on a cot. Suklu pulled off the green cloth to uncover the swollen, purple body. He cut the stomach open. Red worms crawled out. A strange wind emerged from the body with a loud sound. 'Dead bodies become like balloons. When you cut them open, they produce a sound like flatulence,' a CRPF soldier explained. As relatives held the corpses and turned them sideways and upside down, the doctor examined them, poking and prodding with a twig he had picked up from the ground, and made a record in his register.

You were before a similar set of corpses, almost exactly a year ago. Another village in the same district. On the night of 28 June 2012, a CRPF contingent had fired at the forest dwellers when they were celebrating Beej Pundum in Sarkeguda village. Nineteen people were killed. You reached the village after the post-mortem but before the cremation. In Ehadsameta, you witnessed the corpses being cut open.

Indian laws make it mandatory to conduct the post-mortem of people killed in an encounter with security forces, and to prepare an official report on the cause of death. A post-mortem, the Supreme Court mandates, must be conducted by two doctors in a district hospital. Videos and photographs should be taken to ensure that fake encounters are detected. The police may claim that it was an 'encounter killing', which denotes crossfire, but the post-mortem might show that the person was killed from a very short distance, with a pistol to the head. The killer may lie, the corpse may remain silent, but the wound will reveal the trajectory, angle and intention of the bullet.

How did it turn out in Ehadsameta?

'Don't you have another blade? A new one?' Dr Pujari asked his colleagues. The doctor had not touched any corpse so far. Suklu, in his torn green vest and blue underpants, had made several incisions in five corpses with two blades. The doctor suddenly thought of changing the blade. But there was none, let alone any other medical equipment. Suklu was given only one pair of surgical gloves for the whole process. Without changing gloves, he slit open bodies, inserted his hand into the stomachs, pulled out the innards to enable the doctor's examination, before shoving them inside again. The bodies were facing the sky, mouths wide open, teeth darkened.

The villagers watched the public spectacle of their relatives' post-mortem.

Dr Pujari admitted that it was against the law to conduct post-mortems in the open, and that they should never be done in the presence of the police. 'Under certain conditions, an officer with the rank of SDM [sub-divisional magistrate] and above can give permission to conduct it otherwise,' he tried to explain.

SDM Virendra Bahadur Panchbhai said, 'The only requirement for a post-mortem is adequate light. Other things can be relaxed in special situations.'

An obvious mendacity.

So, it's not necessary for the Bastar doctor to personally examine a body. A man will upturn his son's corpse, Suklu will make an incision, and the doctor will 'examine' the bullet wound from a distance. The Bastar doctor, it seems, has an extremely sharp eye, having seen countless corpses being cut open. Armed with deadly weapons, policemen will guard the corpses. One corpse will be wearing blue underpants, its torso naked. Remove the underpants, someone will say. Another man, perhaps his brother, will pull it down. A man, stark naked, his genitals ghastly, like an inflated black balloon.

An hour later, the bodies are ferried on cots to Gangalur police station. The women are already there, having screamed their lungs out for hours and still wailing. Their men somehow persuade them to return. After all, those who have left will have to be given farewells.

The administration has arranged for a tractor, but the terrain is difficult. The hills are not meant for four-wheeled vehicles. The tractor leaves them midway, and then begins the two-hour journey with corpses tied to cots.

Other villagers have prepared pyres at the outskirts of Ehadsameta. Father and son, Joga and Badru, are laid down on one pyre. 'It's not unusual among adivasis. When a person loves someone a lot, we cremate them together,' a villager says.

You have been with the corpses for six hours. The hesitations that had gripped you in a similar moment a year ago vanished today – you took photographs, made videos, came to consider yourself a corpse. When they are laid on the pyre you feel that the day will end only when you are also placed beside them. Surrounded by trees, the logs go up in flames and the villagers leave for their home. In the flames, the pyres of last year flash before you. The road to Ehadsameta began from Sarkeguda.

But it is not an occasion to invoke memories. Evening is about to fall, the news has to be sent to Delhi. The closest internet connection is at the district headquarters, three to four hours away. If these deaths are to be recorded in tomorrow's newspaper, you have to begin the return journey immediately, leaving behind the flames and the memory to the custody of the jungle. That moment is now about to descend, in which every emotion gets converted into news. The bubble of death you have been inside all day is now to be hastily typed up on a laptop with feverish fingers in a mere 800 words, captions for photographs are to be given before the 'send' button is pressed.

death / vii

22 February 2012. Marie Colvin was killed in Syria today. She had been writing against the Assad government.

Wandering through the meadows of Bastar you visualize her death and the many faces of death Bastar carries.

On a dark forested path of Chintalnar at night, some apparitions suddenly emerge before your motorcycle. The edges of their sickles gleam in the headlight. They could be farmers returning from their fields, but they appear like messengers of death carrying an urgent invite from Yamraj.

A month later, as March nears its end, trees shed their leaves, the pond of dry leaves flames up with the tiniest of sparks. A flame slithers through the woods. Has someone laid explosives here? Has a landmine flared up? These are the earliest impressions of a visitor. A fire is a gesture of death in Bastar. A spark that emerges from the dry bamboo leaves and spreads through the jungle creates the illusion of gunfire.

Maoists plant two types of landmines. One is triggered from a distance. The other explodes because of pressure. An explosive of the latter kind has been resting underneath the pathways of this forest – since when, who knows? But these pathways will have to be taken if the forest is to be decoded. It is not necessary that you will be killed in an ambush. A forgotten landmine, hidden under the earth, might also explode at the slightest misstep. You can escape a crossfire, but not a landmine that has been waiting for you.

It can also be during a morning jog. You stop near a pond to catch your breath, and suddenly find a platoon of soldiers marching towards you from three directions. Around 500 metres away. They have rifles of several kinds, 51mm mortars for hurling bombs. The rifles swish through the air, they are fitted with grenade launchers and tele-lenses. You are clearly marked out in the viewfinder.

Are they on an operation? Do they consider you an enemy? Your attire might make you look like a stranger in the forest, but you don't look like an enemy. You may evoke suspicion, but it should not cause a platoon of armed soldiers to rush in with grenade launchers. Surely no one would fire at mere suspicion? But people do. An armed fighter, after all, is the most frightened of all. An unarmed person will seek a hundred ways to escape – the armed one trusts only the bullet. The gleam of brass mutes their thoughts, blinds their memory and deafens their reason.

The distance is 200 metres now. A commander in front, the rest of the unit behind. They are moving across the open field. A soldier stops, kneels down, places the rifle against his shoulder, takes aim. Do they think that you will run away? But you are rooted to the spot. Where, after all, could you run? A big pond lies behind you. But is the platoon really coming for you? Perhaps the Naxals are hiding close by? Maybe on the other side of the pond? Or on the scaffolding, in the trees? The platoon is now closing in. Many soldiers are taking aim. Is an encounter about to begin here? Are you about to be perforated by bullets spraying from all sides? You always wanted to cover a 'live encounter', but when the moment has arrived, you have no notebook or camera. Instead, you are shrouded in fear. There is no culvert, boulder or hill around, behind or under which you can hide. Is it wiser to lie down on the ground before the firing begins? Or to raise your hands, as if in surrender?

* * *

Hundreds of kilometres away, to the north of Bastar, Major Saab lives in a residential neighbourhood of Raipur. He is around fifty years old, and can often be seen sitting on a bench in the park or with the watchman at the gate. He sometimes speaks to a young man, who lives across the road from him. Major Saab has only two complaints. First, he has been unwell these past few days. Making strange sounds, he mentions some unheard-of diseases. He uncovers his stomach, points at a spot below the navel. Second, someone in his family has died recently. Who? Baba, maybe Amma ... He lists a few ambiguous pronouns.

If he doesn't see the young man for a few days, he goes up to the boundary wall of his home, stands on his toes and peeps inside. He never knocks at the gate. It is not in his nature to open the gate and enter. He merely peeps over the boundary wall – the porch, a door and the living room. Like a boy whose ball has landed in a neighbour's home, he cannot gather the courage to step inside but stays at the gate, waiting for someone to come out.

If the door is open and he is able to see the man in the hall, he immediately calls out in a hazy voice: 'Baba died yesterday ... Severe pain below the stomach ... I need to consult a doctor.'

Who was Baba, how did he die? Some 'bhaiya' didn't provide timely medication.

A rusted and near-defunct police jeep is parked outside Major Saab's home. It looks like the home of a junior policeman. Major Saab's brother, perhaps. His terrace can be seen from the young man's porch. When he is on the terrace, enjoying the sun, he smiles, a rare smile, and waves to the young man.

Major Saab loves biscuits, and often comes up to the young man's boundary wall asking for them. There's a curious story to the biscuits. Once, a packet of Parle-G was lying on the dashboard of the young man's car, parked in his porch. Major Saab came to the boundary wall and said, 'I want some biscuits.' The young man went to the kitchen. 'No biscuits at home,' he said. 'They're there.' 'Where?' Major Saab pointed at the car.

After meeting him, the young man thought that he must have been an army major earlier, and if not then, he should be christened Major

Saab now. Soon, however, the name, like any other name, got twisted. The watchman turned Major into Magneto, and he became Magneto Saab – Magneto is a shopping mall in Raipur.

Major Saab's liver is very weak. He is not receiving proper treatment. Whenever the Death Reporter makes a trip to the jungle, his breath hangs by a fragile thread.

death script / xii

The tale of the Bastar journey and the journey of the Bastar tale don't have any companions. Bastar cannot have any companions. You are all alone here. All threads that tie one person to another snap when one is faced with a gleaming cartridge. There aren't many homes in Sukma and Dantewada that have not seen one. Not a live cartridge, but a dead bullet embedded in the flesh.

Crime Reporter in the city, Death Reporter in Bastar. The Crime Reporter traces a murder through bloodstains. The Death Reporter decodes death, gathers the pieces of a corpse scattered like a jigsaw puzzle.

Good novelists, someone said, offer sympathy to their characters in equal amounts, but a great novelist struggles against sympathy. The Death Reporter realizes that sympathy will damage his tale. He writes his tale from exile in Bastar. His rucksack has a few post-mortem reports lifted from a police station, photographs of fresh blood and empty cases of dead cartridges. His notebook is a testament to graveyards.

A fiction writer stays on a word for weeks, even months, overcomes the fear of death by writing a novel. The novel is the ultimate destination of fiction and the fiction writer. Bastar is the last pilgrimage of death and the Death Reporter. He wanders through the wilderness carrying corpses pinned to the tip of his fountain pen. Corpses are his only companions.

* * *

Almost imperceptibly, but profoundly, journalism has mutated your being. You now live in a bewildering haste, in a frenzied endeavour to locate news in every beat around you. The anxiety of missing a possible story trails you. Instead of living in the moment, letting yourself drown in its warmth or coldness, so to speak, you now chase it like a sniffer dog, restless to retrieve any clue or confidential document. This hyper-awakening of your senses has given birth to an unutterable fear that seeps through your being.

In the past few years, you have gathered marvellous experiences that would never have been possible had you not been a journalist. Yet, you have had little mental or temporal space to nourish these memories. You jump from one news item to another, then to a third and a fourth, flit between them, like those who have affairs one after another in their life, sometimes several simultaneously, who want to surrender their entire existence to their lovers but find little space for love as they are doomed to get contentment from merely the outer surface, the body.

The elusive, enchanting universe has been reduced to a mere news item for you, to be reported with a big headline. Almost all human bonds you have had in the past few years are coloured with the brush of 'news'. Even at dinner with someone, the possibility of a story that can be extracted from them never leaves you. 'What is the headline?' is the question that strikes you after meeting with friends. A trader goes to see the Taj Mahal and the first thought that strikes him is how to sell the monument.

You witnessed a similar experience during your romance with fiction, when you found a character in every human being, clues to your ongoing tale in every heartbeat. You were not unaware that there was the protagonist of a movie, a novelist who wished for the ill health of his daughter in order to gain some threads for his narrative. But fiction was a profoundly meditative process. While seeking characters in the world outside, the endeavour was to transcend and efface your own self, to dive into their being and hold an intimate dialogue with them.

A journalist does not enjoy the luxury of meditating over his characters. It may be tragic, but perhaps appropriate, that the English language uses the word 'source' for a journalist's acquaintances. A major part of this beautiful world is merely a 'source' for you.

This, perhaps, marks the difference between a journalist and a novelist. One gets the outer skin, the other delves into the soul. Can you embrace the soul without relinquishing the body?*

* What is the nature of authorship, the elusive creative power that conjures up a magical cosmos of characters and their inner selves? The question has baffled me ever since I became enamoured of fiction in my early teens. Where does the seed of this authority reside?

I lived with this puzzle for years, until I entered journalism and faced another question. Are fiction and journalism two opposing forms of narratives, as the latter is mandated to be based on nothing but facts? Or is there sufficient fiction in journalism? Fiction that's privy only to the journalist. Does a journalist secretly aspire to be a novelist? An aspiration they cannot openly express to anyone, perhaps even admit to themselves. As a fiction writer, I had always been in search of a universe of my own. As a journalist, was I also in search of an alternative world? As a journalist, I certainly did not invent facts, but the interpretation – the final word – was mine. I was now shaken by the question – was it journalism, or a novelistic narrative?

A part of my experiential world, I realized, that did not find the novelistic soil suitable for its flowering had quietly made its home in my news reports. Just like the protagonist of Stefan Zweig's novella was cruelly split between the black and the white pieces of chess, I was now a spectator to the contest between my two selves – journalist and novelist. In popular perception these two are always neatly divided, whereas I found them to be in a coterminous existence.

Several impressions that writers gather are quietly kept aside by their writerly selves. But what if someone has not one but two writerly selves, seemingly opposite ones? And both of them are engaged in a tussle to acquire and appropriate the raw material for their respective yearnings? The unceasing conflict between them often gets bloody – at times, the schism deepens to the extent that one doesn't hesitate to assault the other.

dream / xii

My initial days in Bastar often come back to me. 13 September 2011. My first visit to Dantewada. My first month in this state.

Two memories etched upon my soul – the rains of Bombay and the landscape of Montana – were overwritten within fifteen days of my arrival in Chhattisgarh. Relaxed, self-possessed rains. Raindrops that take no rest even in the sunshine. Such a diaphanous drizzle that, unless you remain in one spot for a while, you won't feel it, and will be surprised later when you notice that your clothes are wet. And the landscape? Thick groves, waterfalls, hills. Walk for miles in the jungle, and you will not hear even a whisper. Your steps are halted, caressed and examined by rivers and streams.

Dantewada stands on the confluence of two gorgeous rivers, Dankini and Shankhini. Their names carry opposite meanings. Dankini is the one who stings, Shankhini blows the holy conch. Such wondrous names the rivers here carry – Dankini, Shankhini, Udanti, Talperu. Ganga, Yamuna and Narmada could only be mothers. Their names evoke respect. You will take a dip in the Ganga to absolve your sins, but Dankini will sting you, tempt you, fill you with yearnings. Shankhini will invite you by blowing her conch. The residents gave their rivers such names very thoughtfully. One can only love and get obsessed with such a landscape. The river with the most lethal name is Jonk, meaning 'leech'. It flows through the Raipur and Mahasamund districts. Take a dip in its water and it will stick to your body forever. It will never leave you, nor let you live, will suck your blood day and night. There are rivers here that could be named after bees, hornets and wasps...

Ten days ago, the dusty river Iriya crossed my path three times on the way to Balrampur. A lot of sand had gathered in the stream after the rain, making it look grey. A river returns to embrace your steps, and also to thwart your way.

* * *

A month later, the midnight of Sharad Purnima in Dantewada. The annual fair called Murga Bazar that the adivasis hold after Dussehra is in progress in a large field along the road from Jagdalpur to Dantewada. Boys and girls, men and women are dancing in circles. An old woman, gathering her sari, comes prancing into the ring. A man high on mahua is rolling in the middle of the field. A collective tune rises up, pierces the sky, drums are beaten, frenzied dance movements shake the earth.

The feverish commotion will continue through the night, and the next night as well. Gambling, playing cards. A game of throwing rings around objects like soap and pencil boxes. Another game that is a local variation on roulette – not circular but square. How did roulette reach Bastar? Some men are rousing their red-crested roosters, stroking their feathers, tying sharp blades to their claws. Cockfighting is a sport of valour. Muscular roosters launch flying assaults on their opponents, pierce their chests with the blades. The owners of the surviving roosters take home the dead ones.

Security forces are deployed along the road in case a brawl breaks out. Uniformed soldiers rebuke mischievous youths, but in jest. This night belongs to the adivasis. The full moon of Sharad Purnima has descended upon these boys and girls. Fear has vanished tonight. The women have brought mahua and rice brew in big pots, and they offer it for free to everyone. Girls drink mahua out of leaf cups.

Given the celebrations tonight, can one say that a police vehicle might hit a landmine on this very road a few days later? That a little further in the jungle, underneath a tarpaulin tent, preparations might be on for the next assault?

Blood and intoxication are twins in this geography. This forest couldn't have avoided weaving a tale of rifles and deaths. These woods were perhaps fated to become the battleground for armed fighters.

* * *

Ruins of schools and hutments. Deserted ghotuls. Faded slogans of the revolution on crumbling walls. Burnt-down bushes. Empty bullet casings embedded in tree trunks. Dried and darkened stains of blood on the ground. Large swathes of land in Bastar betray the traces of a lost culture. People migrated away during the Salwa Judum years. Wild animals vanished in the wind. Walk for several miles – not even a crow crosses your path.

On one such evening, when my eye has not caught sight of a single bird all day, it occurs to me that a poisonous seed has entered the earth of this jungle, a seed whose origins it cannot determine. Many years pass by. The seed has not yet sprouted above the surface, but it has spread its roots underneath the earth all over the jungle. Like a parasite, it draws nourishment from trees, hills and streams that, unwittingly, continue to guard it and, in turn, get depleted.

* * *

I recall another image. April 2012. Two birds are in his gentle grip. He has tied their legs and wings, and softly crushes them. A little cry, the pressure increases slightly, and the neck of one bird collapses. His friends clap. Now it's the turn of the other one. It flutters and shrieks, but cannot resist for long.

The child is just around five years old. His friends are also of the same age. The toys and sports of Dandakaranya. The beaks of birds. Snake hide. Buffalo horn.

At a little distance, women and children fetch water from a ditch, a muddy puddle. The ponds have dried up in the summer, and this is the only source of water for several villages. People have fenced it with logs to keep out cattle, which nevertheless manage to breach it. A dead snake lies rotting close by. Its stench doesn't affect the villagers. They draw water from the ditch. After some time, a woman gestures to two boys and they lift the snake with a long stick and throw it away.

* * *

The residents of Bastar had never cared about death. They had been living in its eternal embrace. They did not want to escape it, nor did they have the desire to defeat it. A curious custom among some adivasi communities perhaps aptly reflects their bond with death. When a respected elderly person dies, the body, draped in fresh cloth, is laid on the floor. A number of women joyfully somersault over the corpse. Some land on the body, some fall aside. They believe that a perfect somersault will ensure them a rebirth in the deceased's family.

Such an intimate and affectionate bond with death is now eroding because the last four decades have sown a death wish in them. They lived a life unencumbered by the burden of the past and the responsibilities of the future. Now, they are not averse to destruction. Their death wish wanders in the infinite sky.

But the adivasis are not alone. They share their forests with revolutionaries who dream of an epic death and storytellers who dream of an epic tale. Their dreams take them beyond death, but also set them ablaze in an insatiable fire. The dreams simultaneously nourish and consume them; sustain them, while quietly eating away at them.

Bastar is not a mere wailing of the dead, it is also a tale of their yearnings. Some yearnings, the memory stones whisper, lead to inevitable ruin. Not a dry and cold ruin – it is permeated by an all-consuming romance. The call of impending death, Bastar is also the lure of a love that forever remains elusive and ethereal, its shadow slithers like a maze of mahua.*

---

* Though what many often seek is not love but the shelter of its comforting assurance, in order to legitimize their misadventures which stand in fundamental conflict with love.

displacement / vii

6 December 2015. Balibeda village, Abujhmad. A luminous sunshine is pirouetting upon the river. It's hard to believe that the entire forest had been enveloped in fog a little while ago. At around 6 a.m., we crossed the river Nai Berad and reached the grove to collect salfi. Thick, white fog. Even the river was barely visible. Five villagers and me. A man climbed up a long wooden ladder tied to a tall tree, the top of which was lost in the foggy clouds. It seemed as if he wouldn't stop before reaching the sky. The salfi had dripped into an earthen pot tied to a branch. He brought the pot down.

Mahua and salfi are the national drinks of Bastar. Marriage, love or the killing of four in a family, including a ten-year-old child – men and women drown every moment in mahua. It helps them embrace life as well as death with dignity. Many treasures of this forest have been destroyed in the past three decades, but mahua has survived. In the absence of mahua, the residents of Bastar might have disappeared long ago. Mahua blooms for just around a month in March and April, but its scent pervades the forest for the entire year.

We return to the village. The drunk men are lazing around. The radio is playing '*Meri desi look*'. At this hour, the song seems to have arrived from another planet.

Last night, Simri told me about her family. She had conceived before marriage, when she was just sixteen. The villagers called a 'meeting' – this word has entered the vocabulary of Bastar through the Maoists – and asked her, 'Who is he?' Soon, she came to live with Mangal. They had another baby later. There was no need to have a formal wedding. 'We give birth to many children,' the villagers say, 'because many die early. If we have seven or eight, a few of them will certainly survive.'

Mangal's elder brother Sanku lost a baby last year. A yearly death is not uncommon in a family.

Mangal's father Vetti Mandavi was paralysed a few years ago. He looks like a crumpled bundle of cloth, lying on a tattered dusty blanket near a fire that simmers through the day. A loincloth, a lungi and a thin blue shirt. The clothes seem heavier than the man. The smoke emanating from the fire makes him cough repeatedly, but he doesn't move. A dog ambles about lazily, chickens hop around him. The thatched shed has gathered innumerable layers of soot.

He is in severe pain, but I never hear him complain. Not a single word comes out of his mouth. He merely spits from time to time. The vocabulary of the jungle doesn't seem to have a word for such pain. Have I ever heard any resident of the interiors of Bastar cry or wail, or even complain? People harassed or tortured by the police do express their pain, but only when they are repeatedly asked about it. It's my third visit to this village in Abujhmad. I have lived in many villages across Bastar, but cannot recall anyone sharing their sorrow with me. Perhaps they don't share it with each other either.

I often find people creating opportunities to regurgitate their grievances – how unfortunate their life is, how hollow their destiny, how their own people have cheated them. But Bastar has an unassuming embrace of sorrow, separation and death. I earlier wondered whether the impossibility of their lives had muted the emotion associated with loss. Perhaps not. Their embrace of nothingness, an all-encompassing nothingness, is absolute.

* * *

A few years later, I found myself in Balibeda again. The village along with several other adjoining ones looked deserted in December 2019. Mangal and Simri had left for Narayanpur six months ago. The family seemed to epitomize the last four decades of Abujhmad. Let me recount their story from the beginning. Simri's elder brother, also named Mangal, was a Maoist commander. He was killed long ago in a police encounter in Gadchiroli. The rebels erected a memorial for him in the middle of Balibeda village. When I first visited the village in February 2014, Simri told me about her brother and took me to the memorial. I found that his name had been scraped off the red stone. Villagers erased the name, she said, fearing that the police would consider them to be Maoist informers.

Undeterred, they continued to live an archetypal adivasi life in the village until a series of tragedies befell them. Sometime in 2018, the District Reserve Guard of the Chhattisgarh police detained Sanku's eldest brother Raju along with several other villagers during a routine patrol, and locked them up in Jagdalpur jail. A year later, on 26 June 2019, the Maoists killed Simri's younger brother Ramji Vadde in a Jan Adalat, accusing him of being a police informer which, villagers said, he was not. The kangaroo court was held in the neighbouring village of Orchha Paar. Several eyewitnesses recounted to me the manner in which the Maoists had asked the villagers to throw stones at the young boy and bludgeon him to death.

Balibeda was now inhabited by the elderly whom the younger ones could not take with them to Narayanpur. As is the tacit norm in a sinking ship, the elderly and the sick are the first to be thrown overboard. The condition of the paralysed Vetti had become precarious; he had been left all alone to quietly die in the jungle. In the next home lived Simri's father Lalu Vadde and her mother Kari Vadde, who fed Vetti. The dogs, the pigs and the hens were still around, and there was a new entrant – a baby monkey. Someone had tied a metal collar around its neck. It hopped around Vetti's cot under a guava tree.

There was another signifiant change: the name of the deceased Maoist Mangal was back on the memorial.

Upon my return to Narayanpur, I went searching for Simri and her husband Mangal. Forced to leave their river and the wilderness, they now lived in a small shack and worked as daily labourers. They had lost weight, and their usual effervescence. Simri, who until a few months ago had ruled over the household and had so wonderfully hosted me in the jungle, now looked like a severed branch of a mahua tree.

death script / xiii

Over nearly ten years – August 2011 to January 2021 – I have made innumerable trips to Bastar. On each occasion, it seemed that it would be my last journey. All the stories and news reports have been written. It's over now.

Whenever I visit this jungle, I remember a magician I met a few years ago. He had many dangerous performances in his repertoire. (He called life-threatening acts 'performances'.) His hands and feet were bound in chains and locked. He was thrown into a huge mound of hay before it was set on fire. But he would come out unhurt. In another such act, he was bound tight with iron chains and locked in a box, before a speeding truck smashed into it. Somehow, he managed to unfetter himself and come out just a split second before the truck hit the box. Was it an illusion? Maya? Were his hands not chained? Why did the escape take place only a split second before? What if there was a slight delay?

'Nothing,' he replied, 'is beyond the laws of science. I can come out earlier too, but my art requires a last-moment escape. There's a risk, but the bigger joy is in defeating death.' The addiction to rewriting his destiny made him play this game again and again. Unknowingly, he echoed a poet: 'Death be not proud … Death, thou shalt die.'

Whenever I enter this jungle, I remember the magician. On each occasion, I am hit by the thought that something will make my return impossible. That I will vanish without a trace. Still, a yearning, intangible, pulls me here.

* * *

I found myself hopelessly lost in the jungle during my last Abujhmad trip in December 2019. My motorbike had broken down in the middle of a river; it was my foolhardiness, wading into waist-deep waters on the machine. It seemed like I might have to leave the damned beast in the jungle and pay the person I had borrowed it from – that is, if I was at all able to return. I had also broken a tooth. Amid the excruciating toothache, the impending loss of the bike, and with no possibility of reaching town anytime soon, I spent a few nights in a village rereading a remarkable book, Jozef Czapski's *Lost Time: Lectures on Proust in a Soviet Prison Camp*. Proust-loving Czapski was among the Polish officers captured during World War II and sent to a Soviet camp. In order to bring some cheer to their prison lives, the captives planned a talk every evening, in which each speaker would talk about a subject. Czapski had chosen to speak on modern French painting, but thought of beginning with lectures on Proust and his monumental novel. Significantly, none of the speakers had any material or books at hand and spoke only from their memory. Thus began a series of great lectures in which a prisoner remembered his impressions of a novel that itself is a feat of remembrance.

Adding his own impressions and interpretations to Proust's work, Czapski recalled the novelist and wrote: 'I observed how distance – distance from books, newspapers, and millions of intellectual impressions of normal life – stimulates that memory.'

Far removed from the world, electricity, the phone and the internet, living with the despair of being lost in the jungle, I read that book at night, recollecting my own memories of the past eight years. And then I came across a paragraph I had overlooked in my first reading. Czapski wrote: 'The slow and painful transformation of a passionate and narrowly egoistical being into a man who gives himself over wholly to some great work or other that devours him, destroys him, lives in his blood, is a trial every creative being must endure.' He then quoted Goethe: 'In the life of a creative man, biography can and must be considered only up to the thirty-fifth year, after that it's no longer his life story, but his struggle with the substance of his work that must become central and, more and more, increasingly absorbing.'

The words sent a shiver up my spine on that cold night, as I lay under an open sky.

* * *

I also recall the knight who wagered his life and played a game of chess with Death to delay his own demise and save his kingdom from the ravaging plague. And the queen who narrated a story every night so that she could see the sun the next morning, defeating death by weaving new stories for a thousand and one nights.

But there are also some tales which, instead of saving you, take you closer to death. Since they are recorded in a doomed script, the narrator becomes their first prey. The tale of a princess who wore the letters of a special alphabet on her eyelids because she wanted to become immortal. The letters belonged to a proscribed alphabet. Each letter killed the reader as soon as it was read. Her blind attendants would write these letters every night and place them upon her eyelids. Her maids shut their eyes when they attended to her in the morning, and removed the letters. She was, thus, protected from her enemies at the time when she was most vulnerable – nobody could assault her while she was sleeping. One day, her maids brought her a special gift of two mirrors – one took you to a few moments ahead in the future, the other a few moments into the past. While she was still in bed and the letters had not yet been washed off, the maids placed the mirrors before her, hoping that the princess would be amused. And thus, she read in the mirror the letters that were to remain locked in her future and her past, and should never have become her present. Her present was impregnable, but not her past and her future. She died instantly, simultaneously killed by the letters from both the past and the future, crushed between the talons of death hovering over her.

The magician who jumps into the fire. The artist who abandons his biography. The knight who plays chess. The storyteller queen. The princess who goes to sleep encased in a blanket of death … Where does the tale of Bastar lie buried?

There's another claimant. The pages of a diary.

14 October 2014, Raipur. Someone in the neighbourhood has died. I don't know who. The security guard gave me a condolence card. It had a name printed on it. I have been living here for over three years, but I can't recognize the man. I have noticed some men with tonsured heads in the last few days. I recognize them. I could make out the deceased's family, but couldn't give him a face.

Yesterday, my neighbour and the security guard insisted that I attend the ritual feast on the thirteenth day after death. I was hesitant, but went to their home after returning from work in the evening. The relatives of the deceased welcomed me, showed me into the hall where food was being served. I tried to look for the garlanded photograph of the deceased, but couldn't find it. They asked me to sit on one of the three rows of mats rolled out on the floor. I could not recognize any of the people sitting next to or around me. I was served puris, vegetables and raita. I was hungry. I was no longer hesitant. I feasted in the memory of a dead man who was an absolute stranger to me.

NOTES

author's note

When I first came to Bastar in August 2011, the roads vanished a little after the Bijapur district headquarters and the forests began. Reporting on a Naxal attack in the forest of Bhadrakali, I had to navigate the river Chintavagu by boat. In those days, one still needed to cross rivers by boat if one couldn't swim. But during my last visit to Bastar in January 2021, I crossed the river in top gear over a new bridge. The forests of the region were now being uprooted for constructing roads and police camps. Perhaps the most ambitious such project was a 650-metre bridge on the river Indravati that connected Fundari village in Bijapur to Abujhmad – a CRPF unit had set up camp along the river to protect it. If you entered Abujhmad from the other side, that is, from Narayanpur district, Sonpur village used to be the last frontier of the state and Kurusnar the last police post. The eighteen-kilometre stretch from Kurusnar to Sonpur, which had earlier been full of streams and mighty rocks, now had a shining road. Sonpur even had a helipad. The state had begun penetrating the wilderness with a road that might eventually connect to Gadchiroli in Maharashtra. If the final battle was going to be in Abujhmad, as they said, its pitch was being prepared.

However, I also found that the jungle had become more impregnable. Several villages in the interior looked deserted. Aided by the Sonpur post, the police had increased patrolling in the area, and regularly rounded up young adivasis who were now in jails. Fearful, many villagers had fled to Narayanpur – perhaps the first mass exodus from these villages which had not yet witnessed any police–Maoist conflict. The forested paths that were once used by villagers to visit the weekly Sonpur market were now obstructed by tree trunks and large ditches, and were effectively an even safer haven for the rebels.

Which is why it is not easy to predict the future of the Maoist insurgency, which is now in its sixth decade. The uprising officially began on 25 May 1967 in Darjeeling's Naxalbari village, when peasants led by Charu Majumdar attacked the landlords. The uprising was quelled within three days by the government in West Bengal, which ironically had the CPI (Marxist) giant Jyoti Basu as the deputy chief minister, but by then the word 'Naxalite' had captured popular as well as intellectual attention. It drew a large number of educated youth in its early years, and found tremendous artistic engagement as stalwarts like Satyajit Ray and Mrinal Sen made movies on related themes.

Months after the first uprising, guerrilla zones appeared at several places in West Bengal, Bihar and Andhra Pradesh. Alongside, the All India Coordination Committee of Communist Revolutionaries (AICCCR) was also formed, before its leaders dissolved it to form the CPI (Marxist–Leninist) on Lenin's birthday, 22 April 1969, with Charu Majumdar as their leader.

Since its inception, the movement has been marked by fratricidal battles between various Left groups, with the first armed clash between the CPI (M) and the CPI (ML) cadres taking place soon after the latter was formed. Even the leaders who favoured an armed struggle found no consensus over strategy, as several of them continued to form separate outfits. One such leader was Kanai Chatterjee who formed the Maoist Communist Centre (MCC) in October 1969. The MCC would carry out armed struggles in Bihar and Jharkhand for decades. Another leader, N. Prasad, formed the CPI (ML) Unity Organization in Bihar in 1978, while Kondapalli Seetharamaiah founded the CPI (ML) People's War in 1980. With a large number of young and bright students from top colleges, the PW was soon to become the most disciplined and intellectually sound organization to lead the struggle in Dandakaranya. The CPI (ML) Unity Organization was later rechristened the CPI (ML) Party Unity, before it merged with the PW in 1998.

Meanwhile, a splinter group of the CPI (ML) formed the CPI (ML) Liberation in 1974. It later moved away from its earlier strategy of 'election boycott', opted for a 'course correction' and began participating in electoral politics. The first former-Naxalite MP, Rameshwar Prasad, was elected to Parliament from the Ara constituency in 1989, a trend that would intensify in the coming decades as a large number of former rebels from Bihar and Jharkhand joined mainstream political parties. Perhaps the most striking instance was that of the ex-CPI (Maoist) commander Kameshwar Baitha, who joined the Jharkhand Mukti Morcha and won the Palamu Lok Sabha seat in 2009 while he was in jail. Such politicians had by then renounced their revolutionary ideology only to face criticism from their former comrades.

Amid this, new revolutionary outfits continued to form in central and south India as the PW firmly established its base in Dandakaranya, drew a large number of adivasis to its ranks and established the People's Liberation Army (later renamed the People's Liberation Guerrilla Army) in 2000 to launch a frontal assault on the state. The adivasis were to become the foot soldiers of this battle.

Realizing the need to form a unified front, the outfits scattered across the country began coming together when the MCC and the Punjab-based Revolutionary Communist Centre of India (Maoist) led by Shamsher Singh Seri merged to form the Maoist Communist Centre of India in 2003, which soon after, in 2004, merged with the PW to form the CPI (Maoist). In 2014, the CPI (ML) Naxalbari, which was primarily operational in the southern peninsula, also merged with the CPI (Maoist). There were still several disparate armed groups in Jharkhand and Bihar, but the CPI (Maoist) was now the numero uno guerrilla party.

Though Kanai Chatterjee had established the MCC in 1969, the rebels were mostly called Naxals until the CPI (Maoist) was formed. The word Maoist has gained currency since then, but both 'Naxal' and

'Maoist' are used interchangeably in the rebel zone, as well as in the government and public spheres.

From 2004 began the deadliest decade of the state–Maoist conflict that has consumed 4,337 lives as of February 2020 in Chhattisgarh alone, including 1,046 Naxals, 1,164 security personnel, forty-two police informers, fifty-six government employees and 1,669 civilians. 8,197 people have been killed across the country, as of December 2019. Three major developments together ensured the sudden surge in violence on both sides: the merger of the two biggest rebel factions in 2004, the launch of Salwa Judum in 2005, and Prime Minister Manmohan Singh terming the Maoists the 'biggest internal security challenge'. It was also a time when industries had been vigorously pushing for mining permits in the forests of central India, the bastion of the rebels. Now determined to cleanse the wilderness, that incidentally forms the lungs of the nation, the central government parachuted its battalions into central India.

For over a decade after the merger, the Maoists suddenly seemed invincible. They had intellectual strength, dedicated cadres, as well as ammunition. They could attack the state's security apparatus at will, raid jails and release their imprisoned cadres, abduct district collectors and MLAs. Dandakaranya was now teeming with landmines that were hard to detect and caused massive casualties to security forces.

But the Indian state is too mighty, constitutionally strong and culturally cohesive to collapse before armed revolutionaries. Following the initial setback, the state pumped in more and more of its security forces. At present, over a hundred battalions of the Central Armed Police Forces, besides a large number of police battalions of various states, are deployed in the battlefield. There have been differences among political parties over the strategy to deal with the Maoists. Some state governments have been seemingly lenient at times; in places like Bastar, the BJP entered into conspiratorial liaisons with the Maoist guerrillas for immediate gains. But across the political spectrum, there has been a near unanimity: crush the Naxals without caring about any collateral damage, that is, the destruction of the adivasi life. The United Progressive Alliance (UPA) government, with Manmohan Singh as prime minister and P. Chidambaram as home minister, presided over the most treacherous killing of a senior cadre when, in the middle of negotiations between the government and the CPI (Maoist), the security forces killed the Maoist emissary Cherukuri Rajkumar, alias Azad, in 2010. In November 2013, the UPA government categorically told the Supreme Court that 'the ideologues and supporters of the CPI (Maoist) in cities and towns have undertaken a concerted and systematic propaganda against the state to project the state in a poor light and also malign it through disinformation ... In fact, it is these ideologues who have kept the Maoist movement alive and are in many ways more dangerous than the cadres of the People's Liberation Guerrilla Army.' Likewise, in the last few years, the Narendra Modi government has invented the epithet of 'urban Naxal' to discredit writers and activists, and put several of them in jail.

The record of various state governments in the last five decades, ranging from the Left Front in West Bengal to the Congress in Andhra Pradesh to the BJP in Chhattisgarh, shows that the country's political establishment has never been able to grasp the issue in all its complexity. It has rarely wanted to initiate negotiations with the rebels, or to bring independent people to participate in the peace process – not realizing that it is these people who create a buffer zone between the state and the insurgents and push both sides to shed their rigidity and come to the table.

The CPI (Maoist) and all its units are banned under the Unlawful Activities (Prevention) Act, 1967. At present, as many as ninety districts, from Kerala to Uttar Pradesh to West Bengal, have been classified by the Union home ministry as left wing extremism-affected districts, which receive special assistance from the Centre – in terms of both finance and force deployment.

In the last few years, the Maoist movement has been on the decline. This can be attributed to three major factors: it has not been able to create the next generation of leadership; the internet and the market are pulling away the adivasis; and urban middle-class support, so crucial for any underground guerrilla outfit, is waning.

While the violence has come down, the Maoists have not disappeared. The rebels are preparing a new base area in the forests, along the tri-junction of Maharashtra, Madhya Pradesh and Chhattisgarh. In another development, the Bastar adivasis have now reached the south. Four decades ago, educated Naxals from Andhra Pradesh came to Bastar to make it their guerrilla base and convert adivasis into fighters. The arrest of Ramlu Korsa – a Bastar resident – from Tamil Nadu in October 2019 suggests that the adivasis, equipped with ideology and military expertise, are now in the south to transform another tribal land.

The southern peninsula has seen sporadic Naxal activity over the years, mostly concentrated along the Karnataka–Kerala–Tamil Nadu (KKT) tri-junction. The rebels operating in that forested tribal belt comprise of a bunch of Left radicals from the three states. A resident of Mankelli village in Bijapur, Chhattisgarh, Ramlu Korsa was a senior CPI (Maoist) commander who was sent to the KKT area in 2015 after a decade-long stint in Bastar. In a rarity for an adivasi, Ramlu Korsa speaks six languages, including Tamil, Malayalam and Kannada. The rebels began sending their cadres to the area in 2012. Their documents state that 'this area has as many as fifty tribal communities including Paniyar, Adiyar, Kattunaikkar and Kurichyar' who have been 'living here for thousands of years'. The document details the deprivation and exploitation of these communities over the centuries, and notes that material conditions are favourable for the creation of another Maoist base there. The area has often seen the presence of senior rebels – the Central Committee member Kuppuswamy Devaraj was killed in an 'encounter' in Malappuram, Kerala, in November 2016.

The Maoists still hold large swathes of territory in Dandakaranya, have a good cadre base, and ammunition that should sustain them against the present level of force deployment for at least ten years. Should the material conditions change, as the Maoists have been hoping, the battle will be prolonged, unless the state decides to bomb and raze the jungle and terminate its citizens overnight – a plan the country's top security establishment had indeed discussed and, eventually, wisely discarded a decade ago.

But what could those material conditions be in twenty-first century India? I once raised the question with a veteran Maoist ideologue. He, in turn, asked: 'Nehru was once your most beloved leader. Could you have ever anticipated that your first prime minister, who laid the foundation of independent India, would come to be vilified overnight?'

His words were brazenly rhetorical, and yet I didn't have any answer to the question. All I knew was this: a conventional army loses a war if it doesn't win; a guerrilla army wins a war if it doesn't lose.

endnotes

epigraph

– The quote from the Mahabharata is from Kate Crosby's translation of the Stree Parvan (The Book of Women), 16th canto, published by the Clay Sanskrit Library.
– The quote from the Homer's Iliad is a paraphrase of verse 176–77 from Book XII, based on Samuel Butler's translation.

pre-text

– Vetaal: A corpse hanging upside down from the branch of a tree in a famous Sanskrit tale. To fulfil a vow, King Vikramaditya is required to carry the corpse on his back to a designated place in complete silence. On the way, Vetaal tells him a tale that ends with a probing question, with the condition that if Vikramaditya knows the answer but chooses not to reply, his head will be smashed to pieces. Vikramaditya knows that if he speaks his vow will be broken and Vetaal will fly back to the tree, forcing him to begin the journey all over again.

death script / i

– *The Brooklyn Follies* is a novel by Paul Auster.

death script / ii

– Yaksha prashna: The most pressing questions a yaksha (a semi-divine being) asks the Pandavas in the Mahabharata. Questions that, if unanswered, would bring doom to the person whom they were directed at.

– The butterfly-collecting novelist mentioned here is Vladimir Nabokov, and the novel is *Lolita*. The German writer is Walter Benjamin and the quote comes from his essay titled 'Berlin Chronicle'.

– The protagonist who assists with the execution of old and diseased dogs is from J.M. Coetzee's novel *Disgrace*.

– It is believed that people go to heaven if they die in Kashi, and to hell if they take their last breath in the nearby town of Maghar. The iconoclast fifteenth-century saint-poet Kabir who had spent his entire life in Kashi rejected the belief and shifted to Maghar in his final days.

– The man who played a game of chess with Death is from Ingmar Bergman's 1957 movie, *Det sjunde inseglet* (*The Seventh Seal*).

displacement / iii

– Salwa Judum: A state-sponsored vigilante campaign that began in the summer of 2005, and fizzled out in 2007. The adivasis that comprised it committed numerous atrocities on their brethren – who in turn joined the Maoist ranks in large numbers.

death / ii

– Garuda Purana: A Sanskrit text that is recited in many Hindu homes after a death as a means to console the bereaved family.

death script / iii

– All the quotes from Valmiki's Ramayana here are from Arshia Sattar's translation of the epic.

death script / v

– Kurukshetra: The battlefield of the Mahabharata war between the Kauravas and the Pandavas.

– The Ernest Hemingway quote is from his 1936 essay 'On the Blue Water: A Gulf Stream Letter' collected in the volume *By-line: Selected Journalism*.

death / iv

– The story narrated here is from the Sri Lankan movie, *Purahanda Kaluwara* (*Death on a Full Moon Day*, 1997) directed by Prasanna Vithanage.

death script / vi

– Guru dakshina: An offering made by a disciple to their guru. Incidentally, the most well-known guru dakshina in Indian literature rests on treachery, when the young Ekalavya, a native of the forest who has, thus far, silently worshipped Guru Dronacharya from a distance, is asked for – and offers up – his right thumb to satisfy his guru's allegiance to the kingdom.

dream / iv

– The Ramachandra Guha quote is from his book *India After Gandhi: The History of the World's Largest Democracy*.

dawn / i

– The Russian novel quoted is Leo Tolstoy's *War and Peace*, in Louise and Aylmer Maude's translation.

dream / v

– The Kashmiri journalist referred to is Basharat Peer. The quote is from his memoir *Curfewed Night.*

– The books mentioned here are Larry Kahaner's *AK-47: The Weapon that Changed the Face of War*, and Mikhail Kalashnikov's *The Gun that Changed the World.*

dawn / ii

– The December 2012 gangrape of a woman that shook the nation's conscience.

– *War and Peace in Junglemahal: People, State and Maoists* is a collection of essays by activists and academics, edited by Biswajit Roy.

– The chairperson of Sahara India Pariwar, Subrata Roy, was arrested on 28 February 2014 after Supreme Court orders in a case related to the non-refund of 20,000 crore rupees to investors.

dawn / iii

– Ghotuls: Community centres, of sorts, where adivasis assembled in the evenings. The Maoists discouraged the practice, and many ghotuls were shut down in Bastar, but a few still remain.

death script / viii

– Verrier Elwin's note and Jawaharlal Nehru's letter to the Assam chief minister are quoted from Ramachandra Guha's book *Savaging the Civilized: Verrier Elwin, His Tribals, and India.*

– Quote from p. 118 of the *Yog Vasishtha* (Varanasi: Tara Book Agency, 1994). This rendering of the verse is from Tim Park's translation of *Ka: Stories of the Mind and Gods of India* by Roberto Calasso.

death script / ix

– The first writer to win the Nobel for literature who also happened to be a journalist of great stature was Ernest Hemingway. He covered a range of armed conflicts across the world. Decades later, Svetlana Alexievich won the Nobel solely for her journalistic writing. Gabriel Garcia Marquez also did a considerable amount of journalism, but his fame rests almost entirely on his novels and short stories.

– The quote from Nirmal Verma's novel *Raat ka Reporter* is from Alok Bhalla's translation titled *Dark Dispatches*.

death script / x

– The Japanese movie mentioned in the footnote is *Yume* (*Dreams*, 1990), directed by Akira Kurosawa.

dream / viii

– Aleida Guevara's quote about her father is from her preface to *The Motorcycle Diaries* by Che Guevara.

death script / xi

– The quote attributed to Krishna Baldev Vaid is a recurring sentiment in his journals. Translated by Ashutosh Bhardwaj.

– Nagbhushan Patnaik's letter quoted in the footnote is from *Naxalbari ke Daur Mein*, ed. Veer Bharat Talwar (New Delhi: Anamika Publishers, 2007), pp. 465–70. Edited for clarity and translated by Ashutosh Bhardwaj.

delusion / vi

– I read this short story, most probably by a Pulitzer prize-winning author, long ago in a collection I can no longer recall the name of.

dream / xi

– Varavara Rao: A Hyderabad-based revolutionary poet and Maoist ideologue. He is now in jail with several other academics and activists in connection with the Bhima Koregaon case, on charges believed to be fabricated.

death script / xii

– The distinction between good and great novelists is a paraphrase from *Dhund se Uthti Dhun* by Nirmal Verma – a collection of his diaries, notes and journals.

– The novelist who wished for the ill health of his daughter is from Ingmar Bergman's movie *Såsom i en spegel* (*Through a Glass Darkly*, 1961).

death script / xiii

– Death be not proud... : From John Donne's famous sonnet.

– The knight who wagered his life is from Ingmar Bergman's 1957 movie, *Det sjunde inseglet* (*The Seventh Seal*).

– The story of the princess and the special alphabet is from Milorad Pavić's *Dictionary of the Khazars.*

about the author

Ashutosh Bhardwaj is a journalist, fiction writer and literary critic. He won the Ramnath Goenka Award for Excellence in Journalism for four consecutive years (2012–15). In 2015, he was shortlisted for the Reuters' Kurt Schork Awards in International Journalism. He is the author of several novellas, a short story collection, and a book of essays which won the Devishankar Awasthi Award 2020 for the best work of literary criticism. He received the Krishna Baldev Vaid Fellowship for fiction in 2012, was a writer in residence at Sangam House, Bangalore, in 2013, and a fellow at the Indian Institute of Advanced Study, Shimla (2017–19). In 2022, he will be a writer in residence at Prague – City of Literature. *The Death Script* was awarded the Atta Galatta–Bangalore Literature Festival Book Prize for Non-Fiction 2020, and was shortlisted for the Tata Literature Live! First Book (Non-Fiction) Award 2020 and the Kamaladevi Chattopadhyay NIF Book Prize 2021.